Praise for *Deceit and Other Possibilities*

Winner of the Asian/Pacific American Award for Literature
Finalist for the California Book Award

"This searing debut is about immigrants navigating a new America." —*O, The Oprah Magazine*

"Profoundly moving, and impossible to forget . . . A truly impressive debut." —*NYLON*

"The men, women and children in Hua's moving debut often find themselves straddling the volatile fault lines between desire and shame, decorum and rage . . . She has a deep understanding of the pressure of submerged emotions and polite, face-saving deceptions. The truth comes out, sometimes explosively, sometimes in a quiet act of courage." —*San Francisco Chronicle*

"An intriguing collection . . . Each of her protagonists is never quite grounded, caught between multiple cultures and countries. Each hides beneath layers of deceit, clinging to lies that enable survival . . . Hua is a writer to watch." —*Booklist*

"Hua writes with sophistication and the punch of the immigrant experience today . . . Exuberant stories filled with nuance and fresh detail." —*Literary Hub*

"Exactly what we need to be reading in this country right now, and probably always. If I had to choose one word to describe Hua's writing style, it would be personable—you actually feel like her narrators are sitting across the sofa from you, popping open the tab of a soda can as they prepare to tell you their story . . . Funny and sad, quick-witted and thought provoking."   —*Bustle*

"A great writer, subversively funny . . . Characters that don't look anything like 'model minorities' . . . Readable and human."
—*BuzzFeed*

"Shrewd . . . Hilarious."   —*VICE*

"These . . . stories follow immigrants to a new America who straddle the uncomfortable line between past and present, allegiances old and new."   —*The Millions*, Most Anticipated

"Rare and generous."   —*Bitch*

"The stories here are filled with desperate, confused, liminal people making questionable life choices . . . What lies at the core of the book is the unhappiness that tends to follow secrets and betrayal . . . It's a hard lesson learned, and one that most of the characters . . . eventually take to heart."   —KQED

"Heart-wrenching, implacable . . . Hua draws the reader in with her power of perception."
—*HuffPost*, Book Club Pick of the Week

"These characters may make us want to turn away, but Hua finds a way to humanize all of them." —*Vela*

"Complicated, cosmopolitan and utterly contemporary . . . These stories will jump right off the page into the reader's imagination."
—MARGOT LIVESEY, author of
Mercury and *The Flight of Gemma Hardy*

"Vanessa Hua inhabits in graceful and heartbreaking detail the people of her stories: strivers and betrayers, lovers and the landless, all of them on their way to transcendence in her hands."
—SUSAN STRAIGHT, author of *Between Heaven and Here*

Deceit and Other Possibilities

ALSO BY VANESSA HUA

A River of Stars

Deceit
and
Other Possibilities

STORIES

Vanessa Hua

Counterpoint
Berkeley, California

Library of Congress Cataloging-in-Publication Data
Names: Hua, Vanessa, author.
Title: Deceit and other possibilities : stories / Vanessa Hua.
Description: First paperback edition. | Berkeley : Counterpoint Press, 2020.
Identifiers: LCCN 2019026333 | ISBN 9781640093485 (trade paperback) |
    ISBN 9781640093492 (ebook)
Subjects: LCSH: Short stories, American. | Immigrants—United States—
    Fiction. | GSAFD: Short stories
Classification: LCC PS3608.U2245 A6 2020 | DDC 813/.6—dc23
LC record available at https://lccn.loc.gov/2019026333

Cover design by Donna Cheng
Book design by Wah-Ming Chang

Counterpoint Press
2560 Ninth Street, Suite 318
Berkeley, CA 94710
www.counterpointpress.com

Printed in the United States of America
Distributed by Publishers Group West

10 9 8 7 6 5 4 3 2 1

For my parents

Contents

Deceit and Other Possibilities

Line, Please

Perhaps you've heard of me?

Maybe you've listened to a song by the Jump Boys, a group I fronted, which had three gold records that launched count-less jingles for a remarkable array of consumer products. Or on television, as the host of a reality show where contestants dared to eat horse-cock sandwiches and cling to helicopters zooming over a tropical bay. On billboards, hawking heavy gold watches, cask-aged cognac, or alligator leather shoes, my shirt unbut-toned to reveal six-pack abs.

I didn't think so.

In America, most likely the only reference you've seen of me would be a blurb, news of the weird, along the lines of "those funny Asians, at it again." Video game pets, robot butlers, used schoolgirl panties sold in vending machines, and the sex scandal involving Kingsway Lee, the Hong Kong star whose compromising photos were stolen off his laptop, posted on the web, and played out in the tabloids.

Thousands of shots from my cell phone, scoring with scores of women: the actress wife of my former bandmate; the Canto-pop star and lover of a reputed mobster; and the daughter of a shipping magnate with ties to Beijing and the Red Army.

I've been forced to flee to the safest place I could think of, where no one would recognize me: my hometown.

TRYING TO FLAG down the pork rib cart, Ma waves as frantically as a passenger in a life raft toward a distant light.

"Ma, she'll be back again." I'm jumpy and jet-lagged from last night's sleeping pills and this morning's Red Bull. Her contortions turn vigorous, like martial arts or semaphore, aggressive to assure the best dishes for her family.

Risky, for me to suggest going out and possibly blow my cover, but I am still pretending I returned home this summer for a long-overdue visit. I have yet to discuss what happened with my parents, who don't know that hours after *The Look*, Hong Kong's biggest tabloid, published my photos online, my cell phone began clicking and hissing, and my archived messages mysteriously disappeared—signs that I must have been hacked, placed under surveillance, and my whereabouts pinpointed. Paparazzi swarmed the entrance to my building, a triad offered a reward for my hacked-off hand, and I'd left that night.

Yet on my first public outing in America, no one recognizes me, which hurts more than I want to admit. How dim, my star across the Pacific. Surely, someone in Chinatown might stare for too long, might whisper with excitement, might acknowledge the calamity that swept me to these shores. Evidence of fans, women my parents could blame for preying upon their firstborn and only son.

Ba serves my sister a shrimp dumpling. "Seafood is brain food. For the baby."

"For me too," Ellen says, though we all know her son, in utero, has usurped her in our father's heart.

Hybrid vigor—her genes, bred with her husband's Irish ones, will create superior offspring, healthier and resistant to disease—according to Ba. In retirement, he's become obsessed with orchids: joined a local club, won prizes at shows, and traveled to buy specimens, lavishing more attention on the flowers than he has on his children. A refined undertaking, noble as learning calligraphy or playing the zither, awakening a sense of beauty suppressed during the many years he designed utilitarian freeways and bridges. From his backyard greenhouse, he coaxed elegant blooms from leathery bulbs and debuted them at Ellen's wedding in the bouquets, boutonnieres, and centerpieces.

I'd skipped the ceremony because I'd been on location for a movie in the far western deserts of China. A role supposed to propel me to greater stardom, a swords-and-slippers epic, endlessly delayed and over budget, expected to be a contender for the foreign-film Oscar and attract the attention of Hollywood. The movie flopped.

The scandal hit a few months later, first breaking on the website of *The Look*, whose publisher, Pius Lam, I had once considered a mentor. Sik si gau. Shit-eating dog. Close as family to me and my girlfriend, Vivienne. We called him Uncle Lam. One day we're cruising on his yacht, and the next he's calling me a haam sup lo, a salty wet man, a pervert, on the cover of every magazine in his empire.

A flash fires beside me. Instinctively, I turn to the left, my good side, before realizing the true center of attention: a chubby little emperor, dressed in a dark blue kung fu suit and a round cap, posing for the camera phone. My hands twitch in my lap. I left mine at home in the refrigerator, hadn't turned it on since landing, to keep people from tracking me. My neck feels strange upright instead of tilted in prayer over my phone, checking for messages on social media in between takes, coming off the set at 3 a.m., and on the limo ride home from a club. The endless high-fives online, in-jokes, and easy approval that Vivienne can't supply.

Although I invited my family to various premieres and award ceremonies in Asia, they never came. Not even Ma. Too busy, they said, and after a while, I stopped asking. Ellen offers me a glistening dumpling, her chopsticks crossing in the back, not staying parallel. Her ineptitude cheers me up. She never holds her chopsticks correctly, no matter how often Ba coaches her. Ellen was my first audience, watching with reverential absorption as I conquered video games, clapping when I moonwalked and when I juggled, hobbies of a teenager with a lot of time on his hands.

Full, I block my plate with my hand. Ellen flushes, and the look she gives me—tightening around her eyes, the parenthesis around her mouth—before smoothing into an uneasy grin, makes me almost certain she's seen the photos, seen what no sister should see of her brother.

I can't breathe. Ba fumbles with his chopsticks, the chicken feet splatting on the tablecloth. Ma purses her coral lips. Probably, they know too.

Ma plops a zongzi onto my plate, nimbly unwrapping the leaf with her chopsticks. By stuffing our faces, we can avoid discussion. Though Ma favors me, she finds me suspect, maybe from the time she caught me scribbling answers for my first-grade spelling test in my palm. She scrubbed so hard that my hands were raw for days. She despised cheaters and shortcuts. With honest hard work, you could achieve your every goal. "Xiao cong ming," she'd called me. Clever-clever, trivial victories at the expense of the significant. To her, Hong Kong is a corrupt city that welcomes my sort of thinking, a place where success comes not from diligence, but from deficiency.

My skin goes moist and sticky as though I had plunged into a bamboo steamer basket. In my other life, I'd rarely been at a loss for words, not with scripts and teleprompters. I hand a server the bill along with a stack of twenties and fend off my parents with my elbow. Their generation lives for a showy fight over the check, tugging, sitting on it, and chasing down the server to pay. Neither one reaches for the bill and I can't help but feel slighted.

I bolt, muttering I'm going out for a smoke, and at the entrance, I stop short to avoid barreling into a woman with her back to me. Her arms are attractively muscled, defined, not the pale twigs in vogue in Hong Kong, where women in my circles lack the strength to lift their arms above their heads and have wrists no bigger than a kindergartner's. Her tanned skin has a creamy latte glow. Delicious, not the watery skim-milk complexions to which I have become accustomed.

My neighbor, Jenny Lin.

My family has dined at Legendary Palace since I was a kid, and my parents often bump into neighbors coming from the suburbs to Oakland Chinatown to eat and shop. But the coincidence of running into her feels like another blooper in the gag reel of my life. Jenny Lin. I'd always envied her popularity. How she knew what to say, as though reading from a script, how easily she slid into crowds, clubs, and committees. Since the first grade, teachers and classmates expected us to be friends because we were both Chinese, in a town with few Chinese families, and our last names were Lee and Lin, which meant that our photos appeared next to each other in the yearbook. Annoying, how others tried to get us to play together and, later, expected us to date. A matched set. Who better to squire her to Winter Formal than the Oriental in alphabetical proximity?

Which is why we had steered clear of each other in high school, why we never partnered in biology and never paired off in P.E., why we hadn't stayed in touch in the years since.

A DECADE AGO, Hong Kong had thrilled me like no other place I'd been. Grimy, glittering, pulsing. After my freshman year at Cal, I was visiting my aunt on a stopover on my way to Taiwan. My first passport, my first overseas trip, and though I was jet-lagged, and though I didn't speak Cantonese, I knew within hours of getting off the plane that I wanted to live there someday. My parents didn't know the med school future they'd planned for me was in peril after I'd flunked organic chemistry. In the absence of their ambitions, I was beginning to find mine.

At an outdoor electronics mall, I haggled with a vendor over a video game, via a calculator and caveman English. Afterward, a stranger sidled up and said I sounded like a rapper. A rapper?

"You from California?"

When I nodded, he brightened and asked if I'd ever modeled.

Senior year, I'd appeared once in my yearbook, stiff and pained in my formal portrait, as though I were encased in a back brace. I'd since shed my glasses and shape-shifted with protein shakes and weight lifting, but this question had to be a scam. I wasn't a model. I was a failed pre-med, a fuck-up son. As I turned away, the man handed me his card and explained he was a talent scout.

I didn't know then that my kind charmed in Asia: someone who looked Chinese but spoke and carried himself like a Westerner. The American exotic—beach lifeguards, football, cowboys—made accessible through us. We were chop suey, orange chicken, egg foo yung, Chinese and yet not, American and yet not.

The photo shoot for a bottled grass jelly drink seemed legit. The scout didn't fleece me with an up-front fee, and miraculously, the makeup artist with the smoky voice and smoky eyes seemed to be flirting with me. With me! In high school biology, the teacher had explained that asexual organisms, like the amoeba, divided and reproduced without a partner. When the teacher asked for more examples, someone blurted, "Kingsway."

Until that moment in Hong Kong, I had been nobody,

nothing to no one. When the makeup artist leaned in, enveloping me with her musky scent, when her breasts pushed against my arm, I thought I might pass out. She wasn't interested, I told myself, until she asked what I was doing that night. To be wanted like that made me feel like a superhero, like I could fly or stop bullets with my hands.

After the shoot, the scout asked if I was available for a television show, adding that I wouldn't need to audition because the booker owed him.

Did I need a work permit?

"I get, I get," he said. A favor from another contact. "Rush job." My initiation into Hong Kong's network of connections, shortcuts, and open disregard of rules that my mother would have scorned. I canceled my plane ticket, my ad appeared in the subway, and strangers began recognizing me: a bigger, brighter version, me all along, like a moth's hidden brilliance, exposed by ultraviolet.

I kept thinking my runaway fame was a practical joke, that I'd wake up and revert to the loser I'd been. Instead I became a star.

JENNY GAZES OVER the balcony onto the plaza below where children whoop and chase each other around the fountain. Over the loudspeaker, the hostess squawks "eighty-nine" in Cantonese and English. Jenny checks her slip of paper, and I wheel toward the elevator. Catching sight of me, she calls out my name. I grit my teeth into a smile, face her, and to my surprise, she throws her arms around me. As I return her embrace, a dangerous heat lights in me.

"Back from Hong Kong?" she asks. We break apart. She's followed my career, at least nominally. Her parents, watchful and amused, hover nearby like chaperones at a school dance.

"Taking a break." I wonder what she knows. Someone, or a team of someones, has updated my Wikipedia entry with a blow-by-blow of the blowjobs performed by spoiled rich girls, auto-tuned singers, and cue-card actresses. The sheer magnitude in the aggregate might appear staggering. Nothing on the order of Wilt Chamberlain's twenty thousand women, but three or so each week add up—an equation of no comfort to Vivienne, whose status as my girlfriend hangs in doubt.

"You might have traveled the farthest," she says. "Unless Ben comes from Brazil."

It takes a second to realize she's referring to our high school reunion, our tenth, held tonight in San Francisco. The invitation had piled up with the rest of the mail addressed to me that kept arriving at my childhood home, as though I led a parallel life that fulfilled the expectations of my parents.

Ellen waddles up, rubbing her fist into the small of her back. Jenny hugs her, a squeeze from the side to avoid her pregnant belly. Somehow, she and my sister have become friends. Life here has continued without me, the college degrees and weddings that I once wanted. Jenny asks about the progress of my sister's pregnancy.

"He kicks so much, I wish he'd kick his way out." Ellen sinks onto the bench and slides her swollen feet out of her Birkenstocks.

"Have you tried the foot massage? Across from the library?" Jenny asks.

"I don't trust those cheap Chinese places."

A foot massage parlor, in our hometown? Seeing my puzzled expression, Ellen explains that these shops are popping up everywhere, the latest cut-rate Chinese export.

"Have you picked a name yet?" Jenny asks.

"His first name we won't decide until he's born. But his middle name—Kingsway." Her apology, for ratting me out to my parents? Even still, the honor floors me. A name Ma had chosen, hoping I might follow the king's way. When Jenny smiles at me, I feel something akin to déjà vu. Like a fast-forward hallucination to a time when Jenny and I are paired off, meeting my family on a routine weekend. As if I could trade one life for another, as if I am choosing scripts, tossing aside a drama in favor of a rom-com. I'd done it once already, gone from nerd to superstar. I picture us slow dancing at the reunion, Jenny's head tucked against my chest, my hands stroking her waist. In this flick, I would right wrongs from those years. I wouldn't arrive by helicopter, Porsche, or elephant, but I could talk about filming on location, about projects in the pipeline, vague enough to impress and vague enough for me to believe my future remained in reach.

"We can ride over together." I swallow hard. Carpool: too gutless to ask her out.

Her smile widens, as if she'd been waiting for me to ask, waiting since graduation. "I'll drive."

IN MY ATTRACTION to Jenny, I've betrayed my girlfriend again.

None of the photos posted online had been taken after I started dating Vivienne. Well, almost none. I'd hooked up with my costar, Bobo Sun, a few nights before filming our love scene, to ensure our chemistry on-screen. And every once in a while, with starlets Yoyo, Kimmee, and Cherry. Nothing serious, like my films, which wavered between violin-string sentimentality and slide-trombone silly from one scene to the next. With each rumored affair that I denied, with each inch of ink in Uncle Lam's celebrity magazines, my star rose, shining bright onto Vivienne.

Worldly as Vivienne was—fluent in Cantonese, Mandarin, English, and French, and a graduate of the top business school in Europe, educated among the children of diplomats and industrialists—my fame fascinated her. I'd seen her at the usual clubs, the usual restaurants, and she'd brokered a lunch, seeking a pitchman. We began dating not long after.

The day the scandal broke, we'd been lazing in bed, in sheets ripe with the scent of sex and sweat. I had a business proposal for her, but I was having trouble thinking about anything beyond her nails scratching my back in slow circles, on the edge of drawing blood. In truth, she was a bit of a bitch, with an alluring abrasiveness, like a grain of sand in a pearl, beauty born from irritation. Her temper was appealing after years of compliant groupies.

"Harder."

When I reached for the script on the floor, she propped herself up. "You get older, but the characters stay the same age."

She had a point. I couldn't play a teen heartthrob forever.

With each year, I'd seem more and more like a loser dropout lurking at the high school. Like a pervy uncle who lingers around his niece's friends. My accidental success had been a windfall, a blessing—what I was owed after my early, unhappy years. But I needed an exit strategy before I stopped getting offers for starring roles, before I became pathetic. These days, Beijing toddlers gorged on McDonald's and learned English from Disney, and my Western upbringing was no longer as glamorous.

Vivienne was always pushing me to think beyond the next line and the next script.

"You settle because it's easy."

If I didn't watch out, I could end up in the kiddie movie ghetto. My robot-detective flick had been a box office hit and my fans were getting alarmingly young. Like the toddler who had tackled my legs the other day. I almost hadn't recognized his mother: Uncle Lam's ayi, as stout and sturdily built as a peasant. She wore a clingy black dress, her hair fell in artful waves, and she slung a limited-edition bag over her shoulder, the kind sewn by French artisans, delivered on unpredictable schedules and in scarce quantities. I hadn't seen his housekeeper lately, hadn't seen her in a long while, actually—had it been years? I'd posed with her son, and the ayi had been so nervous that she'd fumbled with her phone. Starstruck, though hadn't she seen plenty of celebrities around Uncle Lam? My own phone had vibrated, and when I checked the screen, the toddler lunged for it. Every kid loves getting his picture taken, and so I obliged, tucking him into a one-armed hug for the shot.

Maybe I'd go into directing, or get out of the movie business entirely. Padding into the kitchen, I grabbed a tin of shortbread, manufactured by the baked-goods company Vivienne's great-grandfather founded more than a century ago. I bit into a buttery, crisp wedge, and began the presentation I'd been rehearsing in my head. "What about different flavors? Chocolate chip. Peanut butter and jelly."

"We're not a kid's snack. You Americans and your sweets." She had an annoying habit of declaring my quirks emblematic of my national origins.

"No preservatives. Moms will love it." I ate another, wiping crumbs off my mouth with the back of my hand.

"We're not in lunch boxes." Her family's signature product sold in upscale department stores and duty-free shops.

"Not yet."

"Not ever." She'd take over the family business someday. Although she often hinted I might help expand the brand overseas, nothing I said appealed to her, and I wondered if I should become a consultant elsewhere, advising Americans on how to sell to the Chinese: how to attract followers on social media, how to navigate the backroom deals, how to position luxury cars and handbags, and which Hollywood has-beens to Hasselhoff.

In Hong Kong, you needed to be underhanded to gain the upper hand, to land the role, the cover, and the girl. I had more choices than my parents, whose only ticket out of Taiwan had been in science and engineering. More choices than my sister, too, who dutifully joined my mother's optometry practice. My phone rang nonstop, a tinkling rendition of my No. 1 single, "I

Am the Sun, You Are the Dawn." When I answered, my bellowing agent directed me to *The Look*'s website. Vivienne peered over my shoulder. Scroll, scroll, scroll—click, and up popped a photo of her best friend, Brigitte, her distinctive star-shaped mole, and her collagen-plump lips around my cock. I might have denied everything if it weren't for the next photo, a selfie in the mirror of me entering Brigitte from behind.

Risky, to take the pictures, and riskier to keep them, but I'd believed that someday, if—when—the cosmic prank ended and I reclaimed my destiny as a loser, I'd have the pictures to remind me of my time in the stars. Clever-clever, never thinking the photos would sink me.

The phone slipped from my hand, hit the marble floor, and ended the call. As Vivienne jerked on her silver sequined dress, I flung open the safe where I stored my DVDs with the only copies of the photos. Still there. How then? Months ago, I'd deleted the original files from my hard drive. Then I remembered my laptop had died. Last week, the technicians, recommended by Uncle Lam, had recovered my files. Maybe they'd found more, for someone else. For Uncle Lam?

Not him, not the man who talked me up to Vivienne's parents and in his magazines. He wasn't Vivienne's uncle by blood, but by long association, and her parents were always hinting she should date his son. I'd overheard Uncle Lam rooting for me. "A pretty girl needs a pretty boy. You don't want ugly grandchildren!"

"Smarts last longer than looks," Vivienne's father muttered.

"Be good to the boyfriend, and he'll be good to your daughter," Uncle Lam said.

I tried to live up to his faith in me. I admired him. Feared him too, a man coarse and self-made, who'd escaped China by clinging to an inner tube and swimming to Hong Kong. Yet I couldn't deny that *The Look* was Uncle Lam's flagship publication, and nothing on the cover would appear without his approval. The repair technicians, hadn't he called them "top class"? His guys.

Vivienne seemed to be searching for her shoes, her body stiff as a mannequin's. I'd ruined everything she'd planned for me. For us. I'd ruined her and yet my regret circled back to Uncle Lam. I brushed my fingers along the spines of the DVD cases. Maybe someone else was going to break the story, and Uncle Lam couldn't afford to get scooped. He might have even published the photos to protect me. Yes. From what I could tell, he'd held back the worst, leaving out the foursome and the leather sling. The more I tried to justify, the emptier the excuses sounded, falling away until only one remained: he wanted me gone because he wanted Vivienne for his son.

She hurled her spiked heel and it spun at me end over end like a throwing star. I ducked and it hit the smoked glass of my windows, which rattled but did not shatter. The sidewalk was a long way down from my penthouse. I begged her to stop, told her that the other women meant nothing, that she was everything to me. I didn't know any other lines. When I tried to take her into my arms, she scratched tribal slashes across my cheek, stomped out sans shoes, and hailed a cab. Her solitary, straight-backed figure would play big in the tabloids, *The Look* with the splashiest spread of all.

ALL AFTERNOON, I'VE been watching the cul-de-sac from the bay window for would-be vigilantes. Restless, hopped up on energy drinks and cigarettes, I've been debating if I should cancel on tonight's date with Jenny. My mouth tastes foul, like an ashtray drenched with the sticky remains of a popsicle.

I spot a Chinese woman, dressed in black, sleek as an eel. Her companion, built like a fire hydrant, reaches into the trunk of their car—for a baseball bat? A silenced gun? They walk toward the house. I drop the curtain and fall to my knees, sneezing after dust puffs up from the baseboard of the living room. Mummified flies stud a thick spiderweb between a pot of orchids and the wall. Behind the couch, I find the celadon-green glazed bowls that I sent as a gift years ago, in the original bubble wrap, along with stacks of bills, held together with rubber bands. Bills past due, bills for credit cards, for the car, for my parents' mortgage. Bills from an orchid grower, and from the hospital for a colonoscopy.

Ba has his secrets too: rare orchids that cost $5,000 a stem, requiring expensive nutrients, climate control, and care that rival a preemie's. My parents are in trouble, and I can't deny a certain bitter satisfaction. Their way of life—that my parents can't forgive me for rejecting—has not worked for them, either.

Ma enters with my bespoke tuxedo. Ba left for the plant nursery while she stayed home, one of them always on call for the next month until my sister goes into labor. Ma's steamed the tux by blasting the shower in the bathroom, but it remains wrinkled; I'd left it crumpled in my suitcase after my last hosting gig. She asks why I am on the floor—confused, suspicious, and faintly disgusted.

Heels click up the walk. The henchman will rough me up or worse, tie up Ma, and trash the house. Leaping to my feet, I hustle her into the kitchen. When I reach for the cleaver on top of the chopping block, Ma backs away, fist to her mouth.

"They're after us!" I let go of the cleaver and push Ma out the sliding glass door and onto the cracked concrete patio.

"Who? Who?" Ma holds on to the tux, its legs dragging on the ground, but when I try to take it, she won't let go.

"Out front." We run, awkward as partners in a three-legged race. The greenhouse, we could hide in Ba's greenhouse. Then I picture bullets shattering the glass, shards raining down, blinding and slashing us. Grabbing a bucket, I push Ma toward the cinder-block wall and tell her to climb over.

The people after us might have guns, hurry, go, I say. Ducking her head, Ma steps onto the upended bucket. I boost her up, my hands tight on her waist as she swings one leg and the next over the wall. I climb over and hold out my arms to catch her. She perches before pushing herself off, the tux trailing after her. She slips out of my arms and pitches onto her hands and knees, the tux pooling into the outline of a suicide jumper. Her blouse slides up to reveal the elastic waistband of her underwear and the doughy flesh of her lower back. Her permed curls, dyed Dracula black, are a mess.

I did this to her. Kneeling, I help her up, asking if she can walk. She nods, spittle in the corners of her mouth. A car backfires—or a gun goes off. I dash to the neighbor's house and pound on the back door, while a dog barks on the other side, its nails scrabbling on a tile floor. Ma bends in half, trying to catch her breath. "Police. Call the police," she gasps.

A terrier launches itself through the doggie door and nips at my calves. I kick it off, and it flies, yipping, legs churning through the air. When the terrier regroups, it goes after the legs of my tux. Shit! We tug, the terrier growling, teeth bared, its brass tags jingling against its collar. With a mighty rip, the terrier tears the hem, whipping the black scrap in victory.

Ma pushes me toward the alley, the terrier in pursuit. I knock a garbage can into the terrier's path, giving me time to unlatch the gate. Diapers, potato peelings, and a bloody meat carton spill to the ground. As I slam the gate shut, the terrier leaps onto its hind legs. I plunge through the bushes and into the yard of Jenny Lin, where she and her mother are climbing out of their Mercedes, their arms stuffed with silver shopping bags.

Back when I resisted friendship with Jenny, so too did my parents with hers. My parents considered themselves scholars, in contrast to the Lins, who ran McDonald's franchises. Junk food, my mother had sniffed. That the Lins prospered—with their luxury cars and remodeled Tuscan-style house—must have galled my parents.

Leaves are strewn through Ma's hair and a twig has scratched her cheek. My suede sneakers stink of rotting garbage, and my tux hangs soiled and defeated in my arms. Jenny rushes over, asking if we need help while Mrs. Lin clutches a plastic garment bag to her chest like a shield.

"I—we—" I say. My hookups—my entire existence in Hong Kong—had been possible because of the camera's omnipresence. Framing the shot, zooming in, I watched as though outside of myself, performing the playboy, on and off the set, in and out of the bedroom. The lens now shuttered, I no longer know how to act.

"Want to come in?" Jenny asks. "Rest for a few minutes?"

"You have to get ready for tonight." Ma pats her hair back into place. She has regained her dignity after being tossed through the spin cycle.

"I'm not home that often," I say.

"Jenny comes to dinner every week." Mrs. Lin says.

"Unfortunately, I have to bow out," I say.

"Kingsway can go." Ma takes my tux. If I were a child, she would have pinched my arm to silence me. She doesn't like Mrs. Lin acting as though Jenny is too good for me.

None of us notice the strangers until they are upon us. Not a henchman, but a photographer and Maisie Chan, senior writer from Hong Kong's classiest glossy. Published by Uncle Lam's rival, a fact I register with perverse satisfaction.

I straighten and attempt a pensive, humbled expression. The photographer snaps Jenny in the doorway, turning her into an instant, unwitting celebrity. Mrs. Lin gives me an appraising look, but Ma seems fed up. A television camera crew, or Hong Kong's Oprah, or Oprah herself would not impress my parents. I could show them my online feed, pictures of my fans, but my parents would never understand what I achieved, would never consider my success honest and deserved, and the longer I remain here, the more I'll come to forget too.

"How long do you plan to stay?" Maisie points her digital recorder at me.

"No comment." My reply to that question and every follow-up. Whether I'd been in contact with Vivienne or the other women. Whether I'd been blackmailed.

Frustrated, the reporter asks if I could comment on the rumored biopic. News to me. Good news.

"Can't say." I add a cocky smile, to imply a major deal, an international cast, and flashy locations. To awe Jenny, Ma, and the reporter.

"By Zen Ecstasy, yes?" Maisie says. An adult entertainment company. "Is porn the best move for your comeback? Or the only move?"

I gape as the photographer clicks away. I grab at the lens, he sidesteps me with a fullback's brawny grace, and I almost tumble to the ground. I must seem drunk and deranged. Bowing my head, I take a deep breath and, when I look up, offer a rueful smile. I softly promise Maisie an exclusive interview, tomorrow at our home. Summoning the dregs of my charm, I shake her hand with my right and stroke her arm with my left. Maisie melts.

"I'll make lunch for you." I promise her never-before-seen candid childhood photos.

After she and the photographer drive off, I shrug with a nonchalance I do not feel. "The rumors are crazy in this business. Crazy."

"Crazy," Jenny echoes.

Taking me by the elbow, Ma says it's getting late. As we leave, I overhear Mrs. Lin asking what I'd done.

"I'll tell you later," Jenny says. I haven't fooled her. She must have discovered the latest details online, but is too polite to back out, she might pity me, her fallen classmate, or she wants a racy story of her own to tell. I can't start over fresh with her. It isn't a chance I'm certain I want, or even a chance I'm certain I had, but the loss stings all the same.

We walk home in silence. In the living room, I wait for Ma to berate me, and when she doesn't, I understand that she has resigned herself to such behavior from her unredeemable son. I envy my nephew's bright blank future.

"Let's go to the House of Prime Rib," I say desperately. The only non-Chinese restaurant my parents patronize, with dark wood paneled walls, white table clothes, burgundy leather booths, and silver carts bearing magnificent sides of beef—fancy and hearty enough to justify the expense. There, I'd tell my parents I would rescue them.

In the slanting afternoon sunlight, Ba's orchids glow with the saturated colors of stained glass in a cathedral, of jewels on the throat of a queen, of the rings of a gaseous giant in space. Our fixations define us, have overtaken us both, and I have to save him as I myself want to be saved.

"I'll get a reservation," I say.

"Daddy's cholesterol," Ma says. No prime rib, not tonight, no longer. In the six years since my last visit, my parents have grown old and the house has fallen into disrepair. She fingers the tux's torn pants. "I'll find a pair of Daddy's to match the jacket."

When I protest, she cuts me off. "Distance tests a horse's

strength." She's decided I dropped out of the race before it began. Our lives have each met failure, though my parents never slid into the shadows that bred darkness. They're probably going to refuse my help, refuse my tainted money, and the loss of their respect hurts most of all.

Ma sighs. "You can only defend yourself with the character you have. The rest we must bear."

WHEN I ENTER Master Wang's Foot Clinic, a bell tinkles, but the masseuse on duty doesn't look up, engrossed in her cell phone. I blink, my eyes adjusting to the dim light. Padded recliners draped in towels take up most of the space, and a water fountain bubbles in the corner, drowned out by the movie on the large flat screen, *When a Wolf Falls in Love with a Sheep*. I'd turned down the lead role. If only I could land a part like that again.

I'm supposed to be on the Bay Bridge by now, awkwardly flirting with Jenny on our way to the reunion. Instead I'm here, dressed in my sponged-off tux jacket paired with my father's pants, inches too short and ballooning at the waist. I had walked to Jenny's house but felt compelled to keep going. As I passed the tennis courts, the bus stop, and headed down the hill toward the village, sweating in my overcoat, I was already telling myself I could catch a train and meet her in San Francisco later.

After I clear my throat, the masseuse drags over a wooden bucket lined in plastic, and returns with a kettle of herbs steeped in steaming water. The smell hits me with the musty, ancient knowledge that I associate with herbalists. A reflexology poster on the wall diagrams the secret pathways coursing through our bodies. The health of our spleen and our eyes rests upon the soles of our feet. Superstition, not science, yet now nothing but this touch will do. I can't remember what this storefront housed in my childhood, but I am amazed China has seeped into the suburbs. It feels like I could be in Hong Kong, Beijing, Bangkok, Tokyo, or Taipei, any city where these copycat foot massage parlors have proliferated. My life in Asia is distinct, a universe apart from my hometown, and this breach seems a violation.

The masseuse gestures for me to take off my shoes and roll up my pants. None of the privacy, none of the luxury, none of the oils or hot stones of a Western-style massage, but only $25 per hour. I toss the overcoat onto the recliner beside mine.

Sullen, with dead eyes, the masseuse might be in her early twenties. With her hair dyed auburn and wearing tight boot-cut jeans, she's in the target demographic of my songs and movies. I wonder how she ended up in my hometown, if she moved for adventure, opportunity, or debt, if she lives illegally in the back, and if she finds the suburbs baffling, boring, or serene?

The foot bath scalds, but when she asks, "OK?" I nod, welcoming the pain.

The movie's music blares. "Could you turn it down?" I ask. She gives me a blank look, until I ask again in Mandarin. "Do you have anything else?"

In her native tongue, the masseuse turns giggly and chattering. She brings out a binder of DVDs, and on the last page, I find one of my early lead roles, playing the undercover bodyguard of a daffy heiress. My fame has reached the land of my birth. I hold the disk gently between my thumb and forefinger, rainbows winking in the silver—light, fragile, and disposable.

She takes the DVD from me. "I don't remember this."

I can't remember much of the plot, or any of the lines. How vulnerable I look, my cheeks smooth, my innocent face topped by floppy bangs. The masseuse, drying off my feet with a threadbare towel, doesn't make the connection. I force myself to laugh, hating the hollow sound, hoping the masseuse might look up, might recognize me, might tremble with excitement, but then the DVD skips.

The shop's phone rings, and while the masseuse takes down information in the appointment book, I squirm, staring at my pixelated face, my voice stuttering, every hidden sin surfacing. In the intervening years, my youthful promise has gnarled, stunted, and I am gutted, reminded of how much I have lost. To my relief, after she blows off the dust, the DVD won't play further. She turns off the television and wipes my face with a hot towel, the steam loosening the tightness behind my eyes, and the practical yet soothing ritual is a hint of Hong Kong. I lean back and close my eyes.

The fountain trickles loudly, but not enough to hide her camera clicking, a sound I can detect from yards away, like a prairie dog turning its ear to the wind. Peeking, I see her snapping pictures from her cell phone. She must have known all along. She slips it into her back pocket, unaware she's been caught. She kneads her knuckles into the soles of my feet, strong but unskilled, each letup sweet after a burst of pain. "Some men's feet are ugly. Toenails black, falling off, calluses thick enough to strike a match on."

Not mine, regularly waxed and nails buffed. I direct her to the hollow area under my ankle that corresponds to reproduction and pleasure. In her hesitation, I sense she knows what the spot represents. She touches lightly, a dandelion on the wind, and all at once my confidence returns. I take her hand in mine and dig my thumbs into her palm. Her hands are small, a child's, and the skin is rough. I pull her toward me. Her lips, slicked with cherry lip gloss, land on my chin, and her eyes are open and startled. Her first kiss? I recoil. Anything more, anything from me, would set her spinning far off course. She kicks over the tub, splashing us with the force of Shamu and soaking the carpet. Mopping up with towels, we knock heads hard enough to go breathless. In a screwball comedy, this encounter would have been a meet-cute, except for the soaked crotch of my pants and the ache in my groin. Except for the lump on my forehand. Except for how young and frightened the masseuse looks, huddled on the ground.

The bell over the door jingles, and a burly man enters. With thick fingers and the stooped shoulders of a mole, he must be Master Wang, of Master Wang's Foot Clinic. He drops his grocery bags and rushes toward us, his fists raised.

"Meimei!" His daughter.

MASTER WANG IS fast, but I am faster. As twilight falls, I take off toward the park, and twice his fingertips scramble for the collar of my jacket. When he grabs a fistful, cursing me and ten generations of my ancestors, I shrug off the tux and race on. I round the corner of the outdoor stage and duck behind scaffolding. He staggers past. Clawing through bushes, I stumble down a ravine and into a dry creek bed, on the run from what feels like every father, husband, boyfriend, and brother I have wronged.

By now, Jenny would have stopped by our house. By now, my parents would know I'd gone missing. I exhale, my heart pounding, and for the first time since I've arrived, I turn on my phone and find hateful messages and posts, with a few supporters—very few—and nothing from Vivienne. All thanks to Uncle Lam.

"Come out and fight!" Master Wang sounds like he's on the verge of a stroke. He wants to avenge his daughter, to protect her now and always from men like me. Like Uncle Lam, who must have intended to drive me out by publishing the photos. Not for the sake of his son, I now realize, but for the sake of Vivienne. He loves her like a father. And hasn't every possible suspicion a father might have had about me been confirmed in Hong Kong and made plain again just now? I can't be trusted with decency or love.

Master Wang taunts me. "Guaishushu." An odd uncle, a pedophile. A pedophile! To him, his daughter will always be his little girl, but she had pressed against me. The women in Hong Kong had followed me into the bathroom, had balled their panties into my hand, calling, "Kingsway, Kingsway!" They'd smiled for the camera.

Uncle Lam has cast me as the villain, and he won't stop until he destroys me. If he were an emperor, he'd kill off my entire clan, and I have to hit him as he hit me. I swipe through the pictures on my phone, of Vivienne, of me and my young fan—the son of Uncle Lam's housekeeper, and quite possibly the son of Uncle Lam, the same watermelon-seed eyes and flared nostrils. I don't have confirmation, but I don't need it. In my pocket, I find the reporter's business card, the one who worked for Uncle Lam's publishing rival. I draft a message, attaching the boy's photo, the love child of Uncle Lam and his ayi. The reporter tracked me around the globe and she'd chase a rumor this juicy.

Easy, to fall back into the dirty water where I thrive. Clever-clever I'd been, and clever-clever I'd always be. Footsteps approach, panting and crashing through the bushes, loud as surf. My fingers hover above the send button. I have time enough to regret all my mistakes tonight, tomorrow, and tomorrow. But not just yet.

Loaves and Fishes

Of all the signs and wonders Prophet Alex Chan had ever witnessed, none stunned him as much as the stranger coming down the aisle during final boarding. The flight attendant had begun to shut the doors when the man in a gray hoodie and sunglasses slipped past her.

Prophet Alex prayed that the man would go by, leaving the middle seat empty on the red-eye from San Francisco to Hong Kong. On flights, the white-noise hum of the engines and the stale recycled air made his mind receptive to God's small, still voice. The window-seat passenger had draped her plaid scarf over her head, trying to sleep, but the stranger most certainly would step over Prophet Alex to sit down and most certainly would crowd the armrest.

He didn't have a carry-on, the unencumbered sort of man who never handled a piece of paper or had to wait in lines. Sunglasses at night: trying hard not to be recognized, he'd turned conspicuous. When the man stood beside him, apologizing in a husky voice, Prophet Alex recognized him. Kingsway—the Hong Kong pop star, Kingsway Lee, in coach! An improbability great as a plague of frogs, great as God descending into a burning bush, great as a man walking across water.

Which is to say, a miracle, when Prophet Alex needed one most. He tried to catch Kingsway's eye, but the star bent his head over his phone, his thumbs pumping like pistons. The flurry of chirping replies alerted the flight attendant.

"Sir." A brittle blonde, with the desiccated skin of a woman bombarded by solar radiation at high altitudes. "Your phone needs to be in airplane mode."

With an apologetic smile—a smile that belonged in the light of a thousand paparazzi's flashbulbs—Kingsway fiddled with the settings. Her stride faltered, and a giddy smile overcame her, as if she'd been gassed with nitrous oxide. She turned her back and Kingsway resumed texting, with an intensity that suggested his fate rested on each tap.

Rain lashed the scratched Plexiglas windows, blurring the lights of the ground crew at SFO. The late-November storm had delayed the flight for forty minutes, and it was windy tonight, had been for days, strong enough to down power lines and blow apart heaps of leaves. The seatback screens, playing an introductory loop, froze and the picture pixelated, a hiccup in the in-flight entertainment system. Last year, Prophet Alex had taken a cross-country trip on which the system malfunctioned, turning the passengers restless and rude. On this thirteen-hour flight, if the system shut down, mutiny might break out. After the flight attendant flipped the latches on a wall cabinet and hit a reset button, white numbers and letters cascaded down everyone's screens, like ancient computer code for a voyage to the moon.

The flight attendant noticed Kingsway texting again, and told him to put his device away. He apologized and slipped the phone into the kangaroo pocket of his hoodie, but within moments, he was texting again. His hands furtive and compulsive, as if he were jacking off on a park bench. Prophet Alex peeked at an incoming message in a cartoon bubble: "Not now, not ever."

Kingsway was an American-born singer and actor who had found fame—and now infamy—in Asia. All those pictures, all those naked starlets in Hong Kong, stolen off his laptop and circulating on the web. After the summer, he'd disappeared from the headlines. In hiding, Kingsway might have tried to carve out another life, gone back to school or attempted a new line of work. Prophet Alex had contemplated the same, and Kingsway must have also realized he wasn't fit for any other calling.

FIVE MONTHS AGO, the world had continued as usual, but Prophet Alex's life had not. For almost a year, he'd told his followers to prepare for an earthquake and tsunami on June 9. He'd dreamed of a massive wave that swamped the Golden Gate, its cables snapping, towers collapsing as a roiling wall of water swept around the Transamerica Pyramid and turned San Francisco's fourteen hills into fourteen islands. After the waters receded, neighborhoods were pulverized, strewn with crumpled cars, smashed boats, and snapped matchstick bodies.

He preached about the coming disaster, and his followers

had stockpiled water, canned food, and medical supplies. Although he didn't have his own church, he traveled the country, staging prayer meetings and revivals at colleges and universities. He stirred people with his message of accepting and not trying to earn God's love, about the difficulties of honoring your parents while putting the Lord first. ("You're thinking, Idolatry? The golden calf? False idols? Your parents on a pedestal are no different.") His fans followed him on social media and downloaded his holy hip-hop hits, "Liteshine" and "U Want Him."

On the appointed day, he and two dozen of the most faithful gathered on Mount Tam to greet the dawn with songs. Prayer warriors clad in work boots, cargo pants, and heavy leather gloves, armed with video cameras to document the disaster and their relief efforts that would open hearts to Jesus. Hawks had wheeled and floated on the wind fragrant with the scent of eucalyptus and sage, in a blessed quiet he would never forget. Far below, June gloom had obscured much of San Francisco, smothering the city like tailpipe exhaust, which he hadn't seen in his dream, but he wasn't nervous, not until early afternoon, when their voices had gone hoarse and they'd run out of songs. People checked their email and surfed the web, the signal strong from a world that carried on. Then they left.

Prophet Alex had been certain, but he must have misunderstood. The Lord meant next year, or a decade from now. After all, John the Apostle's vision of the Apocalypse—the four horsemen, the seven-headed dragon, the sun black as sackcloth, and the moon like blood—had yet to come to pass. Or maybe the earthquake had been averted through prayer; the people of

Nineveh had been spared from destruction after they repented, fasted, and prayed. Perhaps he was supposed to learn that no one could predict the ways of the Lord. Another lesson: he'd flown too high, assumed too much, and God wanted him on his knees.

No one had died, no one had been hurt, and it might have blown over except online commentators posted to a discussion board, picking him apart, calling him a false prophet, a celebrity pastor, a con man not only because of this campaign but the Happiness Project, One Thousand Hugs, Burritos-by-Bicycle to the homeless—every bit of his brand as a preacher, motivational speaker, hip-hop artist, and faith healer. Sales plummeted on his Christian singles and his T-shirts, baseball caps, and mobile phone covers with his slogan "Crazy love." Churches and campus clubs canceled speaking engagements. Wings clipped, back living with his parents, he couldn't sleep, couldn't eat. When he tried to read the scriptures for comfort, for an explanation for his misery, the verses swarmed before him. He couldn't catch them, any more than he could catch cinders flying off a fire. Nothing made sense. It was said such suffering was necessary, to share the pain of Jesus on the cross. To be humbled. To be purified. To shape servants of the Kingdom. Excuses, all. Nothing true but this: God had forsaken him.

Then, like a rainbow over a flooded world—hope. God led him to an online ad for Awaken, a youth revival in Hong Kong, the kind that used to host him as a keynote speaker.

He booked the next available flight on the last of his airline miles, a week before Thanksgiving, though he didn't know where he'd stay, how to get on the conference schedule, or what

he'd say. He'd redeem himself in a city where born-again bil-
lionaires built scale-model replicas of Noah's Ark in the harbor,
where spectacle was a measure of faith.

KINGSWAY GNAWED ON his thumbnail, and he jiggled his
right leg in an electrocuted beat. Prophet Alex suspected he
wasn't returning victorious to Hong Kong—not without an
entourage and not in coach. He seemed shipwrecked, lost. And
Prophet Alex had found him. All at once, he realized why they'd
each boarded this plane. By flight's end, he would share how
he'd been saved. By flight's end, he'd divine secrets known only
to Kingsway—and to God. By flight's end, Kingsway would
agree to appear at the revival, whose organizers would rejoice in
Prophet Alex and his celebrity convert.

Although your mistakes shaped you, you weren't the sum of
them. Judas and Peter had both denied Jesus before his death.
Judas, leading the Roman soldiers to ambush Jesus in the ol-
ive grove. Peter, denying his master three times before the cock
crowed. Both repented, but when Judas hung himself, his betrayal defined him. Peter lived on, served as chief of the apostles,
and his failure of faith didn't become his legacy.

While the airplane pulled away from the gate, Kingsway
jabbed at his phone. If the flight attendant spotted him texting,
if he refused to stop, she'd kick him off.

"Cabin crew, prepare for takeoff," the captain announced.
Prophet Alex unbuckled his seat belt and stood as the flight
attendant approached.

"Sir, sit down."

"I gotta get something—" He stretched his arms, trying to shield Kingsway from her view. "Just give me a sec."

She told Prophet Alex he'd have to wait until the flight reached cruising altitude. Kingsway tucked his phone into his hoodie pocket and nodded at him. Did he understand that Prophet Alex had done him a favor? He might be suspicious of Prophet Alex and his motives, on guard against endless requests for an autograph, a picture, anything that could be sold to the tabloids. Yet he might also resent Prophet Alex, if he pretended he knew nothing about the sex scandal: the photos of the topless tattooed starlet, kneeling on a toilet seat, her back arched like a mermaid's, and the glistening pink shade of Kingsway's erect penis, a wad of watermelon bubble gum, the yawning mouth of a sea anemone.

The flight attendant huffily retreated down the aisle.

"Come fly the friendly skies," Prophet Alex said. Kingsway didn't laugh, didn't say a word as he inserted his earbuds, his message clear: shut up.

Prophet Alex asked God to reveal how he should counsel Kingsway. *Father, hear me. Help—help.*

Tinny music whined from the earbuds as the airplane taxied, jouncing down the runway. Upon closer inspection, Kingsway's glossy surfaces were smudged: a white smear on his black T-shirt, his fingernails ragged, and his shoulders damp with rain. Mud splashed his suede sneakers, stylish but impractical. His movements had a frenetic energy that Prophet Alex recognized—the wired buzz from sleepless nights and too much caffeine.

The engines revved and the plane gained speed, straining, swaying against the gusts. With the shriek of a pterodactyl, the landing gear retracted, and they were aloft, steeply climbing, the world at a tilt. Kingsway had gone pale and clammy as an earthworm. He wasn't aloof. He was afraid to fly.

The plane broke free of the clouds, outrunning the flashes of lightning that had the look of rockets over Baghdad. Kingsway slid his sunglasses off, turned on a movie, and didn't look up when the flight attendants took drink orders and served dinner. As the cabin lights dimmed, Prophet Alex worried that Kingsway might never rise from his movie marathon. He watched so attentively he never blinked, his eyes glassy. Didn't he need to stretch his legs? Kingsway's bent knees brushed against his tray table. Prophet Alex was built like a fighter pilot, and whatever difficulties short men had in this world, sitting in coach wasn't one of them.

On the flight tracker, the plane was cruising along the coast of California, bound for Alaska, crossing over the Bering Strait, Siberia, and speckles of Japan and Taiwan before landing in Hong Kong. Prophet Alex got up and paced, rounding the corner past the galley and front lavatories, praying for divine inspiration.

God. God, please. I have nothing left.

He walked down the other aisle, before turning by the rear lavatories and completing the circuit. Kingsway hadn't budged, and the blue light of the seat-back screen flickered over his handsome face, the sort that launched hit movies, belonged on billboards, and opened hearts to the Lord.

After Prophet Alex made three loops around the body of the plane, lapping an Indian woman in a peacock-blue sari and puffy white sneakers, God answered with an idea so simple, so audacious, he almost laughed out loud. He'd reboot the entertainment system, temporarily disabling it and forcing Kingsway to look up. The system was located in a wall cabinet near the forward galley, where the blond flight attendant bustled with trays. Prophet Alex would have to wait until she left, but the next time he came by, she was stuffing trash into a plastic sack. "Walking all the way to Hong Kong?"

He forced a smile. His armpits and back were wet with sweat. When would she take a break? Nearing the rear lavatories, he caught an oppressive whiff of urine and floral air freshener. The toilet! He'd plug it up and tell the flight attendant, diverting her attention. After locking the door, he stuffed fistfuls of toilet paper into the bowl. He couldn't stand airplane lavatories, the sickly glow of the overhead light, the sticky floors, wet counters, and crumpled paper towels half in, half out of the garbage.

He flushed and the mass disappeared with a violence that made him dizzy. Had he seen a flash of night sky, a glimmer from below, a light on the body of the airplane? He searched for something else to flush. Maxi pads, and also the socks he yanked off and tossed into the bowl. Grimacing as his bare feet touched the floor speckled with bodily fluids, he hit the button and the toilet clogged with the sound of a dinosaur choking on a bone.

Exiting, he noticed the lavatory across the aisle was vacant, which seemed providential. If he caused two clogs, the flight attendant would stay busy, giving him time to figure out the control panel for the entertainment system. His socks were gone, but he could sacrifice his underwear. He dropped his jeans around his ankles, braced himself against the wall with one hand and wiggled out. He caught sight of himself in the mirror, naked from the waist down, above the sign: "As a courtesy to the next passenger, we suggest you use a towel to wipe off the basin." Courtesy? He'd screwed over his fellow passengers, putting the forward toilets out of commission two hours into a transpacific flight.

After Prophet Alex told the blond flight attendant about the mess in both—both!—lavatories, she rushed out of the galley. He checked if anyone was watching, unlatched the wall cabinet, and discovered a touchscreen listing two options for resetting the entertainment system: an individual seat or the entire plane. He swiped "all," closed the cabinet, and returned to his seat. Those awake groaned as numbers and text tumbled down their seatback screens, or looked up from their tablets and e-readers at the commotion. They rubbed their eyes and checked their watches, struck by the unhappy realization they had many miles left before reaching their destination.

Kingsway had slipped off his earbuds and was talking to the passenger by the window, a pretty Chinese girl—Heidi, she said—and judging from her ecstatic expression, she must have recognized him. Kingsway's overhead light was on, but not Heidi's, adding to the sensation that he was shedding his brilliance on her.

"You fly often?" Prophet Alex asked. Neither replied, and he fought back his anger. If Kingsway gave him a chance, he'd see how much they had in common as fallen men. He glared at his tray table, latched crookedly, which he wanted to punch until it lay flat. Everything squeezed him: the seat's dark blue cloth patterned like a casino's carpet, the institutional beige and gray of the plastic interior, the magazines jammed into the seat-back pocket. The rising cabin temperature might have been pleasant in shorts and a T-shirt, but felt punishing now. His skin crawled, his bare feet in his sneakers and his swampy crotch. So thirsty he felt nauseated, he wanted an icy soda, but if he hit the call button, he couldn't look at the flight attendant without confessing.

Kingsway took off his hoodie, his shirt pulling up to expose his abs and the V-shaped cut in the muscles of his torso. He left it crumpled on the seat and waited for the lavatory, in a line that stretched halfway down the main cabin. As the purser made an announcement, warning passengers not to touch the seat-back screen during the system reboot, Heidi leaned over. "What's his name?" she asked. "I know he's famous, but I can't remember his name!"

Carlson Chung, he said. The only other Hong Kong film star he knew of, whose good looks bordered on girlish—flawless skin, a prepubescent gymnast's body, and the huge, surgically enhanced eyes of an anime character—who didn't resemble Kingsway. Cruel, to mislead her, but he wanted Kingsway humbled when she called him the wrong name.

"He's filming a movie in California," Prophet Alex said. A fake detail that would sting if she mentioned the project to Kingsway. "Somewhere by the beach."

"In Santa Monica? We haven't been there since I was a kid."

Her family was wealthy enough to vacation in America. Pills snagged her cashmere sweater, the reddish brown highlights in her hair had grown out, and her shaggy bob was overgrown and greasy. She resembled a lapdog gone missing from its designer tote, about to dash into the street. He understood at once that she—or her family—was struggling. She had a red sketchbook tucked into her seat-back pocket, wedged beside her tablet computer. She might have been a student at that expensive art academy in San Francisco, the one with the bus ads and lax admissions standards, where foreign students paid a fortune for the privilege of a visa.

"My mother loves the ocean," she said wistfully, as if she doubted her family might go again. She toyed with her pendant, a pink crystal ribbon, the international symbol of breast cancer, a logo aiming for the brand recognition of Coke or McDonald's.

"How long has she been sick?" he said, softly, so she'd have to strain to hear, so she'd focus on his words and wouldn't let doubt creep in.

She stared at him. Even the most godless youth were hungry for miracles that might rescue them from a future that held melting ice caps, polluted air, school shootings, a sinking economy, and zombies and vampires bursting through their front doors. Hungry for the meaning and purpose that only God could provide.

"It's cancer, isn't it?" He hadn't planned on giving her a prophecy, but if God touched her, then she might speak on his behalf to Kingsway.

Tears glistened in her lashes, lush and long, fakes applied a hair at a time. "How?" She didn't seem to remember she wore a necklace with an emblem of the disease.

"God knows." Jesus and his apostles performed miracles, revealed secrets, letting their audience experience the Kingdom of God. Then, now, always.

She sucked in her breath. She'd probably confided in no one, crushed under the burden of her family's secret.

"You're an emotional person, with a lot of compassion." A vision of herself she wanted to see. How helpless she must have felt, time zones apart, frustrated by the cryptic communications from her parents, who didn't want her to worry.

When Prophet Alex opened himself to the Holy Spirit, a God-given certainty overcame him, delivering secrets that shocked his listeners. But not always. Sometimes—often—the transmission was garbled, incomplete, or failed to arrive, forcing him to improvise.

His mother, Madame Chan, taught him how. In addition to repairing mobile phones, televisions, DVD players, and other electronics, she told fortunes in the back of their Oakland shop. She charted out lucky dates for marriages and read palms and faces. Thick lips signified honesty and reliability. Thin eyebrows, a cold heart. A wide and deep groove above the lips predicted a smooth life.

As a kid, doing his homework at the shop counter, he'd watched her unraveling their secrets with the authority she lacked in her halting English. She stroked the lines in their palms with an intimacy he never saw pass between his parents, and the clients gasped, awed by this visitation from the gods.

Madame Chan had a gift, they marveled, and for a time, he'd agreed. When she lit the incense, the smoke carried him into the heavens that could not be found in the shrine, draped in red vinyl and buried under plastic lotus flowers and cheap porcelain gods with blurred faces. Many clients traded goods and services for their reading. A grateful stylist permed his mother's hair into a helmet that could have shielded her in a motorcycle crash. Another sent over so many pork buns, to this day, he couldn't stand them. Another dry-cleaned and pressed their clothes, though the sharp crease in his jeans ruined his gangsta style.

If Madame Chan hit upon the truth, worry twisted her clients' faces. If she misspoke, she corrected herself, so quickly the client forgot the error. But if she had a gift, why was her family stuck in the ghetto, working fifteen-hour days? Why didn't she predict the thieves who ripped off their shop a dozen times? She couldn't save her own family or anyone else, and for a short time, before his arrest, he sold weed to give their family the riches they deserved: a designer purse for his mother, a giant flat screen for his father. In juvie, he'd found God, filled with a serenity and love, his heart a kaleidoscope brilliant with light. A first-time high he was forever chasing, that he wanted to share with as many people as he could.

Heidi leaned over her armrest. He probed for conflict, wounds where he might offer solace. "Your father. Some men, when their wives get sick, can't deal."

Heidi frowned, and he backtracked.

"Your father isn't like that. Praise God, he's been at her side from the beginning."

She wrapped her arms around herself. "Is she going to be okay?"

She needed hope, in this life and in the eternal. Hope that she couldn't find anywhere else. He nodded. Amazing, the relief that flooded over Heidi's face, the light in her eyes and her wide smile. "God has a plan for her. For you." Apostle Paul drew followers because he understood their motivations and desires, and adjusted his message accordingly. To the Jews, he became a Jew, to win the Jews. To the weak, he became weak. Becoming all things to all men. Manipulative, but for the highest cause of all: to save their souls.

"You're about to make a big decision," he said. His mother used to say this phrase—for why else would the client seek her out? Heidi dipped her head in affirmation. Most likely, she was choosing whether to leave school and stay in Hong Kong. With each prophecy, he was warming up, like a pitcher going through the windup before a game, preparing himself for visions from the Lord.

The earthquake had seemed like the sacred message he'd been waiting for, but it turned out God hadn't spoken to him. Heidi reminded him of the good he might do. Jolted awake, as if out of a coma, God's grace circling them both. Most passengers were asleep now in awkward positions, as if they'd been hit by knockout gas, and he wanted to tuck blankets under their chins and plump pillows behind their heads. Anyone could find glory in God's mountain vistas, His might in crashing waves, but the spirit was moving in this drab airplane cabin. Pressing a hand to her shoulder, he asked her to pray.

Tentatively, she clasped her hands together—"Like this?"—and closed her eyes.

What he admitted to no one, and would have hid from God if he could, was that the prophecies diminished Creation. A world reduced to types: Good Girls, afraid of their mothers, of life, yet seeking excitement. Mama's Boys, aching for success. Wise Guys, whose defenses fell with enough flattery. But if man was created in God's image, when people flattened and shrank in the eyes of Prophet Alex, so too did God.

He prayed for Heidi's mother, to transform her weakness into strength, but his thoughts returned to Kingsway. With a long line for the bathroom, by the time Kingsway returned, the entertainment system would finish rebooting and he'd plug himself back in, ignoring everyone—unless Prophet Alex swiped his finger across the seatback screen. It locked up, and he felt as Moses must have, parting the Red Sea with a sweep of his hands.

Heidi opened her eyes. He'd trailed off in his prayers. "Let her be filled with patience and joy," he said.

What prophecy could he offer Kingsway? He heard nothing, not even static. Nothing, until he noticed Kingsway's hoodie, cut from the microfiber of an astronaut's spacesuit, left on the middle seat. He continued praying and Heidi closed her eyes. No one was coming down the aisle, but he hesitated. Going through Kingsway's belongings broke the silent covenant everyone made with their neighbors on planes. People believed their fellow travelers would politely pass their drinks and wouldn't stab them in the neck while they were sleeping. Yet hadn't he already violated common decency when he clogged the toilet?

"Restore your servant to full health." He slid the phone from Kingsway's hoodie and touched the screen. He needed a pass code. Lord, oh Lord. Prophet Alex sensed a string of numbers—"1234"—the most frequently used password, he knew, after working at his family's electronics shop. When that didn't work, he tried another combination—"1111"—Kingsway must consider himself No. 1. It worked. Heidi's eyes squeezed shut, her hands clenched together, straining to feel Him. If she caught Prophet Alex snooping, she'd scream. His palms went slick. A few swipes and taps led to vicious texts between someone named Vivienne and Kingsway, each with avatars whose cuteness didn't match the bitter exchange. She, standing on the Eiffel Tower; he, driving a red convertible.

"Miss u," Kingsway had written a day ago, and a few hours later, a pathetic "hey."

"Do me a favor. Delete this number," Vivienne wrote.

His girlfriend? The name sounded familiar, but dozens of women had been linked to Kingsway after the sex scandal.

"im sorry." If Kingsway was apologizing for the first time over text, he didn't have a chance with this woman. Prophet Alex had never snooped like this, but if God had wanted to stop him, Heidi never would have closed her eyes. He peeked at the lavatories and didn't see Kingsway in line. He might return any second, and Prophet Alex put the phone away. "Amen."

"Amen," Heidi repeated after him. She looked refreshed, as if she'd woken up from a massage. She rubbed lotion onto her hands with the scent of vanilla, the chemical sweet of ready-made frosting.

Prophet Alex stepped aside, Kingsway sat down, and Heidi pulled out her sketchbook. She was going to ask for his autograph, ask for the wrong name because Prophet Alex had misled her. Before he could warn her, she blurted, "Carlson, my mother's a huge fan."

Without flinching, Kingsway signed his showbiz rival's name, sparing her the embarrassment, with a kindness and grace that Prophet Alex didn't expect. The entertainment system finished rebooting and every seat-back screen began to work, except for Kingsway's. He rang for the flight attendant.

She pointed at the frozen screen. "You shouldn't have touched it." Another passenger approached, complaining about an overflowing toilet at the front of the plane. In the front? But Prophet Alex had plugged the toilets in the rear. The back of his neck prickled. If all the toilets were connected, then he'd caused an epic clog, his socks, his underwear in a logjam of shit and piss in the bowels of the plane.

Heidi passed the sketchbook to Prophet Alex, asking if they could trade contact information. Kingsway studied him. Until then, he didn't seem to think of Prophet Alex as much of a threat and didn't think her much of a prize. Soon—Kingsway's look said—he'd drape Heidi across his lap, neither the first nor the last of his conquests. Then he seemed to reconsider. Collapsing in on himself, like a rogue wave disappearing into foam, as exhausted and trapped as everyone else on the flight.

"He knows things," Heidi said. "He knew all about my mother."

"Breast cancer?" Kingsway pointed at her pink ribbon pendant. "Your necklace."

Her eyes clouded, the light of her new faith flickering. "But he knew about my father, he knew things no one else knows. He prayed for us."

Kingsway touched her hand. "I wouldn't count on this guy, or anything he promises. He knows what people want to hear. To get what he wants."

"He didn't ask for anything," Heidi said.

Prophet Alex leveled his gaze at Kingsway. "You miss her."

Kingsway rubbed the back of his head and looked around the cabin. "Are you screwing with me? Are we being filmed?"

A flight attendant burst through the first-class curtain, swift and grim as a doctor responding to a code blue, and huddled with the cabin crew by the lavatories. Prophet Alex couldn't hear what they were saying. If all the toilets were broken, the plane would have to land.

"What's her mom's name?" Kingsway asked. "Did God tell you that?"

"Vivienne misses you, too."

"She does?" Kingsway had all but called him a con man, yet he still might believe because he wanted to believe. He shifted in his seat. After his phone slid out of his hoodie and clunked on the floor, he seemed to realize what Prophet Alex had done. "You went through my messages."

Heidi shook her head. "I was here. He didn't."

"You want ten thousand followers of Christ praying for your mother? For you?" Prophet Alex asked. "A million? Come to Awaken this weekend. God will be moving there."

"I'll come," Heidi said. If not for her seat belt, she might levitate through the roof and into the heavens. "My parents too."

"How many?" Kingsway asked.

"Some nights, enough to fill the coliseum," Prophet Alex said. The city's biggest venue. A miracle of numbers, of loaves and fishes multiplied, and the tactic he should have taken with Kingsway from the beginning.

"Who goes?" Kingsway asked.

"High school and college students hungry for the word of God. Hungry to know they're not alone, hungry for God's forgiveness. For God's love."

Kingsway's face filled with longing and desperation, like that of a child reaching for the forbidden on an impossibly high shelf.

A cattle yard smell drifted from the lavatories. The fasten-seat-belt sign went on, and passengers groggily awoke and smacked their lips, dry-mouthed. Prophet Alex suspected the captain would soon announce a change in plans due to the backed-up toilets. He reached for Heidi's hand, over Kingsway's lap. He wanted to form a prayer circle, but Kingsway folded his arms across his chest.

"You may feel strange, up in the air," Prophet Alex said. "But you'll know it, feel it, when you're standing on solid ground."

"Folks, our apologies," the captain said. "We'll be making an unscheduled landing in Anchorage."

Landing. Just as Prophet Alex had predicted. Heidi gasped. The engine noise softened and it felt like the plane was suspended in midair, seconds from plummeting.

"The toilets are inoperable, and we have to clear them. Please stay seated for the remainder of the flight." A few passengers laughed, others muttered in disgust or crossed their legs, regretting the second soda or cup of coffee, jittery and off-kilter from interrupted sleep.

The plane hit turbulence—the straining that accompanied descent, or shaking from the hand of God? A baby wailed, a sound that pierced between the eyes, and the overhead bins rattled so loudly it sounded as if the doors might burst open. Kingsway's breath turned shallow and panicked. His odor gamey and mildewed as a wrestling mat.

If he calmed Kingsway, the star might begin to trust him. But if the panic attack first spiraled, turned into the worst Kingsway had ever suffered, he'd be grateful when Prophet Alex talked him out of it.

"Planes don't crash every day." Prophet Alex dug out the air-sickness bag in the seat-back pocket, and thrust it into Kingsway's face. Kingsway rocked back and forth in his seat as the captain ordered the flight attendants to take their seats.

"We're not going to crash," Prophet Alex said. "Don't think about it. That flight disappearing over the Indian Ocean—that never happens. Almost never."

Groaning, Kingsway dipped his head low, his eyes blank as a drowning victim's.

"Can you lift your arms? Lift your arms," Prophet Alex said. Slowly, Kingsway raised his arms, his fingers limp, as if he were a zombie.

"Up and down. Up and down."

Kingsway complied, though he was panting when told to draw out his breathes for two, four, and finally six seconds. The plane eased off. Prophet Alex rubbed Kingsway's damp back.

A touch that he cherished, whether blessing a newly baptized Christian emerging from the waves, or laying hands on a teenager in the throes of demonic possession. A touch that healed Prophet Alex as much as it healed those he ministered. "I see us on stage." His voice booming, as if he'd never left the pulpit, as if confidence and volume would bring his vision to life. "People are cheering, sending you so much love. They love you, always have, love you even more after you share your story."

He gripped Kingsway's sticky hands. Eventually, Kingsway might believe. Conviction once would have mattered to Prophet Alex, but not now, maybe not ever again. The spotlight at the revival would be bright and blinding as an atomic blast, and the roar fit for Jay-Z. Smoke machines, giant video screens, and purple strobe lights, God blasting like a wall of speakers, he and Kingsway center stage where they belonged. The plane banked sharply and descended. Prophet Alex's ears ached and sounds grew muffled until he could no longer hear himself, only a singsong drone that presumed the voice of God.

What We Have
Is What We Need

Papá could break into any house in the neighborhood.

He would squirt grease and work on the lock, twisting the pins and springs. Although I heard the click indicating that he was in, he fiddled a few minutes longer, so the customers would think they were getting their money's worth. If it was too easy, they looked annoyed and wondered aloud how much the short visit was really worth. Sixty dollars—for less than an hour's work? Or they went into a spasm of fear about how easily burglars could get in.

"Don't worry," Papá would reply, looking at their dusty televisions, black velvet couches, and gilded portraits of La Virgencita. "I think the thieves have other places to go."

The year I turned thirteen, I was learning the trade. I accompanied Papá on weekend house calls in the Mission District, learned the names of the tools, and in a few instances, gave him the right one before he asked for it. He taught me how to file key blanks—but not yet how to pick a lock. That happened only after my mother began to disappear. Up until then, I had been her son. Not my father's.

After one of our house calls that autumn, I dreamed of a magic key that could open all doors. To our neighbor's apartment, to every car parked on the block, and to the doors of a bank vault. No one would be safe before me. Papá laughed when I told him. "Lalo, there's no need for such a key." He could open any lock with his skills, force his way into anywhere. He kissed my mother on the cheek. She put down her wooden spoon and he embraced her, his hand reaching to cop a feel. The leftover refried beans smoked on the stove. My parents broke apart, and Mamá laughed, swatting at him and pulling the pan off the stove. Neither of them looked at me. His grin was smug, possessive, that of a man polishing his gleaming car just to run his hands over the curves. He cupped her butt once more and she leaned into him.

I wanted such powers for myself someday, to win someone like Mamá, but I could not imagine talking to women with such confidence. Even girls my age seemed years ahead of me, with their thick eyeliner, dark red lips, and curves packed into their jeans.

A week later, Mamá and I were walking back from a market when she showed me the flyer for classes in English, math, and computers at a community center, La Gloria Abierta. An unexpected reminder of home, and a phrase my abuelita, my mother's mother, used to say when the money my parents sent her was long gone, when she conjured another meal from an almost empty sack of beans. La Gloria Abierta, or "what we have is what we need." Not the usual meaning of the words, but something deep and old and mysterious.

I should have crumpled the flyer and tossed it into the trash, told my mother that she had no time, that she worked hard enough already and that I needed her more. Mamá cleaned rooms at a big hotel in downtown San Francisco. Before I arrived, she had worked at restaurants and sewing factories, whatever she could find, but the jobs all paid the same: enough for food and rent, and not much to send home, or to save for an immigration lawyer.

The training at the community center might help her get an office job and higher pay, she said. Maybe at an insurance or accounting agency along Mission Street. The plan, like all her plans, was to earn enough money to bring my two younger brothers from Morelia. Jose, dark and compact, with high cheekbones like me and my father, a daredevil who could walk on his hands. Ernesto, the youngest, with a mop of fat curls like my mother's, quiet and shy, my abuelita's favorite. I missed them, but I didn't want them to come here. Not yet. In America, I was an only child, and I liked having all the attention.

My mother and I did our homework assignments together after dinner in the kitchen. The window looked onto the roof of the building next door, covered in gravel and patches of tar, desolate as the moon. A moist, oily smell of grease permeated our apartment, a hint of all the people who ever lived here. Over her books, my mother often paused to rub her eyes and massage her rough hands. We checked each other's homework, but if there was a question of who was right, she deferred to me. She rewarded me with glasses of milk and cinnamon cookies. "Que listo."

As a teenager, my father left Mexico with his cousin. They crept over the border and walked through the desert before piling into a truck that brought them to San Francisco. When he was twenty, he came home and married my mother, the prettiest girl in their neighborhood of narrow streets, concrete houses, tin roofs, and no fathers. After that, he returned to his family at Christmas every other year, back when it was easier to cross la frontera before the crackdowns. He saw each of his three boys in diapers, and the next time walking and talking. He told my mother to work on the house, to make it nice for when he earned enough money and retired in Mexico in a few years. She added a second floor but ran out of money. The concrete stairs led nowhere. In the evenings, she and I watched telenovelas on a tiny black-and-white set. She sighed over the clothes and houses, but scoffed at the women. "That's no maid," she said. "Look at her hands. Too soft." She made fun of the leading men, who were tricked every time by evil women. "Que tonto. Can't he see what's happening?"

When I was six, my mother followed my father. She told me that she was going away to help Papá, but would be back. My father had stopped coming home at Christmas. His money wasn't enough anymore, for the electricity, for my abuelita's medication, for our school supplies. Three of my tíos lost their jobs after the factory closed. Neighbors and relatives came by whenever they had an emergency, and how could my mother turn them away?

Even if she had so little, they had nothing, she said. Everybody, it seemed, depended on my father's pay.

The afternoon that Mamá left, she asked me to watch over my brothers, who were four and two years old. We were sitting together outside on the steps. I could feel a trickle of snot starting in my nose and knew if I spoke, I would start crying. She was no different than Papá. Worse, because she was supposed to stay with us until his return. She kissed me good-bye on the top of my head. Wait. I wanted to wrap myself around her legs to prevent her from leaving. Joselito, he ran so fast. I could still scoop him up, but I imagined the trouble he would get into: darting in front of a bus, into the path of neighborhood bullies. And Ernesto followed our mother everywhere, underfoot and insisting on her lap. What would he do without her?

I tried to run down the street after Mamá, but my abuelita held me back, her arms tight across my chest. I watched as the blue flag of my mother's dress grew smaller and smaller, until it disappeared as she turned the corner. When my abuelita kissed the top of my head, I squirmed away. You'll see her soon, she promised.

Lies, I knew even then.

When I was eleven, my parents finally picked me to go to San Francisco. I was old enough to make the journey on my own, and my parents wanted me to start attending school in America.

My abuelita put me on a thirty-six-hour bus ride. Although I'd been hoping that the coyote wouldn't show up at the station, he was there, in a white cowboy hat, searching the face of each passenger coming off the bus. I was the only boy traveling by myself, and if strangers asked, I was supposed to say that I was going to visit my aunt. We didn't talk much, which I preferred, but was thankful that he asked what I wanted at meals instead of ordering for me.

At the border checkpoint, the coyote told the officer I was his nephew. His accent must have been convincing, from time he spent in the United States, or from the movies, I didn't know. He'd put away the cowboy hat, shaved off his stubble, and changed into a button-down shirt and khaki pants, a disguise like the Dodgers cap and blue jeans he'd given me to wear. He presented our passports. I looked straight at the officer, like I was told, and forced myself to breathe easy and kept my sweaty hands folded in my lap. And in a moment, the officer nodded and the roads turned from bumpy and pitted, swarming with vendors, to fast, smooth freeways along which no one walked. How lonely.

Across the border, he handed me off to a lady with stiff dyed-blond curls, whose car reeked of cigarettes. She chain-smoked, one hand on the wheel, the other ashing out the window. We stayed on the freeway, which seemed a sign she wasn't going to kidnap me, lock me in a room, and ask for more money from my parents. I was asleep when she pulled up in front of the apartment in San Francisco. She shook me awake. The car was warm and comfortable, the seats soft as flan, and I did not want to get out. It was late. The sky hazy black, the stars faint, and the moon a watery crescent. She rang the buzzer. The front door was set back in an alcove covered by a metal gate. Black gaps interrupted the white tiles arranged in the circular design on the ground, a broken smile. I fidgeted, looking at the pink menus hanging off the doorknob, at the wrinkled newspaper on the ground, at the building's flaky gray paint peeling like the bark of an ancient tree. I read the building directory and found our name, Lopez.

I realized then my abuelita would no longer make me lunch when I returned for the siesta. No longer would she tell me stories about her childhood in a mountain village, where the lacy butterflies descended each fall. No longer would my brothers and I climb to the top of our house to spy on neighbors, at the young wife who hung her lacy panties and bras to dry in the window, and la vieja who smoked a pipe while cooking.

Someone pushed through the front door. I went dizzy, breathless, as though I'd been spinning in circles. What would Mamá look like? I couldn't picture her clearly anymore. Would she recognize me? I hadn't seen her in five years, Papá in seven. I jumped to hug the woman, and then stopped short. A chinita, with chubby cheeks and frizzy hair, squinted at me, clutched her purse, and brushed past us. The driver tugged on my arm. Quit it, she said. We waited another minute, and she buzzed again.

And then my mother rushed to the door, patting her hair and smoothing her dress. She looked like my aunt, but curvier, her long curls tinted red-brown, and her features blurred somehow, like a copy of an original left in Morelia. My father followed. He was short, thick and muscled, with a buzz-cut, spark-plug head. I took a step back. We were supposed to know each other.

"Mamá?" I asked.

"Mijo, you're here." She knelt down and hugged me. I saw her two moles, one above her upper lip, on the right side, and one just beneath her eye. Back home, I had loved to rub the chocolate spots, raised dots in her velvet skin. At last, something I remembered.

THAT NOVEMBER, ON my thirteenth birthday, Mamá set the kitchen table for five. For the three of us in San Francisco, and for my brothers back home. She did that on their birthdays and on Christmas, too. Mamá skipped class, maybe the only time she missed a session for me. But Papá had insisted.

She served me first, with a bowl of sopa tarasca and a plate of pollo placero. My favorites, she had learned. Then she served my brothers, my father, and herself. When she said grace, she prayed that the family would be reunited soon. She never had any other wish. Her voice grew hoarse as she held back her tears. She squeezed my hand, grinding my fingers together. Papá bowed his head. He let her speak, or maybe he had nothing to say, his jokes, his stories, his flirtation silenced. Though I hoarded the affections of my parents, I could not bear to see them so broken. I pictured my brothers bumping elbows while trying to eat. Jose would be greedy, picking off Ernesto's plate. Ernesto saved the bits of tortilla in the soup for last, letting the strips soak until soggy and soft. They were probably sitting with my abuelita, laughing in a life that no longer belonged to me. I had no friends here, and kept to myself at school. I took a few bites and pushed the enchiladas around my plate. My throat was tight, as if I had swallowed an ice cube. I could not go back to Morelia, not until we had our papers. The border was tightening, and it was impossible to travel in a group of three. My father ate from my brothers' plates, after the cheese cooled and congealed on the enchiladas, and the crema sank to the bottom of the bowl. Did he have to choke down their food, grown cold? Or was he merely hungry, eating whatever was before him? Did he miss them? He'd left us behind so many times.

We dialed my brothers after dinner. By then, calls home were only on special occasions, two or three times a year. It was hard on my parents to promise to send for them each time. Mamá asked if they had received the clothes and soccer ball that she sent, if they liked them, how she'd been thinking of them, and promised to send more soon. The arrival of the boxes—big enough to climb into—caused much excitement: my aunts, uncles, and cousins hurrying over for their share, and the neighbors marveling over the contents. Staring at the empty bottom had left me hollow, dried-out, reminding me that my mother wasn't there, and I wondered if my brothers now felt the same.

"Comportate bien," my father commanded, then handed the phone to me.

"Orale, qué pasó?" Ernesto's voice sounded weird, disconnected, still a high-pitched kid.

"No más aqui."

That night, unable to fall asleep, I would have many questions. Does abuelita still cough at night, those gasps that shook the house? Do you wish I was there, or that we could change places? But right now there were only faint clicks and echoes on the line. More silence, we said good-bye, and I hung up.

A FEW WEEKS after my birthday, Papá looked over Mamá's shoulder as she wrote a five-paragraph essay about why she had come to America. She puckered her lips in concentration, studying the page smeared gray with erasures. Beside her, I struggled with my algebra, bad at math in any language. I kept my head down, watching them sidelong. It bugged him, I could tell, that Mamá could be so wrapped up in something that she ignored him, that she was transported to a place where she did not need him.

"Want anything? Something to drink?" he asked.

"Not right now." She didn't look up.

Papá stared at her bent head and sucked in a long breath. "Maybe you could get another job, in the afternoon. You said you were too tired, but now you're doing this."

Mamá clenched her pen. "I quit because I wanted to be home with Lalo after school."

"Don't you want to bring all your sons here?"

"They'll get here faster this way."

"Lalo needs his brothers."

"I need my sons too," she said. "You're the one who left us."

Their quiet, tense voices exploded into shouts, and I shrank in my chair, falling into the pit opening inside me.

"It was the only way!"

"The only way you could think of!"

Papá jabbed a finger at her, inches from her face. "You think I liked being apart from you?"

She stalked out of the kitchen and slammed the bedroom door.

Yes. She and I could go back to Morelia, to live with Ernesto and Joselito and my abuelita, and leave Papá and his yelling behind. But maybe she didn't mean that. Did she want to start over? Without Papá? Without us? Other fathers started new families in America, and stopped sending money to their wives and children. At least Papá had stayed with us.

Six months after Mamá began taking classes, La Gloria hired her to be a community liaison. When we shopped in the neighborhood that spring, people stopped her to ask questions about La Gloria, which offered job training and ESL classes for adults.

"There's a computer class that would be perfect for you," she said to a leathery man in paint-spattered jeans and work boots. "It's free. Just once a week."

I tugged at her arm.

"In a minute, Lalo."

She worked at the hotel five days a week, and two evenings at the center after cooking us dinner. She asked if I wanted to come along, to check out the center's books or get on the computer, but I told her no. I didn't want to leave Papá too. When he could not find the paper napkins, or discovered something else we were out of, he shook his head in irritation. With her gone, we did not have much to talk about, and finished eating within ten minutes. It was then that Papá taught me how to pick locks.

"That's it!" He clapped me on the back when I succeeded in cracking the mechanisms spread out on the kitchen table.

I liked knowing that someday, I could get by with my hands. Like him. When we walked through the neighborhood after dinner, Papá pointed out different houses and apartments where he had picked the locks. Sometimes as we passed strangers, he whispered that this woman kept a messy house that reeked of cats, and this man draped laundry across his studio on a clothesline. That shy woman turned crazy, screaming and tearing at her hair, kicking over a chair, when he cracked the lock to find her boyfriend in bed with another woman. Papá knew their secrets, the ones they could not hide before he broke in.

He told me other stories. What he used to do with his brother Eduardo, the one I was named after. How they played fútbol in the zócalo. How they snuck into the zoo. The animals! A rhinoceros. A bear. Zebras. From the excitement in his face, I could see a little of the boy he once was. But I couldn't imagine my tío—who had grown fat and deliberate—running as fast as Papá claimed.

One night we had seven calls—three car lockouts, two key changes, and two apartment break-ins—which meant a big payoff, and at home he offered me a beer. I tried not to cough after I took a sip of the Negra Modelo.

"I can finish it." Papá drained the beer and his smile disappeared. "Lalo, what I'm teaching you. Don't ever use it to steal. If I catch you—"

I nodded. I'd heard this lecture before. He was clean, unlike some old friends who thought they could make easy money selling drugs or boosting cars. They were dead or in jail. But didn't he break the law every time he picked a lock? He had a fake license, sold to him by Francisco who ran a neighborhood locksmith shop. Francisco, who landed amnistía before the door closed, paid my father less but charged the customers the same. He kept the difference, which was fine with Papá because he made more than he could busing tables or painting or in construction.

Papá checked each morning to make sure I wore nothing to

set off the gangs in the neighborhood, no red or blue clothing, though I didn't need him to tell me which intersections and what kind of people to avoid. I had learned on my own. He forgot what he left behind; the gangs in Morelia were far worse than the cholos who stood on the corners here. My brothers were still there, and who would warn them?

Two months after my mother started her job at La Gloria, Papá told me to leave the dishes on the table. I had been getting sloppy, swiping them once with the sponge, and he yelled at me when he found bits of dried food on the plates and smudges on the glasses. I retreated into my room. Why did I ever want my parents all to myself? If my brothers were here, we could sneak out, run around, and get away from their unhappiness. How could Mamá leave me again, when it had taken so much for us to be together?

Papá was waiting for her when she found the mess. I pictured the bits of tortilla and rice scattered on the kitchen table, and the greasy knives and forks crooked on crumpled napkins. I huddled in bed, listening through thin walls. Before, with the same disgust and fascination, I'd heard the sounds of their fucking—the bed banging and squeaking, my mother moaning. But it had been months now since I'd heard them together.

"What's this?" she asked.

"I work."

"I work too."

"I didn't bring you here so I could live like a bachelor."

I bolted out of bed and cracked open the door. Should I wash the dishes? I stood there, unable to go another step. They were both standing, Papá with his hands braced against the table, as though he were holding it down. Mamá faced him, her eyes narrow and mouth hard. Unyielding. I shut the door. I could not fix them, no matter how many dishes I washed.

They argued every night for a week, until Mamá announced that we all would visit the center together. We gulped down dinner, and set off for La Gloria, a building covered in a mural of Aztec warriors, Teotihuacan, and farm workers picking grapes. The lobby had an orange plaid couch that looked itchy as a haystack, piles of newspapers, and a bulletin board with job postings, and the two classrooms were in the rear, each with a large window in the door. I peeked in. In one room, people pecked out essays on computers. In the other, a man with wavy black hair and sleepy eyes, handsome as a telenovela star, was teaching English. In his class, mothers and fathers were taking notes, the people Mamá had been. I recognized where they were. Tricky verbs, where the past had no connection to the present. Go-Went. Eat-Ate. Take-Took.

I walked to the lobby, where Mamá's picture was on the wall, along with ten other staff members. She wore a green dress with gold buttons and stared straight into the camera. Serious, with a hint of a smile, important but also approachable and reassuring, like she would do whatever she could to help you. A guapa I recognized from school sat down on the couch. Martita. She was slender and taller than me, with sly dark eyes. She slipped on her headphones and waited for her father or mother—or her boyfriend?—to finish class. I wanted to show her the picture on the wall and say, This is my mother.

From across the room, I watched Mamá wave at the volunteer teaching English. He motioned for her to come in, but she shook her head no. Who were these people who relied on her, and what did she owe them? She introduced us to Paul, the director, a gabacho wearing a light blue guayabera. In college, he had spent summers in Guatemala working as a church missionary, he told us in Spanish. "Your mother is an inspiration and an example. We'd love her to work full-time," he said. "Please help us convince her."

"She doesn't need another job," Papá said. "She's already working full-time."

"I see. I hope you'll check the schedule of night classes."

"Someone has to look after our boy." He set his hand on my shoulder. I resisted the urge to shrug him off, and we left the center soon after.

"He thinks he has to save the Mexicans," Papá said. "We can save ourselves."

Mamá stopped. "We are saving ourselves. That's why I work here." She walked ahead.

My father stared at her back, then hurried beside her, slipped his arm around her waist, and she rested her head on his shoulder. I was relieved. Papá was trying. From behind, they looked happy. Solid. Strong. United. But you can never see all angles at once.

LATE IN THE summer, Papá got a call for an apartment on Liberty Street. Mamá had quit her hotel job and worked full-time at the center, after convincing my father that her wages would dip only temporarily. If a state grant came through, the director had promised her a promotion and a raise.

That afternoon, he and I walked to the western edge of the Mission, where the streets climbed into the hills flanking Noe Valley. Flyers stapled to the telephone poles warned residents about daytime break-ins in the neighborhood. "Keep your eyes out!!!" The customer introduced himself as Carlos. He and my father appeared to be about the same age, but he was dressed in khakis and a green V-neck sweater, while Papá wore jeans and a faded button-up from the Salvation Army. Carlos looked familiar but I could not imagine why. After Papá broke through the front door, we climbed the stairs to the third floor of the building, and he got us in again.

"You want a soda, or a beer? Grab anything you want from the fridge," Carlos called from the other room, where he was getting his checkbook.

My father said no. It was better that way, he always told me, to keep things professional, but I still wanted those cookies or Cokes that were forever being offered to us. Some women flirted with him and I wondered sometimes what he would have done, when I wasn't there. What he did those years before my mother arrived.

While Papá studied the big television and flashy stereo, I looked around. Carlos had so many video games! My hands itched to play. The black leather couch looked comfortable, softer than the bed I had at home. Then I saw the picture on the bookshelf. A single framed photograph of a woman who looked like Mamá, but softer somehow, the rough edges smoothed out, glowing. She was glancing over her shoulder, smiling, caught by the photographer.

I looked closer and saw her two moles. Mamá.

Carlos. I recognized him as the volunteer from the center, the man she had waved at from across the room. In the picture, it looked like she was at a party, with a piñata and streamers thick as kelp hanging above her. Why did he have her picture? She had no friends here, none that I knew of. It was always her, Papá, and me. Papá came from behind and studied the photo of Mamá. His eyes widened. He squeezed the trigger of the lock gun. *Click, click, click.*

All those special events at the center, nights and weekends. I never thought about who else was there. Carlos wrote a check, and signed a statement that this was his apartment and that he had given us permission to break in. After my father handed him the receipt, I pulled out the black vinyl logbook and noted the address. My hands shaking, I crossed out the entry twice before I spelled the street correctly.

At the door, Papa stopped. "Where do you get a girl like that?"

"Who?" Carlos said.

"The girl on the shelf."

Carlos smiled. "I tutored her. A very good student. I teach her English, and she teaches me Spanish."

"And now she's your girlfriend."

"Well . . . not quite," Carlos said. "Not yet."

Something flashed across his face—happiness or pain or regret or maybe all of that. I knew only that my mother mattered to him. My mouth went dry as paper, and my stomach twisted. I was unable to take a step, another breath, and would have fallen if I had moved.

"Where are you from?" Carlos said.

"Michoacán."

"My grandparents are from Jalisco." Carlos might have thought we were buddies, brothers, with a shared ancestry. "I've never been back, though."

We had nothing in common, no matter what this pocho said and thought.

"Muchas gracias," he said.

"You're welcome," Papá said in English. "Anytime."

My father walked down the block before picking up an empty beer bottle and smashing it against a wall. The crashing sounded like how I felt inside. After staring at the window of Carlos's apartment for a minute, he tossed the jagged shards into a garbage can. Blood trickled down his fingers from a cut on his palm. Did he understand what was happening more than I did? Or was he as lost as me? I offered to carry the tool bag, but he refused.

When we came home, Papá and I sank onto the couch in front of the television, and for once, Mamá didn't nag me to finish my homework after returning from the center, maybe because she could tell she should leave us alone. That night, Papá picked a fight with her over the messy bathroom. The next day, he complained about her overcooked beans; the next fight happened when she woke him when she was getting ready for work; the next was over her cherry-red lipstick.

Desgraciada, he said.

Mamá kept the lipstick on and left for an event at La Gloria, an awards ceremony, she said. Papá waited ten minutes, and then told me to eat dinner without him. He said he had a job, but I knew he was checking on her. In the living room, I traced my thumb over the buttons of the remote. The television flashed unwatched. My homework assignments remained crumpled at the bottom of my backpack, because all I could think of was the picture. Why couldn't we give her that kind of smile? Open, unguarded, carefree. A flash of who she was, not who she had to be.

I had to see for myself. I ran to find the doors of the center locked and the windows dark. Mamá had lied. Papá had already taken off. I bent over, winded, hands on my knees, feeling stupid for helping Mamá with her homework, when all it did was bring her closer to Carlos. Closer to his world: spacious, tidy, and privileged. Away from ours: poor and cluttered with struggle. Those afternoons and evenings she went to the center, she wasn't taking the classes for my brothers or for me. It was for her alone. Puta. The nasty word rang in my head. She wanted another life, without my father and my brothers. Without me.

I had survived by thinking our family had had no choice but to split up. That I had to accept the loss of all whom I loved, but Mamá was messing with that. None of what had happened was unavoidable or inescapable. She had an alternate existence, happier than what she was born to, bound to. The perfect life that she hid from us, the one where she did not cry for her lost sons or get on her knees to clean toilets or argue with her husband. The life she deserved. I walked home and shut myself in my room, heard my father come in a few minutes later, and after about an hour, my mother. I listened, waiting for the fight that never came, and imagined them curling away from each other in bed, pretending to sleep. What held Papá back?

The next day, when a classmate shoved past me in the

hallway, I pushed back. His friends piled on and we sprawled on the ground. I was a terrible fighter. I thrashed around and each time I swung my fist, I thought of Carlos, smacking his face bloody. If my brothers were here, we could have attacked him, bashed in his teeth, and stomped on his neck. Instead I was flat on my back, kicking at nothing. The teachers broke us apart and called our parents.

Papá cuffed me on the head after I returned home. I rubbed my throbbing right ear, and blinked away the white points of light floating across my eyes. What he could not do to Carlos or to Mamá, he did to me.

"Don't hit him." Mamá looked away, out the living room window, through her reflection, at the rooftops, at the hills beyond, transported somewhere far away from us. That destroyed me, her distance. Not the usual hug to let me know that I was forgiven. All along, she was holding part of herself back. "You can't let them find out about you. About us," she said to me.

Left unsaid was how the truth could have ended with us sent back to Morelia. I wondered if that would be for the best.

THE NEXT DAY, I rang the doorbell of Carlos's apartment. No answer. And so I broke in for the very first time. I had to know why my mother came here. Standing in the living room, I could see her everywhere: sinking into the couch, sipping from a glass, and smiling as Carlos pulled her into the bedroom. I flipped over drawers and emptied the closets, trampling the clothes and spilling cologne bottles. I found a string of condoms in his bedside drawer and flushed them in the toilet. I threw the ladder of the fire escape down, scattering false clues. I took a laptop, CDs, and video games and left them on the sidewalk on 16th Street, where they would disappear in minutes, stolen by junkies.

I kept the only thing that mattered.

I GAVE THE picture of her to Papá, which he accepted with no questions. Mamá would slip away, with no explanation, if we did not stop her, and Papá left me no choice but to reclaim the photo. After Mamá found it on top of the television, she swept into the kitchen. I sat frozen on the couch, gripping a scratchy cushion, unable to turn away.

"Where did you get this?" She thrust the picture into his face.

"You know damn well." Papá shoved back his chair and stood. "Who is this pendejo? What kind of guy would sleep with another man's wife? With a mother?"

"It's nothing. Just a friend from the center."

"The center! There was no awards ceremony the other night. You were with him. I saw you leaving his place."

She opened her mouth but no words came out. She bowed her head, though only for a moment before she drew herself up. "He understands what I want. You, you can't stand to see me better than you."

They argued about their failed plans, and he kept saying she belonged to him.

"That's why you had to steal this. You steal what you can't have." Mamá did not know that I deserved the credit or the blame. She wasn't around to see what I was capable of and what I had become.

Papá slammed his hand down onto the table, scattering the tools on the floor. He kicked over his chair, the rungs splintering like matches. "How could you do this to me? To your sons?" His voice cracked and his expression bared a fear and longing that no son should witness in his father. "You are mine. You belong to me. To the kids. Please. We belong to you."

Mamá sagged, the fight gone out of her, and he staggered over and threw his arms around her. The key to my mother's heart: where she came from was worth more than what she could be. The picture slid from her hand, landing with an explosion of glass. I fled but, at the front door, turned to look at my parents. Over Papá's shoulder, she stared at me with huge, wet eyes. I understood later that she wanted me to save her, to forgive her and make the family whole. To defeat her desire to be admired and respected at the center.

But it was my turn to leave my parents behind.

I walked up and down Mission Street, past the storefronts locked tight and the crowded taquerias, past the prostitutes with aqua eye shadow, flamboyant as parrots, and the skinny addicts with balloons of heroin tucked into their chipmunk cheeks, before hiking to the top of Dolores Park.

A squealing Muni train emerged and glided down the hill with the stately grace of an elephant. I sat on a bench, sweatshirt pulled over my knees, my arms tucked inside. I could wait all night. In the shadowed playground below I could make out a family of three, parents and son, bundled against the cold. Mexicans too, it sounded like, by their accent. Hooting with laughter on the swing, the boy was about six years old, the same age I'd been when Mamá left. Did he have a brother or a sister in Mexico? Had he been born here?

"More," the boy said. "More!"

"Five more minutes and then we'll go," his mother said. The father pushed him higher. I willed them to look at me and wave, giving me their blessing. But they never did.

The Bay Bridge pulsed with cars, shining white coming in, red heading out. The lights of the apartments and skyscrapers glittered gold, beautiful and at a remove. Messy, painful, and ugly up close. That was what you lived with. I knew then I would always remember my parents this way, locked in the embrace of one who cannot let go and another who cannot get away. Their struggling would change shape, disappear, and I would see only mutual devotion in the story of their long marriage. This was their choice. Their sacrifice.

I NEVER TOLD my brothers or my American-born sister, Rosalie—the one with all the privileges, the most loved and most loving in our family—about what happened before they arrived. What happened before we got our papers, before I got the desk job my parents wanted for me. It is my gift to them. My burden.

Carlos didn't connect us to the break-in, as far as I know. There had been burglaries on his street and maybe he figured it was his turn. He seemed like the type I've come to know, who take a certain pride in arriving before the bodegas transform into tapas restaurants, before the dive bars are overrun with hipsters. It would become his war story, though he could replace what he lost with a single swipe of his credit card.

Almost everything. My mother quit her job at the center and worked double shifts at an electronics factory in San Bruno. I don't know what she told Carlos, or if they said good-bye. A family emergency, the director at La Gloria would have said. She had to go back to Mexico.

Years later, I am often tempted to use my father's training. Twice, I broke into the houses of men I suspected my girlfriends were sleeping with. Although I wanted to see if there was any trace of them, their perfume, a bra, or a photo of their true selves, I found nothing. It was wrong, but I liked rifling through drawers, closets, and refrigerators, their lives laid out before me. Call it an insurance policy, a warranty, whatever.

Just now, my girlfriend found the picture of my mother in a shoebox in the back of my closet. Nosy, like me. "What's this?" she says, not recognizing her.

"Someone special."

She's poised to start yelling, when I tell her it's my mother.

"Can't you see the resemblance?" I stroke her cheek.

"That's twisted." She rubs her hand along my back, down my thigh, kneading her fingers into me.

I keep the picture as a reminder of how that smile can disappear, if you take for granted what you can never possess. You must make her yearn only for the life she already has. To want nothing more.

For What They Shared

Ba struggled to unfold the canvas chairs while Ma stood by with a stack of Chinese newspapers and a thermos of black tea. Lin frowned. Should she do it, or let her father figure it out? He could if he tried. Her mother could help. Ever since her parents arrived from China a month ago on their first visit to America, they had depended on Lin for everything, as if to show that they could not adapt. Her parents perched on the edge of the chairs, which tipped forward.

"Aiya!" Ma exclaimed as Ba threw out his arm to stop her from falling.

"Lean back," Lin said. "Lean back!"

They were camping in Big Sur, with brand-new equipment purchased by Lin and her husband, Sang, on an evening shopping spree at a sporting-goods store. They were software engineers, and consequently respected good design: to every feature, a purpose. Money-back guarantee, Lin still marveled, though they had lived in California for close to four years. No wonder products made in China cost so much more here. They splurged, knowing they could return whatever they did not like. No purchase final: that was the American way.

They were learning how to use the gear. The Leatherman radiating its pliers, wire cutter, nail file, scissors, screwdriver, and bottle opener. The green Coleman lantern. Four sleeping bags, soft as steamed buns. In China, camping was considered a Western idiosyncrasy. People did not buy expensive gear to sleep on the ground. Why strive to be uncomfortable, when you had a bed that your ancestors could only dream of?

Although her parents had grumbled at the strange idea, Lin wanted to share this new experience with them so they could see what life here meant to her and Sang. Her parents wanted Lin to return to China. The economy was booming there while her future in Silicon Valley was uncertain. Even waiguoren, foreigners, were flooding into China to make their fortunes. After earning her master's degree in computer science, Lin had worked at one failing startup after another. Sang's company was struggling, with rumors of massive layoffs, maybe later this month. If he lost his job, he would have to find a new employer to sponsor his visa, or else be forced to leave. He had long wanted to return to China, but she convinced him to stay until they obtained green cards. Here, her bosses gave her credit for her hard work, instead of expecting her to serve tea and defer to senior staff. Someday, she could start her own company. She couldn't guess at what she might do with no limits.

None of them knew Lin had lost her job not long before

her parents arrived. Instead of going to work, she hid at the library, searching online for jobs and reading Chinese novels. She had been unable to find another company willing to sponsor her work visa—which meant that her papers were now expired. If she left, she would be unable to reenter. She was supposed to return with her parents at the end of their visit to attend her cousin's wedding, but Lin had decided that she and Sang would stay, no matter what. She would work as a babysitter, a house-cleaner; he could be a waiter, a handyman, anything until prosperity returned. This trip to the redwoods had to convince Sang as much as her parents that they would prosper in America.

Lin would always belong to dirty and cramped Beijing, but here she could give herself away. If she returned to China, she could already picture the rest of her life. A baby, living in a high-rise apartment near her parents, she and Sang advancing toward middle management, growing old, and playing with her own grandchild someday. Comfortable but predictable. Here, there was discovery, uncertainty, and possibility.

WHEN JANEY MENTIONED she practiced Buddhism, Aileen cringed. White people who were more Chinese than her made Aileen feel guilty.

She had a Chinese character tattooed on her biceps, which Aileen didn't know how to read but it probably meant "peace," "courage," or "woman."

Everyone at the campsite in Big Sur had been drinking since sunset, downing microbrews and plastic cups of Cape Cods and rum-and-Cokes. After dating Reed for about six months, Aileen was meeting his old friends for the first time, the ones he did not see often now but who starred in his strongest, fondest memories.

It turned out that she and Janey lived four blocks apart in the Mission District. Janey told her about a meditation class in the neighborhood.

"I'll have to try it sometime." Aileen stared into the fire, her cheeks flushed from heat and embarrassment. She almost didn't come on the trip. She and Reed had been arguing all week, their biggest fight yet, after she discovered a stash of porn on his hard drive, in a folder labeled "MiscPix." She had been snooping for photos of his ex-girlfriends and found naked leggy redheads, chesty blondes, and smoky-eyed brunettes. No Asians. Why not anyone like her? She couldn't bring herself to ask.

"You disgust me," she had said, and stormed into the bathroom. Through the locked door, he promised he would delete the files, and he proposed going to the redwoods a day or two early before everyone else arrived. A getaway. She could hear him breathing and imagined him with his ear to the door. She let him in.

Reed had never dated anyone Asian before her. Never learned to say "ni hao ma" or "ni piaoliang," never decorated his house with paper lanterns, and that appealed to her. He didn't have yellow fever. But were these women on his hard drive what he desired most? Or maybe she had to admit she was moody because she suspected something worse. Her period was late by two weeks.

Aileen wasn't sure why she had agreed to go on the trip. Maybe it was easier to put off knowing for sure about the baby, or maybe it was a test. If they could survive the days-long intimacy, she could tell him. If not, she would know that it was over.

As a kid, she never went camping or did Girl Scouts or Indian Maidens. Her parents' idea of getting back to nature was to drive to a vista point, take pictures, and check into a Best Western or Motel 6. She and Reed spent the first two days hiking to waterfalls and hot springs and making hobo stew and s'mores. He taught her how to start a fire by collecting redwood cones for kindling, and setting the logs into a pyramid. "It's tinder-dry here," he said. Aileen had helped neighboring campers, a Chinese family, pitch their tent. She was pleased to share her small measure of expertise. After they finished, the Chinese woman ran her hand down the spine of the tent, like she was petting an oversized cat. They were about the same age. What was it like to start over in a new country as an adult? Like her parents. Aileen didn't think she had the same courage.

By the campfire, she examined the group. Reed had given her a rundown: Gretchen worked at a nonprofit, something to do with tennis lessons for inner-city kids, and had once dated Chuck, before switching to his roommate, Dan. Gretchen and Dan were still a couple. Sean was a prankster who had launched hard-boiled eggs with a slingshot through the dorm windows at Wesleyan.

"Roberto will be there too. We met the summer I interned in D.C. Overlapped a couple days until I took over his room. He'd saved his dirty laundry from spring semester and took it home in giant duffel bags," Reed said.

"He's Latino?" Until then, Aileen had assumed everyone would be white.

"I'm not sure," Reed said. "Maybe. His last name is Gonzalez. I never asked. But he has red hair."

A collection of people in their late twenties, clean-cut and athletic in jeans, fleece pullovers, baseball hats, and designer running shoes, who clustered around the campfire. The kind of people, Aileen couldn't help but think, who went to parties she wasn't invited to in high school, to keggers where they played Steve Miller and Santana, and then drove home drunk and crashed their SUVs into the garage door and received new cars the following week. Who rushed sororities and fraternities in college, and majored in poli-sci and anthropology, and didn't grind away in pre-med or engineering. Their histories were jumbled in Aileen's mind, about what she was supposed to assume and what she could not let on that she knew. What if they shut her out? What if she could not stand them?

"Aileen's a San Francisco native," Reed announced to the group, by way of introduction. Everyone else hailed from the East Coast or the Midwest, he'd told her.

"From San Francisco?" Sean asked. "You don't meet many natives."

Aileen felt a surge of pride, though it was an accident of birth, a decision made by her parents to settle in the Sunset. Talk turned to taquerias, to the city's best burrito. That question that marked your authenticity, your sense of belonging in San Francisco.

"La Corneta." Aileen had taken Reed to the taqueria around the corner from her apartment and now it was his favorite too. "The shrimp super baby is awesome."

"Eh," Sean said. "El Farolito is much better. More authentic."

This often happened—transplants trying to out-local the locals. Men like Sean prided themselves on knowing every hole-in-the-wall and would dismiss any suggestion for a restaurant or bar as being too touristy or too popular.

With each drink, the conversations grew noisier, sloppier, and indistinct in everything except the decibel level. Mike, Janey's boyfriend, threw the paper box that held the firewood into the pit. For a moment, the flames died down and then flared three feet high. The heat was intense, almost painful, the flames turning the group of twenty-one a maniacal orange and casting blurry shadows onto their faces. Someone cranked a portable stereo and the ominous beats of Metallica's "Enter Sandman" thundered, the lyrics summoning the night and never-never-land. Roberto and Sean hooted, flashing devil signs.

After a beer, Aileen found the jokes and stories more entertaining. She could feel herself getting red, the "Asian flush." Her goal was to get buzzed without getting sick or stumbling drunk, which could be the difference of one or two drinks on an empty stomach. It also might be better to stop drinking if—if she was pregnant. She switched to water, drinking out of the same red plastic cup so no one would notice. Shh, shh, Janey said. The park's curfew was 10 p.m. Each time, the group silenced for a moment before growing louder than before. A light flicked on in the campsite across the road, circled like a firefly, and then disappeared.

AT SUNSET, HEADLIGHTS swarmed into the campsite across the road. Lin's family was finishing dessert, a freeze-dried apple cobbler that delighted her father.

"It's like astronaut food." Ba was proud that China had sent someone into orbit.

Her mother deemed the cobbler too gooey and sweet after a couple of bites. "Don't you prefer nian gao?" Ma asked. The chewy rice flour cake was Lin's favorite dim sum treat.

"You can get that here, as good as in China. You can get whatever you want here," Lin said.

"Bu tong. Bu yi yang," Ma said. Not the same.

"In China, you can get whatever you want from America," Ba said.

"You can get it first, here," Lin said. "It may not even get to China."

"Everything is made in China." Ba flipped an insulated plastic mug upside down, its bottom stamped "China." "See?"

Lin reddened. He knew how to defeat her. Growing up, she lost her arguments and her confidence within minutes, and if she returned to China, she would revert to being that person.

Now music from the neighboring campsite thumped through the ground, jarring her with each beat, a buzz filling her ears. They were laughing, a growling rumble pierced by giggles and shrieks. If she closed her eyes, she could see a million cars honking, a riot breaking out in a market, and the earth cracking apart. Though she burrowed into her sleeping bag, she could not escape. Sang rolled over and whispered in her ear. "So loud. So rude. It's not right."

"What should we do?"

She wanted to impress her parents, but could not have predicted this outcome. How could she claim to know what was best for her and Sang? Maybe her parents would be more comfortable sleeping in their sedan. Or she could sneak off and complain to the park ranger on her cell phone after dialing the phone number posted in the bathroom. Sang could tell the strangers to be quiet, but that could be dangerous. Lin knew the country was violent. The Chinese government had warned her before she left and local television news affirmed her beliefs. Her people were targets in America. Home invasions. Stabbings. Rape. She clipped the worst stories and kept them in a box, a talisman against the evils here. All the risks and prospects of America were a consequence of its disorder. Once, she had taken the wrong exit, onto a street of run-down houses with boarded-up windows. A man with gold-capped teeth came toward her. Terrified, she did an immediate U-turn, barely missing an oncoming car, and sped onto the freeway.

What if these campers had a gun? Americans were crazy for guns. Only thin walls, and faith, kept them safe from the outside. The Leatherman was on the picnic table, its short knife their sole defense. Lin jerked on her sweatshirt.

"Where are you going? Lin?" Sang asked.

Lin stumbled to the picnic table, where she waved the flashlight until she found the Leatherman. She clenched it in her right hand, running her fingers over the casing and the twin grooves in the center. She pictured a fist falling to strike her, and the knife on the Leatherman rising to protect her and her family. Her curses. Wanbadan! Turtle's egg! She turned her flashlight toward the noise across the road, at the many standing around the fire, laughing. Carefree. Careless. Lin could not see their faces, only long shadows that bled into the darkness. A towering man, outlined by the fire, jumped, whooped, and looked straight at her. They'd tear up the hill and trample the tent. She ran.

Sang grabbed her into a hug. "Are you okay?" They stood silent for a few minutes until he kissed her neck. He smelled of soap and minty mouthwash, of American progress and hygiene. She turned her head away, wanting only to be held. Back at the tent, her parents asked no questions. They lay awake for a long time as the clamor outside escalated, and Lin muffled her tears by pulling the sleeping bag over her face.

"Mei you guanxi." Sang stroked her hair. No matter. It has no connection to you.

Lin hated hiding her job loss from Sang, and the distance the secret put between them when she needed him most. She had a sudden, sharp longing for the routine of Beijing. Playing mahjong in her parents' living room. Riding her bike home in early evening and breathing in the smell of roasting meat from roadside stands. Taking walks with Sang in the park where the old men brought out their caged songbirds.

And yet. She remembered the cool air against her cheek tonight, the smile of the honey-colored moon, and the soft, springy ground beneath her feet. She could have run on and on.

AILEEN AWOKE WHEN the sunlight shafted onto her face. The sleeping bag, which promised protection against sub-zero temperatures, was overkill for summer in the coastal redwoods. She squirmed in the bag, sticky and thirsty while Reed, in the shade, slept beside her. Aileen unzipped the tent and stepped out. The tents were circled around the campfire, like pioneer wagons fending off the natives. Empty beer bottles and half-full plastic cups littered the campsite. She unscrewed a bottle of water and was about to take a sip until she noticed a cigarette butt floating in the neck. She emptied the bottle, glugs splashing into the dust. Her head ached, her hair stank of wood smoke, and she was nauseated, a hangover or morning sickness, she didn't want to know.

Janey, after assembling the green stove on the picnic table, cracked eggs into a metal bowl and tore open packages of sausage and flour tortillas for breakfast burritos. A morning person, Aileen thought, and then stopped herself from being dismissive and envious at the same time. They settled into the camaraderie of the first people awake. She liked Janey. When Aileen winced, her knee sore from running, Janey showed her some stretches.

Aileen met Reed while training for a half marathon in San Francisco. She wanted to see how far she could go. None of her friends—who wanted to avoid muscular calves—would train with her. She joined a local running club filled with women on self-empowerment kicks, and Reed was one of the few men. They began dating about a month after they met, following a morning race that led to a boozy brunch that led to afternoon sex.

She had dated other white men. "You're too Chinese," one observed, soon before he dumped her. (Too polite? Too inscrutable? She never knew.) Three years ago, she had decided that finding a Chinese American, with the same upbringing, would be best for all concerned, but after a few months, each relationship collapsed under the weight of expectations. "You're not very Chinese," another said, soon before he left her. (Too loud? Her steamed rice too soggy? She never knew.) And so she made an exception for Reed, for the long lines of his sinewy body, for his crooked nose and their nicknames for other people. The Poor Man's Tom Cruise. Pool Boy. Garfield Eyes. But if she stayed with Reed, he would never know what she had given up: comfort from a shared background, in-laws who understood each other and children who kept their heritage. He did not enjoy the pleasures of eating thousand-year-old eggs like savory Cadburys, chewy chicken feet like E.T. fingers, and dried shredded pork like sawdust. He was not lulled by the sound of Mandarin, her first, now mostly forgotten tongue, the rising and falling tones and rhythms that she could pick out of the noisiest crowd.

She rubbed her hand over her belly. What would this possible clump of cells inside her grow to become, a baby who looked like her? Or would the Chinese roots disappear, transform into a child who looked somewhat Italian or Native American? One-half, one-fourth, one-eighth, one-sixteenth, one-thirty-second Chinese, erased in successive generations until only an echo remained: glossy black hair or tan skin. Aileen would be a distant exotic ancestor, claimed with excitement or else diluted and forgotten.

While others took over making breakfast, she and Janey headed to the bathroom to brush their teeth. A stringy Chinese woman squatted by the faucet across the road, filling a Nalgene bottle. The one Aileen had helped with the tent. A FOB, she could tell, by the woman's colorful plastic slippers worn with athletic socks and the baggy sweatshirt over bright leggings. The woman had pale skin, stippled with acne scars on her cheekbones. When she saw Chinese immigrants with bad haircuts swarming onto city buses, she stood back to avoid being associated with their shoving, alien desperation.

The woman stood. Behind smudged glasses, her small eyes were puffy, and her black hair was pulled into a messy ponytail. Apparently, she hadn't slept well.

Janey smiled, for she'd had a proper upbringing. "Good morning," Janey said. "I hope we weren't too noisy last night." Asking for an apology was easier than seeking permission.

"You ruined our trip." The woman's voice was thin and high with anger. Her lips were chapped, and her teeth were crooked.

"I . . . we didn't know." Janey readjusted the blue bandana that held her blond curls. "We're really sorry." Janey believed the woman should have said "no problem," Aileen knew. They would laugh together, and Janey would invite them to stop by. She would have hosted the whole campground, if she could have. She was that charming.

"Don't you think about other people?"

"I promise it won't happen again," Janey said.

"It shouldn't have happened at all."

Please. Shut up. Aileen knew they had been obnoxious, maybe scary last night, but this woman made her feel ashamed for seeking the group's approval. Should she try to appeal to her on another level? Mutter an apology in her broken Chinese? In theory, they had a bond because their ancestors originated from the same homeland. But Aileen said nothing. She could not speak from a place she had never been to and did not understand. Janey apologized one more time, and walked off without waiting for Aileen. She hurried to catch up. Bitch. The word exploded in her head. Aileen did not know whom she meant: the FOB, Janey, or herself.

HER PARENTS TALKED her out of leaving.

When Lin woke from fitful sleep that morning, she was ready to throw everything into the trunk, unwashed and un-packed, and go home. She fumbled for her glasses and unzipped the flap to find Sang kindling the fire and her parents settled into the camp chairs. They were ignoring last night, she real-ized, to help her save face.

"We don't need to stay. I'm sorry I brought you here. We shouldn't have come." She slammed pans and tossed cans of food into a paper box. A can of beans bounced off the edge and landed on top of a carton of eggs with a sickening crunch. Yolks dripped and spread over the picnic table, and she felt as though she'd vomited the mess. No one moved. For weeks, she and Sang had been preparing. To pack now, to put away the un-eaten food and yet-to-be-used gear, would end a trip just begun.

Sang said they should finish breakfast, and then decide what to do. He was methodical like her, careful to complete every task he started. He unfurled the paper towels and wiped the spilled eggs. Her mom wanted to go hiking again, and her father said he liked sitting under the trees. Like the poet Lao Tze. They could take a nap in the afternoon, maybe using earplugs, he joked. Ma put her hand on his arm to still his reference to last night. Lin suspected that her parents wanted her to get the woods and California out of her system, and to bank every last moment before she left for China. In the past, her parents had employed this strategy, working to convince her, and then pulling back at the last moment to allow her to choose their decision.

After breakfast, she walked to the faucet at the edge of the campsite to rinse the dishes. Running her finger around the bottom of the bowls, scraping off stubborn particles, she noticed a pair of women, one foreigner and one Chinese, from the neighboring campsite. Even while living in America, she called white people foreigners out of habit. She dropped the metal plates with a clang.

The white woman apologized with a smile; Americans smiled very easily. Lin recognized the other woman, the ABC who helped her pitch the tent. Now the ABC looked away, pretending as if they had never met. The foreigner said sorry again, but her mouth was set into a straight line as she departed, her apology as fake as her smile. The ABC followed, dressed in a gray fleece and jeans, and her shoulder-length hair was streaked with auburn highlights, all attempts to hide the peasant within.

Traitor, Lin wanted to tell her. You will always be Chinese. You are not one of them.

"There's no use yelling at foreigners," Ma said, after Lin returned to the campsite. "They won't listen."

"Don't provoke them. There are so many of them," Ba said.

"I'll call the ranger," Sang said. "He can take care of this."

Her parents were storing reasons for why she should leave, for they could see what a place like this could do to her, and the longer she stayed, the more she would forget who she was.

THE RANGER WEARING a Smokey Bear hat strode into the campsite. Sean muttered "busted" under his breath, which made some people snicker. He informed the group that people had complained about the noise, and warned that if he had to return tonight, the group would have to leave. Janey promised that everyone would be quiet. After the ranger was out of sight, she told them about the run-in with the neighbor, some Asian lady.

"What's their problem?" Roberto asked.

"They could have told us to quiet down, instead of running to the ranger," Gretchen said.

"Damn furriners." Sean affected a hick accent. "Why don't they go back to their own . . ." He glanced at Aileen and trailed off. The others looked at their feet, at the trickle of a creek, at the brown needles, twigs, and cones scattered around the red-woods, at the campfire ring, everywhere but at her. She hated Sean for trying to be sensitive but instead singling her out. Why did he look at her and not Roberto? How alone the Chinese woman had seemed. Aileen wanted to apologize for failing to reach out a hand to someone else who did not belong.

Janey dispersed the silence with a wave of her capable hands. "Who wants to go hiking?" Everyone drifted away to get their daypacks. Aileen kicked at the dirt beside their tent, which erupted into a quick puff and then settled down as if nothing had happened.

She and Reed had never talked about the slights, the little judgments and assumptions people made. *Your English is excellent. Your eyes look tired.* Would he ever understand that the world saw her differently? Maybe he thought they had moved beyond the need for discussion. What she feared was that he didn't think about it at all.

"Don't let him get to you," Reed said. "Sean likes to tease, but he's harmless."

Harmless.

He was sorry that she was upset, but he would never experience what she felt. That would always be the divide between them. She had to accept that to stay with him or else let him go. From the center of the campsite, Janey marshaled the hikers together. Aileen shouldered her backpack and handed the other to Reed. She was not ready to give him up, not before she knew what else she could abandon. "Let's go."

LIN CAME PREPARED this time, bundled in a sweatshirt, windbreaker, and hat, before taking watch in the dark at the picnic table. Sang and her parents were in the tent. All day, the three of them did their best to appease her. They deferred to her on where to go hiking, when they should stop for lunch, asking her opinion on the best spots to take photos and how to pose.

They didn't want more broken eggs. As a child, Lin had erupted into anger, squalled with her younger brother over the last dumpling, and screamed at a classmate who stepped ahead of her. Her mother slapped her into obedience, and now Lin's temper flared only a handful of times each year, when pressures built and deadlines converged at work. It still surprised her each time she flew out of control, when she shattered a glass in the sink of the office kitchen, when she kicked aside the row of shoes by the front door.

Before long, Sang would come out and fetch her, when he judged she was satisfied with her duty, squeeze her shoulder, and lead her back to the tent. He was a good husband, tall for a Chinese man, with the wide cheekbones and pointed chin of a cat, who understood her without explanation. They had paired up in graduate school. She was a better programmer, Sang said, not jealous or competitive as other men had been. A smart wife meant smart kids, he often said. She knew that he wanted to return to China but toiled here for her, and many times she had reconsidered: Was she making the right decision? Or was she a selfish wife, unworthy of a man like him? Listening to the laughter drifting from the neighboring camp, Lin rubbed her hand on the unlit lamp, wishing for a spirit to command.

LATE THAT AFTERNOON, after the hike, Aileen and Reed made love in the tent, the space between them becoming small, smaller, smallest. The heat of their nakedness warmed the tent to body temperature, and the sunshine through the red walls bathed them in a rich glow. This was what she wanted: the world shrunk down to the two of them.

On their last night in the woods, after their collective naps, the campers drank steadily and heavily. As the curfew approached, Janey reminded them to be quiet, but a large group can whisper for only so long. When she shushed them, a few glowered toward the neighboring campers. Sean toasted them, tipping his beer bottle in their direction. "Sweet dreams."

That drew a big laugh from the group. "Please, Mr. Ranger, can you tuck us in?" he said in a nasal, simpering voice. His freckled face, open and friendly in daylight, was splotchy and sly in the campfire.

"Yeah, we're afraid of the dark," Roberto chimed in.

"Of monsters." Sean drained his beer, flung the bottle toward the paper box filled with empties, and stumbled to the cooler for another drink.

"Easy, turbo," Reed said. "Slow down."

He squeezed Aileen's hand. She squeezed back.

The trouble began with the spongy Nerf football. A few men played catch, launching it high over the fire. Aileen craned her neck, trying to follow along. After Sean's lob smacked Roberto on the shoulder, the men aimed at each other on purpose, each hit rewarded with rowdy laughter. She darted her eyes to the other campsite. What did they see? Her hand went sweaty in Reed's and she let go. Reed bounced the Nerf off of Sean, who howled in protest, and a free-for-all with the marshmallows followed. Aileen waited—would she be included in the game? A dirty lump landed in her lap, a toss from Janey, and Aileen heaved it at Reed. He caught it with one hand and threw it into the fire, which flared from the sugary fuel. The flames enthralled her.

Sean threw his bottle at the neighboring campsite. The bottle disappeared into the darkness and exploded on the road. Aileen jerked her gaze from the fire, jarred—and gratified—by the sound of tinkling glass. Others threw their beer cans, plastic cups, empty bottles of tequila and wine, kindling, rocks, whatever they could grab. Aileen jumped to her feet. United, they were unstoppable, the crashing skittering in the night.

"Stop," Janey shouted. "Stop!"

Aileen wobbled and sank into her chair. She stared at her right hand, which a moment before had held her third bottle of beer. Throwing with all her might had been ecstasy, to let loose against what troubled her.

A BOTTLE WHIZZED into the campsite. Lin leaped to her feet. She and her family were under attack. Sang was struggling to get out of the tent. She would have to hurry. Grabbing the lantern, she ran to the middle of the road, smelling the sticky sweet of the alcohol as bottles and cans rained down. If she did nothing, they would never stop. They would swarm like locusts, consuming and destroying. She picked up a triangular shard of glass, rubbing her thumb in the hollow. One slip and she could slit open her hand. Backlit by the fire, the foreigners looked huge and spiteful, but she was invisible to them, another patch of darkness in the road.

With steady hands, she lit the lantern and threw.

Janey scolded the group. The tightness of her voice betrayed her fear. "You have to clean up and apologize to the people next door. The ranger is probably on his way. We'll get kicked out."

Mike put his arm around her. "What the fuck?" he said. "Not cool, guys."

Everyone shouted, arguing who was to blame and what to do next, too ashamed to look at the other campsite. Aileen could imagine her own parents cowering with the Chinese family. She had switched allegiances in exchange for nothing lasting. Reed rubbed the small of her back, which ached from sleeping on the ground, from an oncoming period, or from the creature within her, dividing and dividing. He and a baby would always remind her of her complicity.

Gretchen screamed first. A tent was ablaze, a shuddering mass of flames, and people tripped over themselves as they rushed to get up. The ground was covered with dry leaves and redwood cones, which fed the flames that licked at an SUV parked next to a tent. Reed grabbed a jug of water and poured it onto the fire. Others scrambled for their Nalgenes and bottles of Gatorade and cranberry juice, and with frenzied shakes flung the liquid, arcing and glittering in the firelight like writhing water snakes.

Reed shoved a bottle of water into her hand. Stunned to realize she had not moved, she poured the water. The flames grew higher. She backed away from the searing heat as others jostled past her. By the time the fire truck arrived, they had beaten down most of the flames that had consumed three tents, singed a redwood, and melted the tires on the SUV. An acrid, chemical smell permeated their clothing, their hair, and their skin. The medics wrapped Gretchen's ankle, which she sprained when she fell, trying to run for help. Officials questioned the rest of the group in an investigation that would later determine the fire was accidental, caused by a lamp tipping over.

Afterward, people packed, dismantling their tents and tossing their sleeping bags and air mattresses into their trunks. The disembodied light of their headlamps bobbed as if will-o'-the-wisps had taken over the campsite. She and Reed hugged Janey good-bye, climbed into his car, and drove away on Highway 1. One false move and they would plummet from the cliffs and into the ocean. No one told the ranger about the run-in with the other campsite. No one but Aileen saw the lamp flying through the air, a beacon, a firebomb. No one but she could have imagined that look of defiant pleasure. For what they shared, the woman deserved her silence.

At last, Lin could sleep. With Sang at the wheel and her parents nodding off in the back seat, they were safe together. She wondered if they had seen her throw the lantern, an act she watched outside of herself in disbelief and with a frightening glee. The bright lights of the fire investigators and squawking radios made sleep impossible at the campsite, and they packed while her parents waited in the car. As they pulled away, their headlights swept over the neighboring campsite. An arm, a leg, tents. And for an instant, she saw the ABC—eyes downcast, shoulders slumped, body like a snapped rubber band—then trees and dark spaces. Did shame twist the other woman's face? They were not so different after all.

They drove a few miles on the winding roads before Sang pulled into a turnout at the edge of a cliff. Here was quiet and the stars that the redwood trees had hidden from view. In her seat, she snuggled under the sleeping bag, which she intended to return, along with the tent and everything else from the sporting-goods store. Camping had fooled her into thinking that she belonged where she did not, as if the equipment alone could guarantee happiness and safe passage.

The Responsibility
of Deceit

We arrived in Napa Valley at night, after battling Friday rush-hour traffic and dodging oncoming cars on the two-lane roads. Our headlights illuminated snatches of rolling hills, fences, and metal stakes in the dark vineyards.

It was all last minute. A friend of Peter's prepaid for a stay months ago at a bed-and-breakfast but broke up with her boyfriend last week. Planning in advance jinxed things. This trip was our first to wine country. We had stayed in Russian River and sunned poolside with the other men at Fife's, but Calistoga offered gauzily romantic activities: hot-air balloon rides, couples' massages, and bicycles built for two. We needed to get away. In the last month, after our fight in the car, we had avoided each other, spending time apart at lab, at work, or at the gym.

The GPS told us to go left, right, right, until we were parked in front of Whitmore Manor, where everyone else appeared to be tucked away for the evening. The owner had left the keys to our room and to the house taped to the tall front doors, along with a note written in tight, small cursive script: *Quiet hours begin after 10 pm. Extra pillows and blankets are in the armoire. Breakfast served from 8 to 9:30 am.*

She had signed the note, "Mistress Goodnough."

"She sounds like a discount dominatrix," I said.

"Or a pilgrim."

We crept into the house like bandits, our eyes adjusting to the glow from the moon and the night-light in the front parlor. There was a plate of chocolate chip cookies on a side table. Reaching for one, I tripped over a cat, which yowled and darted under the table. Laughing, Peter stilled the quaking table and righted the chubby porcelain figurines toppled next to the cookies. I wasn't used to house pets. My immigrant Chinese parents saw no use in feeding an animal that lived in the house, or for that matter, any creature not bound for the dinner table. Practical, they saw themselves undisputed at the top of the food chain.

As a result, I was uneasy around dogs and cats, never quite sure what to do with myself or their sentience, and nervous around goldfish, wondering if I should tap the glass tank or leave them alone. Peter bonded with animals, extending his curled hand to their noses, getting on his knees to play with them, and letting them lick his face. "You're too easy," I once said, teasing him about his loose affections. "You're too cautious," he replied.

We took careful steps on the creaking staircase to our third-floor room, the Hedgehog's Nook, dominated by a huge four-poster bed, hung with watercolor sketches of the misty English countryside, and scented with lavender. A pair of stuffed hedgehogs, kissing, sat against plumped pillows. One was wearing a lace dress and a bonnet, the other wore a checkered cap and short red velvet pants on its stubby legs. A magnet held their lips together.

I set the pair on the mahogany nightstand, turning their heads to the wall. I didn't want them to see what we were up to. When I turned around, Peter was sprawled on his stomach, wearing only his boxers. Like Clark Kent, he could shuck off his clothes in a single bound. Tall and lean, he had curly brown hair starting to thin that we were debating whether to shave off. I was shorter, stocky, and strong from lifting weights.

He was more comfortable than me stripping down in strange places. In locker rooms, I kept a towel wrapped around my waist when I changed. At clubs, when men tore off their ribbed undershirts while dancing, I kept mine on.

"Calvin, I wonder how many couples have put this to use?" He tested the springiness of the bed with his hand, his query both scientific and flirtatious.

I slid in next to him. "Is that including the hedgehogs?"

At sixteen, he came out to his mother after his car broke down in the Castro. He'd spent the evening groping strangers in a club he'd entered with a fake ID. Although she picked him up with no questions, he told her over fries at the Bagdad Café. She had suspected, she said, but was waiting for him to tell her.

With me, Peter worried about dating someone still coming

out, and that he served as a training wheel that I would cast off when I came into my own.

"You'll marry a woman to please your parents," he had said as we drifted off to sleep one night. I held him tighter, but said nothing. I did not want to promise what I could not predict. In three years, I had revealed myself to my sister, Jeanne, to my friends, to coworkers, and to our neighbors in Berkeley. All dry runs for when I would tell my parents.

Last year, my family had watched an evening newscast that featured the Pride Parade in San Francisco. Drag queens, dykes on bikes, and so on. Then an Asian Pacific Islander group walked by, waving rainbow flags and beating drums.

"Those are Thai and Filipino." My father walked to the television and scrutinized them, inches from the screen. "Not Chinese."

Behind him, my sister had smirked. My mother glanced at the ancestral shrine on our mantelpiece, piled with oranges and fragrant with incense. "Their poor parents."

A THIN SHAFT of light through the heavy velvet drapes meant it had to be morning, probably early. Peter stirred beside me. I envied how he could immediately plunge into deep sleep, and then awaken ready to go, no matter where we were or how late we had stayed up.

His hand drifted across my stomach and down my thigh.

Mornings used to be our specialty, a quick romp before we headed out. We fell into each other. Afterward, I listened to the sound of water running somewhere in the house, and footsteps through the walls and the floor. Very soon, we would no longer have the whole place to ourselves.

"Let's go for a walk." Peter bounded over to the window and pulled open the drapes, letting in blinding light. I turned my head toward the wall.

"I think we're in a historic district. We don't have to go far." Whenever we traveled, Peter was out the door first, headed toward whatever looked interesting while I trailed behind with tour books and maps. I was in no mood to explore this morning, preferring to curl in bed with Peter, and try to reclaim a little lost sleep. "I don't feel like getting lost before breakfast," I said.

"Come on—live a little."

I pushed off the covers, willing myself to get out of bed. Peter flipped through a magazine on the coffee table, and then threw it back down.

"Never mind. We have all weekend." He disappeared into the bathroom and started the shower.

He was the only person I had ever been with, and I was still learning how to act in a relationship. My teenage years passed by without the usual sexual fumbling and confusion. Studying was enough for me, and for my parents, and in college, I continued as a sexless engineer, seeking comfort in the cold order of circuits.

As a graduation requirement, I took a biology seminar on animal behavior. I wrote a paper on homosexuality in animals, about rams that butted heads, male monkeys that rubbed one another, and boy dogs that licked each other. There were fags everywhere in the animal kingdom, exhibiting similarities that looked like the truth.

It had been obvious that I was struggling with myself. Peter had been amused at my awkward attempt to understand, but also had admired my logic, my drive to think through the matter. He hoped to see how I would turn out, he told his friends. He could want the kind of man I would become.

We ran into each other a year after graduation and only then did I admit to myself I was attracted to him. Even then, I thought it was because I found his field of study, biomechanical engineering, interesting. Later, when he kissed me, the years of calculus and physics fell away under the simple proof of his lips.

"In the animal kingdom, geese mate for life," I told him on our one-year anniversary. We were parked in a turnout in the Berkeley Hills, looking at the dark water of the bay and the glittering lights of San Francisco.

"Yes, but they also lay eggs and fly south for the winter," he said. "They're birds; instinct is all they know."

PETER HAD SEEN my childhood home only once before, last month when my parents were visiting my aunt in Los Angeles. He wanted to see where I grew up. I agreed, but only on the condition that we wore baseball hats and sunglasses. Lavenida was a small town, and we risked running into people who knew me.

"Why do I need to hide?" Peter had asked. "No one knows who I am."

"But then I'll look out of place, if I'm the only one covered up."

On the tour of my childhood, we first stopped by my elementary school, where the metal play structures had been replaced with a fancy climbing wall, and the sand with rubber mats. Then we visited the library, where I found a haven of science fiction books as a teenager. At my favorite novelty store, Peter bought sour apple bombs and a handful of green army men, one of which he marched over my arms and shoulders as I drove.

After we turned off the main strip of small shops, I followed the road to my neighborhood, passing through a tunnel of trees. I kept an eye out for deer and wild turkeys, whose population flourished here with no predator but car bumpers. Many houses were set back from the main road, glimpsed over hedges and through lush trees. Peter twisted around, looking in all directions, as if we were on an African safari instead of a ride down a suburban street.

"Did your parents change the house much?" Peter asked.

"After I left for college, Mom turned my bedroom into a guest room." My mother took over the closet space, but kept the same twin bed and plaid comforter. "She left my Academic Decathlon trophies. Jeanne calls it 'the shrine.'"

"Impressive. The same posters, too, on the walls? Let me guess. A black-and-white shot of Einstein, with his tongue sticking out? A map of the solar system? Or maybe an Oakland A's player you were fascinated with, but didn't know why at the time. You wanted to know all his stats."

The soldier lingered on my ear, circling, toying with my lobe. I took my right hand off the steering wheel and ruffled the back of his head.

"If you already knew everything about me, why did you want to come?"

"You might surprise me," he said. "There's a small chance."

"Am I that predictable?"

"Not predictable, Calvin. Just transparent."

I swatted away the toy soldier, machine-gunning against my ear. "I'm trying to drive."

I was turning onto my street when I spotted a familiar blue station wagon—my next-door neighbor's car—coming from the opposite direction.

"Get down, get down!" When he hesitated, I reached over and pushed him below the dashboard. He complied, hunching, his eyes level with the radio dial. I rested my hand on the back of his neck, where I could feel the tiny hairs and our sweat pooling beneath my fingers.

I looked away as I drove past the Volvo, and then back onto the main road into town. Not until we were back on the freeway did I tell Peter he could sit up. He rubbed the back of his neck, glaring at me.

"I'm sorry, but I thought I saw the neighbors." I punched up the AC.

"How would they even know we're together?"

"They would tell my parents they saw me, and my parents would ask why I came by when I knew they weren't there and who I was with. Questions I'm not ready to answer now."

"Or maybe ever."

He was not asking me to come out, only pointing out a possible truth. In this potential future, I would never acknowledge him, or myself, to my parents. And that would be the end of us.

———

DOWNSTAIRS, THE MISTRESS greeted us with a plate of cranberry scones. Wearing a striped dress that buttoned up to her throat and a frilly white apron, she told us buttermilk waffles and homemade sausages were on today's menu. She curtsied good-bye and stepped backward into the kitchen.

I broke apart a scone and gave Peter half, hoping that breakfast could help us start the morning over. He wolfed his share and held his hand out for more, smiling. He curtsied, imitating the mistress, before we took our seats at the long polished table across from an older couple. Tom and Diane were scouting Napa and Sonoma as a potential place to retire, maybe to raise alpacas or angora goats on leftover land no good for vineyards, they said. The fleece was soft, warm, hypoallergenic—all natural. "It's a better investment than emu." Tom resembled a gunslinger, with his bushy gray mustache, scar over his right eye, and battered cowboy hat. "They have a bad temper."

"Alpacas don't bite, but they do spit." Diane was tanned and wiry as a leather whip, with ropy muscles in her arms and neck. "When they get angry. Or agitated. You never know what might set them off."

Were people also one way or another in terms of temperament? Some were rude, some polite, some flamboyant, others bookish—it was in their nature. Biology was fate. If being gay was a trait like eye or hair color, then ancestor after ancestor had passed this inheritance down to me. It couldn't be helped. I could accept who I was if I had no say in the matter, and in this way I hoped my parents would understand, all of us released from responsibility.

I was pouring syrup on my waffles when Mr. and Mrs. Woo, my parents' favorite karaoke partners, walked into the dining room. The top fell off the miniature jug, and blueberry syrup flowed off the waffle and onto the plate. Peter took my hand and righted the jug. Looking where I was looking, he took his hand off my knee.

Why were they here? Middle-class Chinese immigrants stayed at glitzy hotel towers in Las Vegas, not at quaint bed-and-breakfasts. They didn't drink wine, comparing vintages; they sipped Rémy Martin at Chinese banquets. They wanted their own spacious suite, with a view, a luminous pool, and a buffet piled high with king crab and jumbo shrimp.

They were looking through brochures about wineries, hot-air balloons, and couple massages spread out on the antique sideboard. I wanted to slip out of the room or slide under the table, but it was too late. I couldn't hide.

"Woo Tai Tai, Woo Xian Sheng," I called out, using the Chinese titles of respect.

Mr. Woo looked around the room, confused at who was speaking to him in this unfamiliar place, before he recognized me.

"Xiao Hu!" He used my childhood nickname, "Little Tiger." My reserved parents, and their generation, showed rare affection to their children with such endearments.

"How are your parents?" he said in Chinese. "Your sister?"

He wore an argyle sweater vest, dress slacks, and wingtips, a banker even on weekends. He and my father were not the sort to wear shorts and sneakers and play basketball in the driveways with their sons. He and Mrs. Woo sat kitty-corner across from us.

"I'm having dinner with them tomorrow night," I answered in English. I didn't introduce Peter.

For years, I had attended Chinese school on Saturdays with their sons, learning stick fighting and how to cheat on tests. Victor was married to a filial Chinese daughter, a pharmacist, and Ernest was dating one, my mother reminded me at dinner each Sunday.

My parents were zero for two, in terms of arranging the proper relationship for either of their children. They matchmade with friends over karaoke and at Chinese wedding banquets, but their schemes never worked. My sister and I begged off dates, with busy schedules as an excuse, or consented at most to one dinner. My parents adhered to strict Chinese traditions that we learned to circumvent. Over the years, we shared the responsibility of deceit, the big and little secrets that oiled the machinery of family expectations.

Peter and I lived together on the second floor of an old house. We alternated between the two bedrooms, depending on the mood—either to bask in the glow of a tropical fish tank in his room, or to snuggle in my feather comforter and flannel sheets. I kept the doors to the bedrooms shut when my parents visited. Ever polite, they never asked to look inside.

A year ago, my sister had moved in with her boyfriend, Phuoc, whose parents were refugees from Vietnam. They lived in San Jose, more than an hour away, too far for my parents to drop by unannounced. As far as they knew, her roommate was a medical student always at the hospital. Phuoc was a hardworking line cook bursting with ideas for artisanal dishes, farm-to-table-to-pun—but not Chinese.

"Victor and Ernest sent us here for our thirtieth anniversary," Mrs. Woo beamed beneath her permed hair and gold-rimmed glasses, much like my mother's. She was proud that her sons, a doctor and a software engineer, were successful enough to pay for the trip.

"They're making it tough for the rest of us," I said. "My sister and I will have to send our parents to a place like this, on their anniversary."

Mrs. Woo laughed. "Where's your girlfriend? My sons said, very romantic."

"Big beds," Mr. Woo said. "Comfortable."

"I'm here with my roommate."

The conversation halted at the inadequacy of the title. Mr. and Mrs. Woo looked at Peter, me, and then at each other as if to say, *We'll continue this later, in Chinese.* As oblivious as my parents and their immigrant friends were to pop culture or social revolutions, they knew that male roommates did not spend weekends together in wine country.

"They told us you had a good friend," Mrs. Woo said after a minute. Her husband busied himself by pouring a glass of cranberry juice.

"We met in college," I said. "We like traveling together."

"You're just like Victor. Always liked to go out with his friends. Go to ski, go to Vegas, go around everywhere," Mrs. Woo said. "Finally he settle down."

She was giving both of us an out. She did not have to recognize what was before her, if I did not. It would have been easy. I had done it many times before, putting just enough distance between us when I saw someone I was not ready to out myself to. On guard in public, putting Peter on edge all over again. He had already settled on who he was, but I had forced him again into hesitancy. I hung my head and closed my eyes, trying to relieve the pressure building.

Looking up again took an immense effort. Exhausted from last night, and from pretending, I put my hand on top of Peter's. He rubbed his thumb along my pinky, on display next to the butter dish. Our hands splayed together looked like a strange species of crab, one half pink and hairy, the other smooth and tan.

The Woos glanced down and kept talking about their plans for the day. Golf, Mr. Woo said. Mud bath, Mrs. Woo said. Wine tasting for us. Maybe they did not understand our precise relationship, or they disagreed with who we were, but they kept chatting with us. Small as the talk was, it left me hopeful.

I also knew that dealing with me was easier for the Woos than my parents. I was not their son. When I was nine, my paternal grandfather had died after wasting away in our spare bedroom for several months, and I came to associate the smell of herbal brews with decay and decline. My father cried that afternoon, standing over the body, choking gasps from a quiet man. I hid in my bedroom, covering my head with a pillow and scratchy Garfield comforter, but I could not escape the sound.

Soon after, he was on the phone, arranging for motels and airline tickets for relatives. I understood then that sons repaid their fathers at the time of death. And that sons had to have sons to carry on the family line.

At the funeral, taped Buddhist chants played on a portable

stereo. Incense drifted from the brass pot in front of the casket. The family took turns, each person bowing at the waist three times, then kneeling on the ground and touching their head to the floor, starting with the eldest son, my father, and ending with the youngest male grandchild, my cousin Louis. After my turn, I sat next to my mother and put my head in her lap, something I had stopped doing a year earlier, because it seemed too babyish.

"He's responsible for everyone now." My mother had stopped stroking my head and sat me upright, smoothing her hand down my back. I stared at the dark paisley carpet. If I looked at the casket, I might fall in, the lid closing over me. "Just like you will be."

I could guess how my parents would react in the abstract, but could not bear to imagine the details if I told them I was not whom they assumed. Would my mother wail about the shame to the family, would my father walk away? Would they tell me to leave and never return?

As much as I concealed from my parents, I needed them to be there to hide from. Worse than any rejection would be their absence from my life.

WE WERE AT our fourth winery, and I was getting buzzed. Although there was a silver spit bucket at the end of the counter, it seemed a waste of fine wine not to drink.

"Imagine what that tastes like." Peter tipped the bucket and peered inside. The mixture of wine and saliva sloshed against the sides, stinking of grape juice and yeasty ferment.

"This is much better." I swirled the rest of the Merlot in the back of my mouth.

Other couples stood at the bar, sniffing and downing their $10 glasses of wine. The wineries had different themes, tricked out as farmhouses and French chateaus, with outdoor sculptures, peacocks, aerial trams, whatever the rich founder fancied. You could be anywhere. This winery had the décor of an Italian villa, with a whitewashed exterior, red tile roofs, and bottles of olive oil sold beside the raffia-wrapped wine in the gift shop.

"Winemakers do it in barrels," he said, reading aloud from the front of a $40 apron. "That can't be comfortable."

"Or hygienic."

"Or romantic." Peter took my hand and we walked outside, up the hill, to a gazebo that overlooked a duck pond. We stumbled upon a couple necking inside, a man and a woman, both wearing tight black shirts and jeans. He had one hand up the back of her shirt, the other on her butt. She was stroking his face. As I tugged at Peter to walk away, the couple turned to us. Both slender and long-limbed, they were a matched pair of greyhounds.

"We're finished." The man motioned for us to come back.

"Your turn," the woman added. They walked back to the main building hand-to-butt, their arms crossed behind their backs and slipped into the pocket of their lover. They were like teenagers making out at a party, outdoing the ardor of other couples. I felt shy, inexperienced, and unable to meet the challenge.

It had taken a long time for me to hold hands with Peter in public, before graduating to pecks on the lips good-bye. My parents did not express themselves through hugs and kisses, and I had learned how to accept Peter's.

He walked to the far end of the gazebo, which overlooked a pond where a fleet of ducklings followed their mother. Bees buzzed on the overhanging honeysuckle. The wine and heat suddenly hit me. Woozy, I sat on a bench beside him. We had said little of our encounter with Mr. and Mrs. Woo. I touched his wrist, and he looked down at me. "So we're roommates."

"What does it matter what I call you?" My head throbbed.

"It matters. What would you call me if no one else was around?"

"Someone's always around. With my family, it's never just us."

EVER SINCE I left home, I returned without fail on Sundays. Coming back from Napa, we drove past the suburbs that had grown from sleepy to self-satisfied in the last decade, as the wealth seeped eastward along Highway 24. The plan was to drop him off at the BART station and for me to go home for dinner, but I accelerated past the exit. I knew now I could not give up whom I loved most for my family. My parents made me the man with whom Peter fell in love. Peter made me the man I wanted my parents to love. Without both, I could have neither.

Peter, engrossed in a science journal, did not notice where we were until we turned onto my street. I parked across from the house, behind Jeanne's car. My sister had beaten me home.

"You forgot to drop me off," he said.

"I didn't forget."

What I wanted sank in. "Are you sure?"

"Are you?"

He snapped the journal shut. The cooling engine ticked, solemn as a metronome. "Are you worried that your parents' friends will out you?"

"I don't know how the Woos would even bring it up. It wouldn't be very polite, to get into family business."

"This is something you should do by yourself. They'll want to talk to you alone."

"If you're there, they can't deny you exist."

"I don't want to be a prop." He dropped the journal on the floor. "They'll blame me for making you gay."

"Please." My back was sticky with sweat and my mouth tasted skunky.

He ran his hand along the diagonal seat belt strap, but hesitated above the buckle. I pressed down with both hands on his, releasing him, and embraced him clumsily, inhaling his musky scent, which I could identify from a lineup of dozens.

I could see the silhouette of my mother in the kitchen window of the white ranch-style house, maybe washing off bai cai in the sink or filling the battered tin teapot with water. My father was laid bare in the living room window. The television flashed against his face. He was frugal, turning on the lights in the last minute of sundown. The scene was routine—their life, the moment before they learned that their only son was gay.

Much confusion and blame tumbled out afterward. My parents shut me out, with my sister forced to act as a go-between, the messenger of their accusations and their pleas—first hurt, then hopeful—for me to be normal, to marry, and to have children.

My mother consulted a Chinese fortune-teller, seeking cures. When told that I would not change, she vowed to jump in front of a bus. My parents stopped boasting about me to their friends, who understood not to ask questions. Two years later, they did not go to our wedding in San Francisco's city hall, but sent us a red envelope of crisp $100 bills. Three more years followed and they came back into our lives after we designed a website to attract a birth mother. Both of us smiled so hard in our pictures that our cheeks throbbed as if punched. My parents offered to pay for an egg donor and surrogate to carry our child—our son. A baby they could understand and get behind.

I knew none of that, then. But as I watched my parents through the window, I knew it was my responsibility to tell them. If I did not, all the other duties I tried to fulfill meant nothing.

That night, the moment my key goes into the lock, my parents rush to the door. My father shouts to my mother: "Lai le, la le!" He has arrived. I hear the television turn off, the running kitchen faucet go silent, and their quick steps on the tile floor.

Peter and I stand apart, flanking the welcome mat. I hold my breath until the door swings open, and my parents greet me with smiles. I slip my hand into Peter's, and we go in.

Accepted

It occurred to me that I'd become too comfortable with breaking and entering.

Back from field training, I'd leaped onto the windowsill in a single bound, no awkward scrambling, as though onto a pommel horse, despite my combat boots and my Kevlar. I crouched, resting my hands lightly on the frame. My ponytail bobbed and then went still. In perfect balance, I could have carried a stack of books on my head, a debutante but for the stench of dirt and sweat.

I tiptoed in the dark until realizing my roommates were out. As I set down my ruck, an RA in the lounge shouted an invitation to join a group headed to Flicks. A door slammed, and a basketball thudded down the hallway. From the floor above, reggae blasted, competing with the howl of a blow dryer. No sign of the dorm settling down Sunday night, not with the last of the weekend to enjoy.

Too tired to shower, I collapsed onto the futon for a nap before my all-nighter. A sudden, strange lull descended, so complete it seemed like I was in one of those sensory-deprivation chambers that drive test subjects insane. I couldn't shake the feeling that everyone in the world had disappeared. "Hello?" I called out. "Hello, hello." No one answered, and I fired up Julia's laptop to fill the void with light and noise.

We met fall quarter, after I studied her for a half hour while she sunbathed. Her body long and lean in a black sports bra and board shorts, on the lawn outside her dorm, the new one with spacious lounges and nooks for studying, and where I wanted to live most. Julia seemed like the kind of girl who adopted wounded birds and stray puppies, willing to help a newcomer in need.

I told her I had nowhere to stay because of a mix-up in Housing. Officials said they might find something within a week or two, but until then I'd be sleeping in the twenty-four-hour room at the library. What a way to start freshman year! Julia, a sophomore, invited me to crash in the room she shared with her best friend. One night turned into a week, another and another, and then we were at the end of the quarter, Dead Week, finals, and saying our good-byes for the holidays. Without their knowledge, my roommates had aided and abetted me. My classmates considered me no different than them, these student body presidents, valedictorians, salutatorians, National Merit Scholars, Model UN reps, Academic Decathletes, All-State swimmers and wrestlers, and other shining exemplars of America's youth.

———

THE REJECTION FROM Admissions was a mistake. That's what I told myself after I clicked on the link and logged on to the portal last spring. Stanford had denied another Elaine Park, another in Irvine who'd also applied. I waited for a phone call of apology, along with an email with the correct link.

I hadn't meant to lie, not at first, but when Jack Min donned his Stanford sweatshirt after receiving his acceptance (a senior tradition)—I yanked my Cardinal red hoodie out of my locker. When my AP English teacher, Ms. Banks, stopped to congratulate me, I couldn't bring myself to say, not yet. She'd worked with me on a dozen revisions of my college essay and written a generous letter of rec, and I didn't want to disappoint her.

Another week passed, and I posed with Jack for the school paper. A banner year for the church our families both attended, and for Sparta High, with two students in a single class admitted to Stanford. When I showed my parents the article as proof of my acceptance, Appa held the newspaper with his fingertips, as if it were bridal lace he was preserving on a special order. He reeked of chemicals from the cleaner's, the stink of exhaustion and servility.

"Assiduous." His praise for my hard work. My vocab drills, which began nightly when I was in kindergarten, had fallen to him. For years, he'd been reading the dictionary for self-improvement, and the words we'd studied together coded what otherwise might remain unsaid.

"Sagacity." I thanked my father for his wisdom.

In June, with graduation approaching, I politely alerted Admissions of its error.

"You haven't received any notification?" the woman asked on the other end of the line.

"A rejection. For another Elaine Park." Only then did I realize how ridiculous I sounded. Could I appeal the decision, or get on the wait list, I asked.

No, she gently said. She explained that those chosen off the wait list had been notified two weeks ago, and wished me the best of luck.

All those hours, all that money. The after-school academic cram programs. The cost kept us from moving out of our tiny two-bedroom apartment, whose only amenity was its location in a desirable school district and the stagnant pool where my neighbor taught me to swim. Other sacrifices: Appa put off visiting the doctor until his colds turned into bronchitis and then pneumonia. Umma's eyes going bad, squinting at the alterations she did for extra cash at the dry cleaner where they both worked.

Stanford was the only school to which I'd applied, the only school my parents imagined me attending. On our sole family vacation, before my junior year, we piled into the car and drove to Stanford and back in a single day, a seven-hour trip each way—enough time to eat our gimbap rolls in the parking lot, snap photos of Hoover Tower, buy a sweatshirt, and pick up a course catalogue and a copy of the *Stanford Daily*, all of which I studied as closely as an archaeologist trying to crack ancient runes. I was supposed to become a doctor and buy my parents a sedan and a house in a gated community. A doctor had a title, respect, and would never be brushed off like them, never berated by customers, and never snubbed by salesclerks. My sister, who sulked the entire ride to campus, wasn't to be counted on. Five years younger than me, a chola in the making, with Cleopatra eyeliner and teased bangs, she'd turned rebellious in junior high. She could take care of herself, and I'd take care of our parents.

When I asked the Admissions officer if I could send additional letters of rec, her tone turned icy. "We never reverse a decision officially rendered." She hung up.

The problem, I came to understand, was that my story was too typical. My scores, my accomplishments, and my volunteer work were identical to hundreds, maybe thousands of other applicants, and Admissions had reached its quota of hard-luck, hardworking children of immigrants. I'd been too honest, straightforward where I should have embellished, ordinary where I should have been fanciful. My classmate Jack had launched his own startup, sending used cell phones to Africa. If only I'd been a homeless teen or knit socks and mittens for orphans in China. If only I'd had cancer.

I couldn't tell my parents the truth, not after my pastor announced my Stanford acceptance at church. If my high school classmates found out, I'd become a joke. But if I spent time on the Farm, I'd discover the secret of how to talk, how to act, how to be. When I became a full-fledged student, no one had to know I had been anything but. I searched online to see what incoming freshmen said about forms, housing, tuition, and classes, and told my parents I'd been awarded a government scholarship, and a work-study job to cover the rest.

At the bus station, Umma pressed her papery cheek against mine and gave me a sack of snacks, puffed rice and dried seaweed.

My parents wanted to caravan with Jack's family, but I told them not to waste a day's pay by taking time off. My sister wished me luck, less surly upon realizing she'd get my room after I left. Appa handed me a prepaid cell phone and gruffly reminded me to call on Sundays.

"Cogent," he said. Other words described me more aptly, that I didn't dare say: *legerdemain, reprobate.*

EARLY MONDAY MORNING, the room phone rang, Julia's mother. I was typing notes for Hum Bio on her laptop, preparing for a test I'd never take. Not strange at all, considering there was a word for it—*auditing*—learning, but without credit.

Covering for Julia, I told Mrs. Ramirez she was at practice. She had probably spent the night at Scott's, from the men's crew team. They'd been hooking up, but he was also hanging out with other girls.

Scott. He couldn't be trusted. Not after last night, when he'd come looking for Julia. It was late, late for her, usually asleep after dinner, on the water at first light for crew practice. I expected him to leave, but he'd sprawled onto the futon—my bed—and asked about my weekend.

"At the pool." I'd learned how to turn my pants into a personal flotation device. Wriggling out, knotting each leg like a sausage, my fingers cramped and slippery. Jerking the pants overhead in a single motion, to fill the legs with air. How to swim on my side, raising my dummy rifle out of the water. The calm I felt, as splashes ricocheted around me. "Water combat training."

"Badass," he said.

He wasn't making fun of me. He was checking me out, his eyes following the line of my legs, up to the powerful curve of my thighs in a pair of running shorts. My body had changed under PT, turned harder, stronger, faster, and the hours I used to devote to studying I now spent jogging on Campus Drive and lifting weights.

I blushed, trying to fasten the buttons of the shirt I'd tossed over my sport bra. Scott had long eyelashes, so lush he could have been wearing mascara. The air between us had thickened. His deodorant had a woodsy, musky smell that made me think of plaid and lumberjacks. His phone had buzzed, a text from Julia. She was waiting for him at his place, he'd said, and loped off.

Although I'd dreamed I would find lifelong friends at Stanford, women who would be my bridesmaids and men to pal around with and maybe date, I remained apart as ever. Except for Julia. Because I was a cul-de-sac, not in her circle of jock friends, she trusted me with her secrets. Her fears about Scott, her complaints about our roommate Tina, so spoiled, so careless with her money.

I pushed Tina's mess away from my corner. She'd begun encroaching, her textbooks, her crumpled jeans, her energy bar wrappers, and hairballs swirling like the Pacific garbage patch. Tina was Chinese American, the daughter of immigrants too. From Grosse Pointe, she was used to being the only Asian and had run with a popular crowd in high school.

Before break, I told them that Housing had found a spot for me. When the new quarter began, I said it fell through. A few times, I'd walked into the room and the conversation stopped, and I knew they'd been talking about me. Although it might seem strange that they never locked me out, they were too polite, too trusting of a fellow classmate in need.

My stomach growled. Security was lax on campus, but the dining hall at this hour wasn't busy enough to sneak through the exit for breakfast. Freeloading didn't seem like stealing, not exactly, with more than enough food and classroom seats to go around. I only took what would go to waste.

I dug through my ruck, searching for my ROTC assignment due that afternoon. Although the corps had been banned on campus during Vietnam War protests, Stanford students took classes and trained with battalions at other local colleges. I'd slipped through a loophole, able to sign up because of the informal communication between the schools about the program.

I hitched a ride three times a week to ROTC with a pair of Stanford seniors, who'd both committed to serving eight years in the army. Friendly but not looking to make another friend, not with graduation and a likely deployment to the Middle East looming. Still, I was grateful for the assignments in military history some treated as a joke, and grateful for the rank of cadet. Grateful for the ruck, and the Kevlar that gave me a look of purpose, compared to the Stanford students dressed in shorts and sandals all the time, like they were going to the beach. BDU—battle dress uniform. LBE—load-bearing equipment, harness, canteen, first-aid kit, and ammo pouch. I was proud to speak the language of ROTC, proud I could navigate in the dark, armed with a map, compass, and a piece of paper. Finding the point, finding the code, finding the pirate's buried treasure.

Flipping open my binder, I found a flyer urging Stanford cadets to apply for the ROTC honor roll with the attached form and an unofficial transcript. A reminder I didn't have grades, and wasn't enrolled, a reminder I should give up and go home. I wasn't a legacy, and didn't have a family spending thousands—millions—to get me in. Surviving day-to-day brought me no closer to becoming an official student. I imagined my father's disappointment, my father's words: *ignominious, mendacious.*

After reapplying, I was waiting for my acceptance from Stanford. Sometimes in lecture hall, biking through White Plaza, shuffling through the dining hall, and at my café job, I sank into the illusion that I belonged here. No different, common among the uncommon. My fingers moved over the keyboard, typing out my classes from first quarter and a grade for each. Three A-minuses, and a B-plus and a B: I wasn't greedy. If only I'd been given the chance, it would have been my transcript. If—no. The problem sets were impossible and I probably would have flunked out of pre-med. I hurled the binder across the room, hitting Julia's dresser, knocking over a corkboard plastered with photos of her friends and family. Propping it up, I tried to straighten the crooked picture of us goofing around, wearing sunglasses and singing into hairbrushes.

Julia burst into the room, back from crew practice. With her broad teeth, broad smile, and glossy chestnut hair, she'd make a good show horse. She swept past me, grabbing her birth control pills. As she broke the foil and tipped one into her mouth,

I shoved fallen photos under the futon with my foot. When she reached for her laptop, I slid it away, snapping the lid shut. She reached again.

"Sorry." I didn't hand it over. I said her mother called, hoping Julia might thank me for covering for her. She didn't. She hovered as I restarted her laptop, its hard drive whirring and hanging.

"Never mind." She grabbed her dining hall pass and left.

The day had barely begun, and I'd pissed off the one person who cared about me here. The laptop woke up, and the file popped open to my fantasy list of grades. If only those could be my marks. That's when it hit me: an unofficial transcript was easy to fake, without requiring a watermark or school seal, Courier font in Microsoft Word. With it, I'd apply for the ROTC honor roll. I'd never become Dr. Kim, but with a résumé listing my honors and awards, I'd get an internship, and later on, a job to support my parents. Weren't tech startups full of dropouts? I hit delete and lowered my A to a B+ in Hum Bio. It didn't seem fair to give myself an F for a class I wasn't enrolled in. I decided the grades should reflect my efforts and no one, knowing the lengths I'd gone to, could question mine.

OVER THE NEXT few weeks, my luck turned. With my faked transcript, I made the ROTC honor roll, received a ribbon for my uniform, and sent the newsletter listing my award to my parents. It wouldn't be long until I received my acceptance from Admissions, I told myself. Scott was coming around more often, too. Flirting, when he brushed a leaf out of my hair or when he helped himself to dry cereal from a bowl in my lap. His casual touching, as if I were a prized possession. Nothing could happen between us, not if I wanted a roof over my head, and yet I found myself hoping that each knock at the door meant him.

When Julia tried to tell him she loved him, he'd acted weird and left in a hurry, she'd confided. Just before I left for weekend field training, I found the futon folded up into a couch, heaped with dirty laundry, sweat-stained athletic bras and balled-up panties, a move territorial as a dog pissing on a fire hydrant, potent as a radiation symbol not to touch. Julia stood in the doorway, Scott behind her. She drew herself up, and told me I had to be out by next Friday, when their families were visiting for Parents' Weekend.

What if I spent those nights away and returned after the weekend? "From now on, I'll stay out one night a week," I pleaded.

She bit her lip.

"Two nights. Please. I'll keep out of Tina's way."

Mentioning our roommate seemed to remind her of their arguments against me. Julia straightened. "It's Housing's responsibility. Not ours."

I tried to catch Scott's eye—she'd listen to him—but he was intent on his texts. Had I imagined his attraction? For him, a game, a reflex.

"I could pay." I had a couple hundred dollars saved from my job at the café. Although their room and board had been covered at the beginning of the quarter, I could give them spending money.

"I have no choice," she said.

"You have more choices than me." I shouldered my ruck and left.

On the drive to field training, my head ached, tender as an overinflated balloon.

I stumbled through the mission, to clear an abandoned house on the training course. First the squad leader forced us into a ditch. Soaked, our BDUs clung and chafed, then stiffened in the rising heat of the day.

"Cover me while I'm moving!"

"You got covered!"

"Moving!" I ran flat out for three seconds, my heart pounding in my ears. I cleared my head of everything but the task ahead, hurled myself into the dirt, into the rocks and burrs, a hard landing that stole my breath. When I swiveled my dummy rifle, scanning for enemies, Julia appeared beneath a tree. I aimed. I'd never felt so bright, like ten thousand flashbulbs going off, and then she vanished, quicker than I could have pulled a trigger.

WHEN I RETURNED to campus late Sunday afternoon, red and white balloons had sprouted, along with vinyl banners, temporary stages, and areas cordoned off for Parents' Weekend. The window to our room was locked, the shades down. I jogged to the dorm entrance and waited for someone to let me in. I fidgeted in my muddy boots. If I were a cartoon, a gray cloud of stink would have trailed me. At our room, I reached for the doorknob and then dropped my hand. From now on, I had to knock first. Julia told me to come in.

I discovered the futon folded up and my belongings missing. I sank to the floor, everything I'd been carrying these past
months crushing me. Julia rushed toward me, her arms out, with
the same concern that had welcomed me to campus, a concern
that I'd have to kindle if I wanted to remain her charity case.
I lied. "There's been a fire." The cleaner's burned down earlier
this month, I added. I could almost smell the blackened rem-
nants of the shop, see the collapsed roof and charred timbers
and smashed glass, and the melted plastic bags. Taste the sickly
sweet ash floating in the sunshine. My parents were out of work
and sticking them for the bill for room and board would bankrupt them. She hugged me, enveloping me with the scent of
laundry detergent and clean living. I felt guilty for aiming at
Julia's mirage during field training, even if I hadn't meant to,
even if near heatstroke had put me in a trance.

I became aware of my stench, its density, crowding out the
air in the room. Julia said she would take up a collection around
the dorm to help my family get back on our feet. Tina hadn't
budged from her bunk. *Bullshit*, her expression said.

"We can talk to the RA in your new dorm, too," Julia said.
How easily she thought she could get rid of me, how little I mattered. She'd showered me with goodwill until she lost interest
in me, as if I were an Easter chick sprouting scraggly feathers.

Stiffening, I drew away from her. She was wearing an oversized Stanford crew sweatshirt—Scott's. The song ended and, in
the silence, Julia added that my sister had friended her online.
"She wanted directions to our dorm."

My sister and I had never been close. Umma had promised

me a baby brother, and when Angela arrived sickly and translucent as a tadpole, I had been disappointed.

I jumped up. "What did you tell her? Did you tell her I was moving?"

"For Parents' Weekend," Julia said.

Tina opened the window, breathing through her mouth, making no effort to hide her disgust at my reek. Both their sisters were going to spend the night here, she said. "We'll be on top of each other. But we're used to that."

"I didn't think you'd be psyched to see Tina's family," I said. "Doesn't she get whiny around them?"

Julia gaped at me. The secrets she'd whispered to me in the dark were on fire, sticky and searing as napalm. Fighting back, I felt as exhilarated and terrified as I had been on the training mission. As Tina lit into her, I fled outside. My weekly calls home had dwindled to once or twice a month, from a half hour to a few minutes. My sister answered on the first ring.

"Don't do this to them," I said.

"To them?" Angela asked. "You think I want to spend all weekend in the car with them?"

Bedsprings creaked, and I pictured my sister on her back, her narrow feet propped on the wall. "They bragged at church about the honor roll, and Jack's parents asked if they were going to Parents' Weekend. Got them excited about visiting their number one daughter."

"I have midterms," I said. Gas prices. The expense. The drive. The hassle of registration.

Each excuse sounded flimsier than the last.

"I get it now," she said. "Why I couldn't find you in the school directory."

I had nothing to negotiate with, nothing but the threat of what would happen if the lies came to an end. "If I move home, you'd be back on the foldout," I said.

Silence. "Maybe they'll stick you there. Or kick you out." She paused. "It's time they stopped thinking you'll save them."

Time I stopped thinking it too.

AT THE DORM, I found my stuff in the lobby. I wouldn't have a chance to apologize. It took a couple of hours, dozens of trips with an overstuffed backpack to the library—carrying all my books and clothes at once would make the clerk at the front desk suspicious—but I managed to hide everything deep within the stacks. I was a mess, drenched in sweat, and my hair matted against my scalp, and still filthy from field training. In the restroom, I splashed water onto my face and into my armpits. My shirt was soaked, and after I leaned against the sink, the crotch of my pants too, as though I'd peed myself. When the door swung open, I hid in a stall, trembling. Opprobrium.

My sister had relented and promised to keep quiet, but I had to find another place to live within a few days, before Parents' Weekend started on Friday. When I canvassed dorms in search of roommates, people weren't as friendly to strangers, not like at the beginning of the year. Cliques had formed. Eventually, I might find a way in, though not before my family arrived.

My routine saved me. Although I could have stopped going

to class and ROTC, I would have had too much time to think about Julia, and how she'd turned her back on me. Blessed with so much, she'd accomplish everything she set out to do. I'd slip into insignificance, a footnote, if anyone remembered me at all.

I saw her once, by an ATM at Tresidder, and debated whether I should confront her, or convince her to take me back in. When Scott showed up with smoothies, we locked eyes. After he kissed the top of her head, I fled. Her—his—their rejection felt like Stanford rejecting me all over again. Everything here was sunnier and brighter, with an ease that blinded people, that made them forget about imperfection and turned them heartless.

The day before Parents' Weekend began, the notification arrived from Admissions. I logged onto the portal, feeling as though no time had passed, as if I were again a high school senior on the cusp. The screen flashed. "It is with great regret that we are unable to offer you admission . . . you are a fine student . . . want to thank you for your interest . . ."

Denied. Everything, everything, for nothing. I didn't belong at Stanford, never did and never would, in limbo, not here or anywhere, not of the present and lacking a future. Denied. I must have logged off, must have exited the library, but what I remembered next was Jack, my classmate from high school, calling my name. He rolled up on his bike. I hadn't seen him much, except in big pre-med classes, and by mutual unspoken agreement we never sat together. He'd gone preppy, with floppy bangs, khakis, and untucked button-downs after joining an Asian frat. He mentioned that our parents were driving up together and would take us to lunch tomorrow at a Korean restaurant.

The news of my deceit would spread through the church, among the only people my parents trusted.

"You can wait a day, can't you?" He grinned.

"I haven't had Korean food since winter break," I said weakly.

After we parted, I narrowly avoided a collision with another cyclist and a wooden bollard. No one loved me like my parents, and I'd returned their love with lies. I collapsed in the grass, watching students and professors zooming by on their bikes, and joggers in sunglasses and tight, shiny workout gear pounding past.

I couldn't stop my parents. But I could stop Parents' Weekend.

Though people here pretended to be laid-back, they couldn't, wouldn't be stopped from reaching their destination. Calling in a bomb threat wouldn't be enough. The situation called for something bigger, something louder, a credible threat, of the kind we'd been studying in ROTC: insurgency.

EVERYTHING FELL INTO place, except for one detail, one that had nothing to do with what I planned but explained everything I'd been driven to do. Minutes before dawn, I crept outside my old dorm, where I found the window cracked open and the room empty. After crawling inside, I searched for the picture on the corkboard of me and Julia lip-syncing, the only hard evidence of my months here.

Gone. Trashed, like she'd trashed me.

The room phone rang and rang, but I didn't answer. Julia's

cell phone buzzed, forgotten and left charging on the floor, and when I noticed the caller ID indicating her mother, I answered. I'd been making excuses for Julia for so long, I couldn't stop. Mrs. Ramirez said they were starting their drive and wanted to know if Julia needed anything. For a second, I almost said she was at Scott's. Mrs. Ramirez didn't know her daughter was hooking up with Scott, who Scott was, or that he wasn't much for relationships, but I said Julia was on the water, and promised to leave a note.

I stared at the background photo on the phone, her and Tina, their heads tilted together, eyes crossed, sticking out their tongues. Friends, best friends. Julia was certain of her love, and her family's, certain about everything, everyone but Scott. The tighter she clung, the more he pulled away, and if she lost him, then she might feel as abandoned as me.

From her phone, I texted Scott: "I love you." Now we were even.

THE SKY WAS starting to lighten. In the center of campus, nothing stirred but squirrels. At the base of a palm tree outside the Registrar's, I planted a liter bottle of gasoline stuffed with strips of a T- shirt. The golden gasoline sloshed back and forth, a storm in a bottle. Back home, palm trees were common, but not like the ones on campus, which were rumored to cost a year's tuition. The fronds were lush, a country club's, and fallen ones whisked away before they hit the ground.

I heard the whine of an electric cart, I ducked behind a post, and a groundskeeper went by. I'd have to hurry. I set down the letter, sealed in a clear plastic bag and held in place with a brick. Though I'd written it at the end of a very long night, the words had rushed out, with the inspiration I wished for in my college entrance essays. I ranted against rich kids and the parents who spoiled them, acting like they owned the world. Like they were the world itself. I taunted them, implying I'd scattered booby traps and bombs around campus.

Dousing the tree with gasoline, I lit the wick, which sputtered with the delicious hiss of a lawn sprinkler. The syrupy fumes made me giddy with the happiness I once thought I might achieve here. In White Plaza, I left another copy of the letter and lit a second firebomb.

I might have predicted the investigation, news stories, the online fan pages—"Elaine Park rocks!" At the jail, my mother in near collapse, propped up by my sister. Her face, awful and old, marked by grief as all her hard years had never marked her. My father asking why, not in Korean, not in SAT words, but in the plain English he reserved for customers. For strangers. His hope—his hope in me—would do me in. "I can't," I would say, my voice breaking. "I can't lie anymore."

His caved-in expression. "You have to tell everyone the truth. Telling me won't help."

Yet if I had been thinking clearly and stopped, if I had retreated, I would have missed the moment when I became mighty and billowing. The smoke drifted into the stratosphere with the crackle and roar of a wildfire. The dizzying smell of gasoline, of charcoal, of ash come alive. The flaming palm tree the most spectacular of all. An enormous Fourth of July sparkler, a gold-orange celebration burning on and on, a monument, a memory that would far outlast my time here.

The Shot

With the whistle of mortar fire, the golf ball strafed their heads and landed with a *thunk* on the green. Sam ducked, along with the two players in his group. He stared at the foursome behind them, resisting the impulse to hurl the ball into the creek that trickled through Hidden Valley.

"Fore!" the asshole shouted belatedly and shrugged his shoulders. The first time, Sam had given the man the benefit of the doubt. The man might not realize how far the ball would go, or maybe the trees had hidden their group from view. Now Sam knew that the man was hurrying them along. He looked familiar, but that was impossible. Sam had picked this course for its cheap greens fees and its distance far from anyone he knew.

He squared his shoulders, preparing to putt. He'd leave the man's ball alone. He didn't know the other two players—a grandfather and teenage grandson—and he didn't want to alarm them. They had met early that morning in the tee box, a pair looking for singles, and so far, Sam found them friendly, if quiet. He preferred quiet to buddy-buddy, to the men who shared their marital problems, tried to sell him car insurance, or offered him a toke of marijuana in between holes.

The dry, hot Santa Ana winds rustled in the skinny palm trees that lined the edge of the course. After Sam left this breezy oasis, the temperatures would go up twenty degrees. It was a week before Halloween, and the winds were vicious, overturning trucks and tumbleweeds on the freeway and fanning errant flames around Southern California.

As Sam focused on the dimpled ball before him, the image of his real estate agent popped into his head. Big teeth, big hair. "Number one seller in Rancho Cucamonga! Your home, your dreams!" Garrett Williams proclaimed from billboards, bus stops, and calendars that he sent to prospective clients. He'd sold Sam and his wife, Ani, their new home on a Jack Nicklaus–designed golf course. Faux Tuscan architecture, wall-to-wall carpeting, four bedrooms, an outdoor fireplace, and a wet bar in the living room. Garrett had also referred them to the local bank, where they took out a home equity loan to pay for their future: a good life, nursing school for Ani, while Sam taught tae kwon do at his own studio.

Sam swung and shanked it, hitting the ball almost out of bounds. He squinted at the golfer behind them. He wasn't Garrett. Garrett belonged to a country club in Chino Hills, the kind with a bar in the men's locker room, dark-wood paneling, brass rails, and paintings of fox hunting in the English countryside.

Garrett wouldn't play at Hidden Valley, a public golf course lo-cated in the heart of the Inland Empire. East of downtown Los Angeles, with parts so desolate the desert landscape resembled Tatooine, and as beautiful too, with its steep mountains and brilliant blue skies when the smog lifted in winter.

Not-Garrett waved at Sam, pleasantly, though as if to say, *Hurry up.*

With his right hand, Sam touched his holster. The gun was tucked into the hem of his pants, under his blue windbreaker. Sweat was pooling under the holster. He wasn't sure why he had taken the gun to the golf course, why he slipped on the holster this morning before he left the house, but he'd grown used to its presence, reminding him to stand straight, to be a man worthy of a gun. A man worthy of Ani.

He wasn't a nut, not like some of the men in the sheriff's reserve, eager to get their department-issued Beretta 92FS, who gleefully sprayed paper targets on the practice range. He had joined the reserve to help with the bills. The bank loan paid for the tae kwon do studio, for the renovations and the equipment, but the dojang didn't have enough customers to cover the rent and utilities, let alone monthly household expenses. Sam had heard that his military background would help him get hired, and the reserve had flexible hours. He liked the camaraderie of men and the sense of justice, of public service. And the badge— Ani had liked that, and the uniform too, at first.

Soon she complained that the work was dangerous, and she never got to see him. She was pulling double shifts at the hospital where she worked as a medical technician. She didn't like a gun in the house, either, though Sam protested that he was an excellent shot. "I could dot an *i* on a highway sign."

AFTER HOLING OUT, he walked to his cart. The red flag perched beside the hole snapped in the scorching wind.

"You laddies need anything?" the cart girl asked, after she rolled up to Sam and the two players with whom he'd been paired. *Cart girl* was a charitable term. She had the stout body, gray curly hair, and the reassuring yet domineering air of a junior high gym teacher.

Not like Ani, who was working weekends as a cart girl when they met six years ago. He fell hard for her curly brown hair gathered into a cheerleader's high ponytail, the tiny mole above her lip, and her teasing about his powerful but graceless swing.

She was the only daughter in a large Armenian family. Her five older brothers taught her how to play golf and to drive stick shift. At first, her parents didn't trust Sam; they wanted her to date someone from church, but she told them that Sam was Serbian, and that Serbians and Armenians had both been screwed by the Turks, and didn't that count for something?

Serbian looks dominated in Sam—that noble nose, that caveman's brow—and most people couldn't tell his mother was half Chinese but for his elfin eyes he'd inherited. Sam loved the big rambunctious dinners held by Ani's parents: the huge platters of lamb and pilaf and börek; being urged to eat, eat, eat, a sign of how her family looked out for each other, even if that sometimes meant meddling and unwanted advice.

One evening, after Ani's nephew rammed into her legs, she had cuddled him, stroking the boy's curls.

"Do you want another cousin?" Sam asked the toddler.

Ani glared at him, and Sam went silent, but it was too late, for her mother had heard and she launched into a plea for grandchildren. Ani didn't argue with her mother then, but Sam knew she was furious by the tight set of her shoulders. She didn't want her mother's life, forever sacrificing, in the kitchen, her worth dependent on her children. In the car ride home, Ani said, "I wish you could stand by me."

Now Sam looked down the fairway. The course marshal—a ruddy-cheeked, round-faced man in aviator sunglasses—was nowhere to be found. Not-Garrett climbed onto the rise and Sam decided to make him wait a few minutes longer. He bought a round of drinks: a beer for the grandfather, Juan, and a lemon-lime for Tony, the grandson. Juan nodded in thanks, his movements small and precise, nothing wasted. Tony dropped the soda, lunging forward to keep the can from rolling down the slope. He was clumsy, not yet grown into his body.

Sam hadn't known either of his grandfathers and probably would never have a grandson. He had only a few memories of his Serbian father, with his beaked nose, bushy eyebrows, and fairy-tale-giant height. At the annual blessing of the house, in celebration of his family's patron saint day, a bearded priest in velvet robes had chanted prayers.

His father left when Sam was six, and though his mother cut off ties to the Radulovich family, Sam never lost the longing for that which made him different. On his own, he sampled slivovitz, a harsh plum brandy, read up on the war in Yugoslavia, and found Serbian curse words online. His favorite was Yebachu ti sveca, or "I'll fuck your saint." When Sam repeated those curses, he felt an ancient power—almost medieval, with clanking armor and skulls on spikes—that he couldn't otherwise summon out of his suburban existence.

He clinked cans with Juan and Tony, lanky replicas across generations, down to the same protruding ears. Serious and cautious, they both squatted for a minute or longer to read the slope of the green.

"Much obliged." Juan adjusted his baseball cap on his bushy silver hair.

"Thanks again." Tony raised his can of soda, toasting Sam.

His genes living on, a chance to be the father that he never had—sure, Sam had considered all those reasons to have children, but what had appealed to him most was the fantasy of their family, them together against the world. He got into the cart. The group ahead—two Asian couples, Koreans, probably, the husbands in polo shirts, their wives in huge visors shielding their faces, like welder's masks—were betting on each stroke, exchanging fistfuls of dollars, which slowed down the game for everyone who followed. They should keep a running tally and pay out at the end of the round, but then, they wouldn't have the repeated joy of winning their small stakes.

He drove to the next hole, the wheels crunching on the gravel path. He should call his mother, and tell her what had happened between him and Ani. When he was growing up, she had worked two waitressing jobs, which kept them fed and housed but left time for little else.

He never stopped feeling abandoned, he'd once confided to Ani. She had folded her sinewy arms around him, her grip comforting and confining.

The idea for the practical joke had come to him after he browsed through an old-fashioned candy shop stocked with saltwater taffy, licorice, and other curiosities. He found an unopened packet of pills in the medicine cabinet, slit off the foil backing with an X-Acto knife, dropped in the pale yellow candies—remarkable, how close the resemblance—and glued back the foil. He smoothed the edges with his forefinger. Perfect.

Ani didn't notice the fake pills on the first day, or the next, but on the third, feeling dizzy and hot, she realized what he had done. She'd thrust the pack into his face at breakfast.

"Gotcha!" He realized too late how much he had wronged her. How much he felt she had wronged him, by denying him a family.

She hurled the pill pack, which slid across the table and onto the floor. "I don't want kids."

You don't want kids with me, he had been too afraid to say. He parked the cart. Ani had told him to keep out of the house while she packed today. He said he could help, he could fix breakfast, but she had sighed on the phone. "Please, no." She didn't want counseling, didn't want to forgive him, and he suspected that she'd already been on the verge of leaving him. She wasn't one to hash out a decision endlessly; once she made up her mind, she moved on. He pictured her filling her green suitcase with the rest of her clothes, cardboard boxes with her cookware, and trash bags with old magazines and half-empty shampoo bottles that she would tie and stack beside the garbage can. She'd given him back the wedding ring, closing his fingers around it for safekeeping.

A swift getaway, a clean break: independent, she'd kept a separate checking account and her last name after marriage. She would pack thoroughly and quickly. No one wanted to linger at Palm Estates, where the developer went bankrupt before finishing the project, leaving a hole in the ground for the swimming pool and metal posts but no security gate. Foreclosure signs hung in front of a quarter of the houses.

Lately, the Santa Anas had kicked up dust from the unlandscaped dirt, turning his eyes red and his throat raw. Fifteen miles south, a housing tract much like his own was on fire, sending up clouds on the horizon. Last night the television news broadcast a scarred black hillside, alight with red-gold flames, terrible and beautiful.

Suddenly he realized he should leave to help Ani, she couldn't say it, but that was what she wanted. This gesture would change her mind. He backed up the cart, which beeped with a silly shriek, and the urge left as quickly as it had arrived. He sagged into his seat. She didn't want to see him. Not-Garrett and his gang stood with their arms folded across their chests, glowering beneath their sunglasses. Sam bristled. He'd take as long as he needed.

"What's their rush?" Juan grumbled, and parked beside him.

He recognized the players. They'd tailgated him off the freeway this morning and tried to race around his truck to nab a spot in the parking lot.

Tony grinned. "We got there first."

A doe and two perfect fawns walked out of the oak trees, from the nature preserve abutting the course. The deer nibbled the grass, their heads bobbing in the sunlight, their backs speckled white, and their black noses glistening. Their bodies twitched and their tails flicked at unseen fleas. The thwack of clubs and the distant hum of traffic fell away, leaving Sam alone with the deer, who looked up at him, unafraid and trusting, and continued eating.

A flash went off, and the deer dashed into the woods. "I think the picture's blurry," Tony said, riveted by his camera phone. He wiped the smudged screen with the hem of his T-shirt and showed the picture to his grandfather. "We saw them last month." Tony stuffed his phone into the pocket of his shorts.

"Those guys"—Juan jerked his thumb behind him, at Not-Garrett—"miss stuff like this."

Sam realized that he had been holding his breath. He exhaled. He wished he could have shared this moment with Ani. He lightly touched his gun again, to check if it was secure. He slid out of the cart and shouldered his bag.

After he hit his shot, he wanted the ball to stay aloft forever, for that was when the impossible seemed possible: a hole in one, a prosperous business, a happy wife. The ball sailed up, up, up, streaking across the hazy blue sky, almost there—and into a sand trap, disappearing like a light winked out, like lost hope.

Fuck.

Tony teed up his ball and landed it on the green. He pumped his fist, so full of youthful exuberance that Sam sank deeper into his misery. Sam drove to the trap and spent the next few minutes digging out the ball. He planted his feet and swung shallow, scooped sand along with the ball, but no matter what he did, it rolled to the lowest point of the trap—what felt like the lowest point of Hidden Valley, at the lowest point of his life.

He peeked out of the trap to see Juan and Tony parked on the green. While they waited, Tony studied a thick textbook, highlighting frequently, while his grandfather bent his head over the book, reading along. Sam gritted his teeth. He would not let the ball defeat him.

He mouthed a tae kwon do chant to clear the buzzing in his head. With a buddy, he'd begun training while stationed in South Korea, something else to do besides going to bars, shopping for knockoffs, or eating at the American fast-food restaurants around Yongsan base. Something that marked the time he spent there as any different than if he had never left Southern California. He had impressed his instructor—a tiny, tidy man who marveled at Sam's speed despite his size. The smell of the red vinyl mats, the ritual bow as he entered and left the dojang, the power and control he felt going through the forms—all this, he loved.

He trained during his various deployments to Okinawa and Turkey. After his discharge and college graduation, Sam took a job selling copy machines. Because of his time in the service, he was older than the other salesmen, and always a beat behind their jokes, unfamiliar with their references to music and movies. After his coworkers invited him to the driving range, Sam accepted, grateful for something to talk about, and had taken up golf.

He swung again but the ball failed to clear the trap. He cursed, emptying himself into the expletives, his vision gone hazy. When he blinked, he found the club buried deep into the sand. With both hands, he pulled it out. Face burning, he knew that Not-Garrett and his gang must be laughing at him. He fetched the ball and climbed out.

AFTER THE NINTH hole, they stopped for hot dogs at the clubhouse. They had a few minutes. The Korean group ahead was fast on the fairways, but slow on the green. It was eleven thirty, and Ani would almost be done packing. She didn't have much to move.

Sam wolfed down the hot dog, the relish tangy on his tongue. His back was sore, his calves aching, and sweat soaked his visor, but he felt something like happiness for the first time that day. Although the sand trap had nearly swallowed him whole, golf offered redemption with every shot. Golf's appeal: its possibilities. If not this shot, the next. If not this hole, the next. If not this round, the next.

At the thirteenth hole, the cart girl rolled up and handed them gin and tonics in red plastic cups, and a soda for Tony. "The gentlemen playing behind you sent these drinks." Her expression calm, almost bored, as if she did such things every day.

"I'll be damned." Juan chuckled, a smile spreading across his face.

Not-Garrett gave him a thumbs-up. Sam sniffed the drink, sweet and herbal, cut through with the bright smell of the lime wedge.

"I mixed them fresh," the cart girl said.

Perhaps this drink was a peace offering, and Sam raised his cup in thanks. The drink was strong, just a splash of tonic. A breeze arrived, carrying the smell of cut grass and smoke from the wildfires. They were at the crest of a hill, a viewpoint from which they could see the course spreading below them.

He'd been to Hidden Valley once before, on a sting operation with the sheriff's department. Organizers of a private tournament erected "hospitality tents" around the course, and inside, prostitutes offered a menu of services. Sam, with the other officers, dressed in camouflage and hidden in the brush, spied with binoculars before busting the johns. That operation had earned Hidden Valley the unfortunate nickname "Hooker Valley." A majestic course, and Sam had always meant to come back with Ani. Patient and determined, she was a better golfer than Sam. She hit the ball straight, over and over, until she reached the hole.

Sam tipped the cart girl $5.

"I'm supposed to tell you that he'll buy you another round, if you let them play through." The cart girl fiddled with the lid of the cooler.

Sam dumped the rest of his drink onto the grass and flipped off Not-Garrett. Tony and Juan did the same, and their solidarity lifted the heaviness in Sam's chest. He knew he could count on them, if only for today, if only for this round, and it gave him more hope than he'd had in months.

"You'd think they hated each other, the way they're trying to get through the course as fast as possible." Juan squeezed his grandson's shoulder.

The fusillade began after that, as Not-Garrett and his gang rained down their balls. Sam and his crew took their own revenge, hurling the balls off the course. Not-Garrett seemed to have an endless supply, a golf bag full of balls.

"Christ," Juan said, after a ball twanged against the roof of his cart. He said he was going back to the clubhouse to report the group.

"Don't," Sam said.

Juan sized him up. If Sam told him what he wanted to say—that doing so would amount to defeat, a defeat that might crush him utterly—he would sound ridiculous.

"They might retaliate, if they get kicked off. They might come after us in the parking lot. Slash our tires. Threaten us with their golf clubs. I've seen that kind of thing, I've seen worse, while out on patrol."

At the beginning of the round, when they were exchanging their brief histories, Sam let slip that he was a sheriff, without disclosing that he was actually in the reserve.

Juan's expression softened, and he seemed to appreciate the warning. "You know best, I suppose. We only have three holes left."

Maybe, he added, they should let the group pass?

No, Sam said. "They'll think they can do this every time they play. They'll keep doing it, if we don't take a stand."

They kept playing, although Tony seemed shaken, missing his strokes and jumping out of his seat when balls whizzed by. He reminded Sam of himself as a teenager: big and shy, not quite understanding how he and his body had become so imposing.

A good kid, the kind Sam liked to teach at the dojang. When he opened his studio, he wanted to help his students conquer their fear. About a dozen remained. Debbie, a freckled college girl, who wanted to protect herself against rapists. Josh and Jack, redheaded eight-year-old twins who loved Japanese anime, fortune cookies, and all things Oriental. Leroy, a financial planner. Sometimes Sam thought his students could be enough, standins for the children Ani didn't want.

The economy tanked, people lost their jobs, their homes, and cut back on their visits to hair salons, to restaurants, to dentists, and to the dojang. When the adjacent doughnut shop and the Chinese takeout joint went out of business, Sam knew that he would too. He should have begged the landlord for a break on the rent, found more students from church, so many ideas that came to him too late. That was when he pressured Ani to have kids. When he swapped out her birth control pills.

Sam stretched, raising his arms above his head and bending at the waist to touch his toes. The Koreans paused on the green, passing around bags of snacks. The men didn't nuzzle their wives, no kisses or hugs, but Sam could tell who belonged with whom. The elegant woman in tan plaid passed a napkin to her husband, a stout sausage of a man. The shorter couple had flashy clothing, orange and pink like a tropical drink. Both couples had been married for years, Sam suspected, and would be for many more.

He hit a high, arching shot that landed six feet from the hole. He was playing better now than he had all day. Getting the better of Not-Garrett and his pals had improved his game. When he drove up in his cart, Juan clapped him on the back and Tony asked for pointers.

He would survive without Ani. He would have to. Maybe he would ask Juan for his phone number after the round and arrange to play weekday mornings or at twilight, when the rates were cheaper. He decided he would offer Tony free lessons, among the last he would teach before he shut the dojang.

A careering ball clocked Tony in the head, and the teenager tumbled to the ground. He made a strange, strangled sound and went still. The wind picked up again, the palm fronds thrashing and glistening in the harsh white light.

Juan rushed over to his grandson. "Call 911! Call the police! Please!" He hooked his hands under Tony's armpits and dragged him across the green. He staggered, his knees buckling under the weight. Sam grabbed Tony's splayed legs, trying to keep them together. His legs were damp and unwieldy. His fingers slipped and he tightened his grip around the ankles. Together they carried Tony, his backside sagging against the grass, and with a one-two-three, heaved the teenager onto the passenger seat. Sam held Tony up. Juan leaped into the driver's seat and put an arm around his grandson to hold him up. Sam whipped off his windbreaker and laid it across Tony, whose breathing was fast, faint, and shallow.

"I'm sorry," Sam said, the words familiar and choking.

Juan floored the cart toward the clubhouse and disappeared when the path dipped down the hill.

Tony.

The dojang.

Ani.

Sam clenched his hands, blood roaring in his ears, his chest close to bursting. He didn't know how many minutes had passed when Not-Garrett arrived in his cart.

"Things got out of hand," Not-Garrett said.

Things got out of hand when Not-Garrett hit into them on purpose. When Sam did not stop him.

"We didn't mean any harm." Not-Garrett stepped out of the cart. He was shorter than Sam imagined him, a garden gnome in tasseled golf shoes. "Let's go back to the clubhouse."

"You're under arrest." Sam flashed his sheriff's badge. He almost dropped it, his fingers fumbling with the leather case.

"We're both at fault." Not-Garrett pulled out his wallet. "It's the poor kid who got in the way. We can settle this right now." He held out a wad of $100 bills to Sam. His nails were buffed to a high gloss and his fingers fleshy and pink as piglets crowding their mother's teat.

As if money would solve everything. It did most things. Sam tried to draw his gun. The gesture was awkward, as though someone had pinned his arm behind his back. He trained the gun on Not-Garrett. Sam had hit the bull's-eye many times on practice ranges, but he had never aimed a gun at someone. How strange and alien the gun seemed in his hand. How tender and exposed the sunburned flesh of Not-Garrett's neck.

"Holy shit!" Not-Garrett dove into his cart and hit the accelerator, hunching his body and tucking his head. The cart veered off the path and into the green.

Sam released the safety, wheeled around, and aimed at Not-Garrett's ball, flecked with blood. In the distance, he heard sirens and people shouting. He was overcome with the same feeling of possibility, of perfection as when he watched his golf ball arcing across the sky. If he made this shot, then Ani would take him back, his dojang would be saved, and Tony healed. He realized his folly in the next instant—before the turf erupted, before the ball bounced, before the course marshals tackled him—and wished in that split second he could take back the mistakes that led to this moment.

Like the bullet, some things just couldn't be stopped.

VIP Tutoring

I met Angel while stuffing my family's restaurant menus under the front door of her apartment building. China Fresh was close to campus, and we delivered.

She clutched a map. "Do you speak Chinese?" she asked, her eyes wide and desperate.

This happened every so often, a Chinese man or woman urgently asking me, "Where is the nearest bathroom?" "Where is this street?" Their mounting panic turned to relief upon finding someone with a Chinese face to help them in this college town out on the prairie.

She was trying to get to an orientation event at the Student Union, and I offered to walk her there. She was a FOB—fresh off the boat—but not the kind I grew up knowing, the strivers with their bowl haircuts and thick glasses. The FOBs my parents had been. Her skin glowed in the unreal way of starlets or vampires, and her eyelashes were long and lush as a Disney heroine's.

I took her past the towering sycamores and redbrick buildings with lead-glass windows and avoided the concrete blocks that made much of the campus resemble a minimum-security prison. The air was muggy, and the sky hazy at the start of the school year. Pointing in awe at a storybook turret, she didn't notice when her gold bracelet slipped off her wrist and pinged against the walkway. I retrieved the bracelet, its weight lingering in my hand.

"I'm such a muddle-headed fool!" she exclaimed. She showed me her schedule and I told her to drop Intro to Government and sign up for the musical theater lecture. Both fulfilled the American Studies requirement, but musical theater ranked among the easiest and most popular classes on campus.

"So clever! I could tell you were kind, by looking at you!" Her questions had only just begun, and I could help her. I signed her on as my first client for a business whose name I invented on the spot: VIP Tutoring.

I was a senior at the university located ten minutes from home, and as soon as I graduated, I wanted to escape. A few years back, the school had begun recruiting undergraduates from China. A plan sure to fail, I'd thought. Why wouldn't the rich Chinese, with the country open to them, go somewhere cool in Los Angeles, Boston, or New York? Anyone with the least sense would get back on a plane after taking in the fields of corn and soybeans that stretched into infinity. But I was wrong, and the trickle of Chinese had quickly turned into a flood, scores of eighteen-year-olds fleeing the dorms for luxury apartments with lucky touches aimed at them: addresses and phone numbers brimming with the number 8, in buildings that omitted the fourth floor.

I came to understand that Angel couldn't pass her classes. She wouldn't have passed the third grade here. She must have hired a ringer to take her entrance exams in China and intended to cheat her way through school. I should have been furious at the university for accepting students so ill prepared that they cheapened my own degree—not that officials would have cared. The state had slashed funding, and everyone knew that tuition from these students made up the shortfall. If the university was going to use the Chinese for its mercenary ends, why shouldn't students like Angel use the university for theirs?

And why shouldn't I?

FOR A TERM paper, I demanded a Louis Vuitton purse. For a take-home midterm, a Tiffany bracelet. For other assignments, I took whatever I wanted from my two dozen clients, mining their walk-in closets packed with clothes, shoes, and accessories new with tags. I sold my haul online.

After China Fresh's gas stove and freezer died, I'd spent everything I'd earned to cover what my parents' insurance didn't. Since then, I'd been pulling eighteen-hour days, answering the phone for to-go orders, making deliveries, and taking on new tutoring clients to pay my way to California, where my parents should have raised me and my sister.

My father had arrived on a graduate fellowship to study engineering, and my mother followed a year later to marry him. He began working at China Fresh as a waiter, and later on, he bought a share in the business. Later still, my younger sister and I were born, and he bought out his partners. After crossing oceans and continents, my parents traveled no farther, raising us in a town built along a murky brown river, in a state whose motto—"The Crossroads of America"—made it plain that our chief attraction was that you could go elsewhere.

My parents would live above the restaurant, the scent of soy sauce and sesame oil seeping into their skin, into their tears, and into their dreams until they died. Most people around here worked at the university or at the county hospital, at the tractor engine plant or venetian blind factory. Who knew what I could do, who I'd become, if I moved to California, to the land of six-figure salaries, signing bonuses, free meals, nap pods, and perks galore? I'd find Chinese, Chinese everywhere—Chinese mayors, Chinese prom queens, Chinese founders at startups—so many of us that we weren't considered weird and foreign. My family knew nothing of my plan, and wouldn't until after I bought my plane ticket and signed a lease on an apartment.

Late spring semester, I found someone willing to accept me as a roommate even though I didn't have a job. In two weeks, I had to wire my share of the security deposit, first and last month's rent—$3,500. What a waste, my parents would have said, if they'd known, to throw so much away on rent. More than what they probably paid on their monthly mortgage, but they didn't understand that you had to spend money to make money. China Fresh's rickety chairs, the wood laminate tables, and the fluorescent lighting attracted stingy customers who left pennies as tips and accused my parents of skimping on the wontons.

I told my parents to put in soft, flattering lighting, hang a scroll or two, and call the stir-fried green beans "Dragon Leaves" and the chicken chow mein "Phoenix Nest." "We could charge a dollar, two dollars more per dish," I said.

"Dragon leaves?" my father asked. Rain drummed against the windows in what had been a never-ending spring. "You don't need to lie if you offer good food at a good value." He prized honesty above all else, even when a supplier's mistake would have been in his favor or if a customer overpaid.

My sister smirked. "Don't you know: *A* for is for *American*, *B* is for *burrito*, *C* is for *Chinese*." Like the letter grades from the Health Department, she said. Five years younger than me, Ivy moved with an easy athleticism and was always surrounded by a pack of friends from the cross-country team. "*C* is for *Chinese!*" She might have heard the quip from a friend, the sort who told her, "I don't even think of you as Chinese!"

Ivy didn't seem to understand the joke was on her, or maybe she chose to ignore it, one of many things she let pass to fit in.

"Chinese get A," my father said, stoic as a general on a doomed mission.

SATURDAY NIGHT, ANGEL texted, asking me to come over. In the lobby, I noticed a flyer for a new apartment complex opening next year. The map had to be wrong. How could the building be on fraternity row?

When she answered the door, her friends behind her, peering at me, I could tell they'd been drinking. Her eyes were bright but unfocused and her breath boozy. She was wearing a cocktail dress, and so were her two friends, Clarissa and Crystal. The names they picked for their new American lives seemed straight out of a Regency romance novel or a porn movie.

"Da Jie!" she cried. Big Sister. The title was supposed to be a sign of respect and affection, even if we both knew I was the hired help. By paying me in gifts, we could pretend our relationship wasn't transactional. She was my most steady customer, and she and her friends listened to my counsel with attention and respect, treating me as indispensible, all the ways in which I wanted the world to consider me.

Angel led me inside. "You've arrived in time for the party!"

Party? I was dressed in yoga pants and a sweatshirt, and I'd knotted my greasy hair into a ponytail. A pimple pulsed above my lip. An hour ago, I'd delivered pans of fried rice and chow mein to a fraternity that looked like a plantation house. I knew the guy who paid, Tyler, from an operations management class. He used to peek at the answers on my quizzes, and I never stopped him. I was glad that he didn't recognize me.

Angel now tugged on my arm, trying to draw me deeper into her apartment. "Da Jie, the party is for you!" Her voice had gone helium high-pitched, a tone she and her friends seemed to think sounded cute.

Aside from rifling through her closet, I'd never spent much time in this spacious corner suite with a view of the stubby campus clock tower. It smelled like the bath store at the mall, sweet and girlish, and her carpets were pristine and white. Although I should have taken off my shoes, my socks were mismatched, and my big toe poked through a hole. I was being rude, but I didn't plan to stay for long.

"I'm not dressed for a party."

"We know how hard you've been working!" Angel said. "We want to thank you!"

"We're giving you a makeover." Clarissa had been going to school in the United States since she was thirteen and should have spoken excellent English, but she still lived in a Chinese bubble of foods, pop culture, and language and seemed perpetually on China local time, staying up all night and sleeping for most of the day. The more she'd been excluded by her classmates, the more she'd clung to her own kind. Or it might have been the other way around, and nothing much about Americans held her interest.

"I don't need a makeover."

"We're so bored!" Crystal said. "Please!"

Each presented me a size 00 outfit, little black dresses as narrow as the tailor-made qipao my mother brought from Taiwan and kept packed in mothballs. I waved off the dresses. Raised on meat and milk, I was twice their size.

"You don't like them?" Angel asked. "We can find another."

"I—I don't fit."

"But these are the sizes that you always take."

Clarissa shot her a warning look. "American Chinese, different style, needs color," she said. She alone might have realized that I'd been selling everything off. She reached back into the closet and returned with a loose cotton dress, a beach cover-up, one size fits all. I didn't expect this kindness from her.

Wavering, I decided to try it on. I locked myself into the bathroom, shed my clothes, and examined myself in a three-way mirror. Despite the flattering lighting that turned my skin smooth and poreless, the mirror couldn't hide my flat chest and my lumpy belly, every imperfection reflected and repeated. I slipped the dress on and it floated over me, soft as a breeze.

According to Angel, after carjackers gunned down two Chinese students in Los Angeles, parents had considered the big cities too dangerous and sent their children here. But we had our own menaces: Clarissa's Range Rover had been vandalized; her hood spray-painted "Go Away" in blood-red letters. A man in a supermarket parking lot yelled at Angel, "Go back to China." And I'd overheard other students grumbling about cheating; the Chinese had gotten that reputation. Hadn't that family spent millions to get their daughter on the sailing team? No wonder Angel and her friends left on shopping sprees to Chicago and New York every chance they could.

After I let them into the bathroom, they stripped, sanded, and moisturized me. Angel sprayed on foundation with a special mister that made my skin dewy. I flinched when Clarissa flipped up my eyelid to apply liner. Crystal stroked on blush and lipstick, the three of them conferring over different shades. The ease among them made my chest ache, and as Angel brushed out my hair, my eyes grew wet.

Clarissa dabbed at me with a tissue. "Did something get in your eyes?"

"Am I pulling too hard?" Angel asked.

"It's nothing. Allergies." I was rough on myself, digging my fingernails to squeeze out blackheads or pulling my hair into tight ponytails. No one had touched me like that in years, with such care. My mother had stopped long ago. Starting in the first grade, I had to get myself and my sister ready for the day. In my earliest memory, Ivy sat in my lap as I pulled on her socks. How complete I'd felt, with her in my arms.

How different she turned out to be from me. In the intervening years between our births, my parents had eased up. She didn't remember that I'd been the one who made sure she didn't show up to school dressed like a FOB, and would never understand how effortless her life seemed compared to mine.

Not long ago, when an old family friend had stopped by China Fresh, I overheard Ivy greeting him.

"You've lost a lot of weight," he told her in that blunt Chinese way.

"You are thinking of my other daughter," my father said, just as blunt.

Cheeks burning, I carried in a pot of tea from the kitchen, pretending I hadn't heard. Ivy, who had returned to folding napkins in the back of the dining room, smiled at me but didn't acknowledge his comment either, not then, not ever.

I wanted her to come to San Francisco for college, where she might show me how to be carefree in a new place, where she finally might want to be related to me.

As Angel and her friends debated whether to braid or curl my hair, I closed my eyes and must have dozed off. When Angel shook me awake, she was beaming. She spun me around, proud of their handiwork. I was smiling too. Not because I'd been transformed—I looked like Cinderella's stepsister at the ball—but because I now knew how to solve my present dilemma. Their hands on me, working together at the same time, had inspired me. Just as they'd outsourced their assignments to me, I'd outsource them elsewhere, to multiple writers who could work in parallel. Not to other students on campus, but somewhere I could pocket the difference between our rates, somewhere they spoke excellent English and had an excess of PhDs pining for jobs: overseas.

AT HOME, I submitted my request to an outsourcing website. "Top dollar, for top papers!" I wrote in the headline. I'd figured out what my parents hadn't: the toil of your own hands only went so far. You rose in life the further you got away from the sweat of your own brow. At a knock on my door, I minimized the browser on my computer.

"You're working too hard," my mother said from the doorway. "The light from the computer's not good for you. You'll go blind."

She came up beside me, standing next to the bed where I'd tossed the dress that Angel insisted I take, along with the purse, strappy sandals, and chunky onyx necklace. I usually hid my treasures underneath the bed, but I'd run out of room. My mother balled her hands into fists, unable to hide her hunger to fondle the calfskin. In her wedding photo, she'd seemed like a child bride, her skin pale from too much face powder, her puffy dress so big it wore her, and yet she'd had such a candlelit glow before the years wore her down.

"I was going to ask if you had anything for graduation," she said. "If you wanted to pick one of my dresses from Taiwan. But Daddy said it was old-fashioned, not your style."

The silk and rayon qipao were more elegant than anything I could have bought in a two-hundred-mile radius. She'd never had the occasion to wear them here.

"I don't have a style." I turned back to the computer. "I have to finish."

The sooner I set my plan into motion, the sooner I'd get us what we all deserved. After my sister graduated, I'd find her a job in California too. With the money we sent back each month, my parents could hire help at the restaurant, buy a car that didn't break down so often, and vacation for a night or two.

"Not too late," my mother warned, and left.

THE NEXT MORNING, I had more than a hundred applicants from the Philippines, South Africa, Nigeria, Pakistan, and India. Some were incomprehensible, as if they fed their words to a website that translated without regard to syntax or meaning. Even the best applicants' offshore English was off-key at times, riddled with formal diction or antiquated phrases.

New applicants kept submitting by the minute and my head throbbed as I tried to keep track of the different time zones. Shouldn't they be asleep? Their desperation made me squirm, but I couldn't worry about everyone who applied. I picked the top five: Valentina from Manila, Raj from Bangalore, Sweetie from Nigeria, Sabina from Islamabad, and Tessie from Cebu. If this took off, I could hire more.

They answered my emails within minutes and must have been dozing with their phones in their hands, tucked beside their pillows, dragging themselves up with each beep and buzz signaling an opportunity. In the weeks that followed, my team remained just as eager. I didn't feel guilty about paying them less—the dollar must go further in their countries, and I marveled at how fast they filed their assignments, always ahead of time, and asked for more. Soon I wired the rent money to San Francisco and started saving up for my plane ticket.

"You're still up?" Tessie wrote me when I was pulling an all-nighter. Her concern seemed almost sisterly, from the big sister I'd never had. "Get some sleep!"

IN THE FINAL weeks of the school year, as the first hot days arrived, my classmates stripped down to shorts and sundresses, threw water balloons across the Quad, waded in fountains, and jumped in bouncy houses that sprouted like mushrooms on the lawns of fraternities and sororities.

I was working the cash register at China Fresh when Tyler showed up with a friend. With their pastel polo shirts, fraternity baseball caps, and perfect teeth, they exuded an air of legacy and entitlement. They asked if they could buy two hundred takeout containers. I named a price, triple the wholesale cost, which they paid without question.

"Thanks, Tyler." He seemed shocked that I knew his name—shocked and exposed—even though I'd sat by him all semester. He and his friend's great-great-great-grandfathers had probably immigrated from Sweden to till the land. Their kind dominated the university, which had not one but three agricultural fraternities and a swine genetics program among the best in the world.

"Party favors?" I asked.

"Kind of." He was straining against his good breeding, knowing he should invite me out of politeness to whatever it was that they were planning. His friend bowed his head, covering his mouth, stifling a laugh.

My sister walked by with a plate of noodles and a flash of recognition passed between them. Tyler nodded, and she smiled and ducked her head. He might have seen her at a party that she and her high school friends had crashed, or he could have been checking her out for the first time. Hot, embarrassing tears sprang up in my eyes, and I turned away to stack menus.

Tyler and his friend grabbed a handful on the way out, so pleased with themselves that I felt uneasy. My mother emerged from the back office and tugged a scratchy cardigan over my shoulders. "You'll catch cold."

Close on her heels, my father handed me a wad of fives and ones, tips from customers. When I tried to open the till, he told me to keep it.

"I don't need it," I said.

"For clothes. For graduation."

I slid it into the pocket of my jeans, knowing that I was acting like an ingrate. My mother's purple tracksuit was faded and frayed, and I couldn't remember the last time she'd bought new clothes.

"Put it in your wallet," my father said. Always chiding and anxious, a part of him still a starving grad student who turned down the heat, wore parkas inside the house, and never passed up free samples at the grocery store.

He'd never stop nagging me. And yet at that moment I missed my family with a sudden fierceness, missed them before I'd even left.

WHILE I DROVE my parents' battered sedan, Angel and her friends passed around a bottle of vodka in the back seat. The prospect of leaving made me fearless, and the parties on campus beckoned. As we walked toward Tyler's fraternity, speakers blasted "China Girl." I hadn't been here in weeks because Ivy had taken over deliveries at the end of the semester. The mess of new construction next door surprised me, the bulldozers parked crookedly beside heaps of dirt. For years, the fraternities had annexed the vacant lot for their volleyball tournaments, their Slip N Slides, and their one-story ice luge. I realized then that the fancy new apartments were going in here, a Chinese invasion that the neighbors surely couldn't stand but couldn't stop.

On the front porch of the fraternity, people in cone hats swayed under garlands of Chinese takeout boxes—the ones from China Fresh. Some guests had embraced the party's theme, wearing plastic buckteeth and silky kimonos, and making their eyes slanty with makeup. The disco hit "Kung Fu Fighting" thumped out next. "Those fists were fast as lightning!"

Someone wrapped me into a bear hug, sloshing beer all over me—my sister. Ivy wore one of my mother's pink floral qipao over skinny jeans and had thrust chopsticks in her hair. For her, the costume was no different than putting on a cowboy hat or riding a witch's broom for Halloween.

I wanted to grab her by the shoulders. Didn't she understand? They were making fun of us. Past and present, over treaties or over beers, Americans despised the Chinese. But maybe she didn't even feel Chinese. Maybe no one treated her differently—yet.

"Do Mom and Dad know you're here?" I asked, and immediately felt ridiculous. Of course they didn't.

She put a finger to her lips—"Shhhh!"—and giggled.

"Who's that?" someone behind me asked.

I turned to find two freckled blondes shouting into each other's ears.

"I didn't know she had a sister," the tall one said.

Their eyes flicked over me, and then they grabbed Ivy by the elbow and swept her away. "I love this song!" Ivy shouted over her shoulder.

A trio of guys followed. I could go after them, telling them that the girls were underage, and warning my sister to resist their drinks and their invitations to go upstairs. Maybe they already knew how to hold their own. The joke was forever on those on the outside, where I stood and always would. I'd been foolish to think Ivy would give up her home, foolish to think we could find our way back to each other in San Francisco.

Angel and her friends were giggling too. How funny, how strange! They didn't think of themselves this way—not the music, not the clothes—so how could they know they were the butt of a joke? They'd suffer no lasting harm from this party, and after graduation their parents would help them get positions that were as ceremonial as their time at the university.

Someday, over cocktails in a glittering tower far, far away, they would recount these odd Americans and their drinking and mating rituals: bumping and grinding in outlandish costumes, screaming like madmen. But someday was a long time from now, and so we pushed inside the house, the music vibrating through us, the floor sticky with spilled drinks, and the air humid with possibility. Our bodies thrashed and pushed, our arms raised in surrender or in ecstasy, until we forgot ourselves.

BACK IN THE car, Clarissa blasted Mandopop from her phone, the melody frothy as champagne shaken up. Not yet ready to go home and more than a little drunk, I steered away from campus, past the water tower and onto roads winding past the fields. The breeze through our open windows carried the scent of turned earth and the tang of fertilizer.

In search of french fries, my sister and her friends had dashed off too. "See you at home," Ivy had whispered conspiratorially, with the closeness I wished we'd shared before now.

Clarissa nudged the bottle against my arm, the vodka sloshing merrily. "Here."

I took a deep swig, letting the warmth seep through me.

"Da Jie, I don't understand." Angel passed her phone to me.

Glancing at her phone, I read the email from the school's academic council. The language was veiled, but the accusation clear: She'd plagiarized her paper in her postwar American history seminar. The one that Tessie from Cebu had sent me. I'd corrected grammar and spelling, but never thought to check if she'd copied it from somewhere else.

Headlights blinded us, and an oncoming pickup driver leaned on the horn. Our eyes met. If I did nothing, the accident would take its course, the terrible crash of glass and metal. Blood roared in my ears. Seconds, centuries passed. I veered onto the shoulder of the road, the tires skidding in the gravel. The driver honked again, and in the rearview mirror, I watched his brake lights flash red as though he might reverse and return to berate me. Instead he gunned his engine and sped away.

The pop song played on, horribly upbeat, until Clarissa turned it off.

"Why did you give her the vodka?" Crystal whined.

Angel reached over the headrest. "My phone—give me back my phone."

I thrust it back at her and with fumbling fingers I searched on my own phone for the title of the paper that Tessie had submitted to me. As Clarissa got out of the car, followed by the others, I discovered the paper for sale in a massive database, written by someone in Sri Lanka, priced for less than what I'd paid Tessie.

Stomach churning, I dry-heaved until I caught hold of myself. Crystal and Angel were studying their phones now, their heads bowed in unison, their faces lit blue. Tessie had also completed their assignments. They showed their screens to Angel, their alarm apparent. The university must have caught them too.

Angel teetered back toward my open window, and started reading the email, stumbling over the words. "At your Student Conduct Conference, you will have the opportunity to respond to what has been reported and review evidence that is the basis of my concern. I have placed a hold on your record until the meeting occurs. You may have an advisor or other counsel present during the conduct conference . . ." She trailed off.

"Evidence?" Clarissa asked.

"Counsel? A lawyer?" Crystal asked.

"That notice? It's nothing," I said. Although I couldn't fend off the truth for long, I needed time to figure out what to do. "You're all supposed to meet with counselors to discuss the majors you're declaring."

"Da Jie?" Angel asked.

"Have I ever led you wrong?" I asked. "Out of everyone you've met here, could you trust anyone more?"

They wandered off again to confer, huddling a few feet away before gazing up at the sky, seeming to take in the profound darkness of the countryside. The sky thick with stars that made you understand the vastness of space and time. You were a speck, less than a speck.

I could claim I'd urged them to model their work after these papers, persuade Angel to say she'd cut-and-pasted notes that she'd forgotten to take out. Clarissa could say she'd suffered a mental breakdown, and Crystal could explain she'd misunderstood the rules. Maybe I had a way out.

No. As soon as they opened their mouths to defend themselves in their broken English, the Office of Academic Integrity would know the truth. And of course Angel and her friends would turn me in. They had no reason to protect me, a servant who'd betrayed them.

Someone more daring might have treated it as a minor set-back, bought a one-way bus ticket to San Francisco, lied on her résumé about graduating, and talked her way into a job—maybe resumed the business, this time with safeguards in place. But getting caught wasn't why I felt gutted, gasping. If I couldn't hack it here, I'd never survive San Francisco. Your character was your fate, and mine was as washed out, washed up as the landscape around me.

Clarissa and her friends would get expelled too, though university higher-ups might be inclined to put them on probation to keep the word from getting out that the school was anything but accommodating to its international students. They'd remain enrolled, even though I'd worked ten times as hard as them, even though I'd forgotten more than they'd ever learn.

Maybe the university would take pity on me, too, if I pleaded our family's financial hardship, if I did community service to make amends, and if I pledged I'd never stray again.

I doubted it. No one had ever shown me much mercy. And why should they? I'd considered myself a good girl, a dutiful daughter, and yet at the first opportunity, my true self had emerged: cheater.

My parents. Their sacrifice had been for nothing. Expelled, with a tainted transcript, I couldn't transfer to another school. With no degree, I'd never get the jobs my parents had wanted for me. I'd never be able to give them a different future. And yet hadn't they also taken money from me without asking how I'd come into so much, so quickly?

I dug the heels of my hands into my eyes. It did no good

to think this way. After I told my parents what I'd done, my mother would collapse in on herself, and my father would turn to stone. I could guess what they'd say: tell the truth. Shivering, I wished I had my mother's cardigan, which I'd tossed onto the floor of my bedroom. Reaching into my wallet, I brushed my fingers against the cash my father had given me, cash he and my mother had come by honestly.

I flicked the headlights and Angel and her friends climbed back in, subdued. As I swung the car around, I snapped on the radio. I didn't know if they believed me, but we collectively, silently, decided that we weren't discussing the future for now.

When the song hit an operatic crescendo, I punched off the headlights and everyone screamed with terror and glee.

"It's like flying," Angel said.

I turned on the headlights again, the beams sweeping over a hulking tractor and bales of hay.

"Do it again! Again!"

We zoomed along the dips and turns that were as familiar to me as the lines in my palm.

In the dark, we could be anywhere, together for a little while longer.

The Older the Ginger

Sometime after lunch, Old Zhang realized he'd been kidnapped.

On the way from the airport, his cousin had taken a detour. If he'd driven in circles, or gone in the wrong direction, Old Zhang wouldn't have known the difference. In the countryside west of Hong Kong on the Pearl River Delta, the rutted roads looked alike and the flash of return, of welcome, hadn't yet arrived. More than a half century ago, he left the hills green with pine and bamboo for San Francisco, and hadn't returned since.

His cousin wasn't the son of an aunt or an uncle, but a relative of some kind from the village, who possessed a wreck of a car, and had volunteered to fetch Old Zhang. The cousin was a former construction worker whose time perched on skyscrapers had inflated his self-importance. Less than an hour into the drive, his cousin parked in front of a concrete building, a restaurant famous for the local specialty: rice flour dumplings pleated into the shape of ingots and deep fried. The air was muggy, swollen as a bruise. They were the only customers at the only table, and the only staff his cousin's daughter, Little Treasure. She brought out platter after platter, pots of jasmine tea, and a bottle of rice wine that Old Zhang declined. She hovered, simpering and smiling like a courtesan.

It was startling to find himself in high demand after his years among the bachelors of Chinatown. When Chinese first left for America to tunnel through mountains for railroads and snatch gold from rivers, most were men. Though few fortune-seekers intended to settle, laws also barred most Chinese women, to prevent families from taking root.

During World War II, not long before Old Zhang's parents sent him to America, the laws changed. Finding a wife had remained a competitive endeavor, and Old Zhang hadn't much to differentiate himself as a suitor, he was just another waiter-turned-cook. Others had gone on to run restaurants, laundries, farms, and factories and move to the suburbs, but Old Zhang never left. By the time families crammed into Chinatown's tenements, it was too late to start his own. The ancients had decreed a man should not marry after thirty years of age, and should not have children after fifty, because the proper time for those things had passed.

Then his mother had written, insisting Old Zhang marry. She was ninety-three, he was seventy-six. Come back, she told him. Come back and find a wife.

Little Treasure dropped off toothpicks and a bowl of lychees, and poured another cup of tea, but he refrained from drinking. He had a long ride ahead to the village, his leaky bladder didn't need more pressure, and the strong brew made him jittery. A few minutes ago, his cousin had excused himself to urinate, and Old Zhang should too. He didn't want to run to the latrines in the first moments of his homecoming, but when he tried to turn the handle of the door, it didn't budge. It must be stuck, the wooden frame warped and swollen. "Hey, hey," he shouted.

Little Treasure tugged on his elbow. "Uncle, eat." She looked at him coyly from beneath her lashes. "Does it taste like how you remember?"

"We filled ours with air." During his childhood, his family ate meat only once a year, during the Spring Festival, but this young girl had never known such want, only China on the rise and none of its turmoil. Turmoil that he had largely escaped by moving to America: the stunted crops and starvation of the Great Leap Forward, the book burnings and beatings of the Cultural Revolution, decades of strife and deprivation that his parents had spared him.

He knocked again and leaned his weight against the door. Locked. He searched for another exit, but didn't see another door, and the sole window was too small to squeeze through. He'd heard of brides abducted by grooms, but never a kidnapped groom! His cousin must want to present his daughter to Old Zhang, to make her the first and most memorable candidate for marriage and the green card that came along with the deal. In time, she could sponsor her parents, her siblings, their spouses, and their children to immigrate. A prize her father wouldn't let slip out of his fingers.

"Uncle, eat." Little Treasure had a broad, plain face, placid as a cow, her beauty residing in the cascade of inky black hair that fell to her waist. In a tight T-shirt and flared jeans, she was as tall as him and twice as strong, with the muscular arms of a model revolutionary. She could level weeds and enemies alike. She could pin him to the narrow bed that he now noticed beneath a calendar of beer models. "Uncle, he'll be back soon. Sit, sit. You've had a long flight."

He settled into his chair. Even if he escaped, he didn't know where he was or how far he'd have to walk to his village. Soon enough, his cousin would understand that love at first sight hadn't transpired. Little Treasure would have to wait her turn to be ranked and compared to the other women whom the village elders had selected for his consideration.

He ate another dumpling, the crust crispy yet chewy, filled with sausage, peanuts, chives, and water chestnuts. Little Treasure dug her fingers into his shoulders. Every bit of him clenched, his jaw, his gut, his toes.

"Uncle, let me." She kneaded the knots in his neck. She might be one of those girls who sold themselves in the cities. On occasion, he had visited those languorous, heavy-lidded women who charged by the hour, by the procedure, in the red-lit massage parlors a few blocks from Chinatown. He hadn't visited in years, not with the dried shrimp between his legs that hardly had the strength to take a piss.

Her hand crept to his thigh, and he pushed it away. "Let me help you," she whispered. Her face burned.

He'd been mistaken. She wasn't a professional. He shuffled away, wondering if his cousin was spying through a crack, trying to catch Old Zhang in an indelicate position. And who could blame him? China was becoming a superpower that launched astronauts into space, put on an Olympics breathtaking in its scale and magnificence, and might soon become the Middle Kingdom around which the world revolved. But for now, his cousin and Little Treasure remained mired in this backwater where Old Zhang presented the best and only prospects.

Little Treasure wept, burying her face into her hands.

"Young maiden," he began.

"Young?" Her cheeks glittered with tears. "You should see who they have picked out for you, girls pried from their dolls. I'm a leftover woman."

Old Zhang guessed that she was approaching thirty and still single. She told him that, after she returned from working in the city as a waitress, she'd had a few marriage proposals, but her father held out, convinced she could make a better match.

"You don't want an old gingerroot like me," Old Zhang said.

"The older the ginger, the hotter the spice."

"When is he coming back?"

"As long as it takes." She sniffled and wiped her nose with the back of her hand. "You're my last chance."

"You're not old enough to be thinking about the end."

"No one wants meat that's gone off." Her bluntness surprised him.

"Call your father."

She pushed the bowl of lychees toward him, which he ate to cleanse his greasy mouth. He spat the shiny pit into his cupped palm, and he had another, savoring the sweetness. His mother used to peel lychees for him, digging in her thumbnail to break the flesh. Long ago, the emperor's concubine had pined for the taste in winter. With lychees crammed into saddlebags, imperial soldiers galloped north, handing off the precious cargo to the next rider each time the horse tired, completing the journey of two weeks in two days.

Old Zhang had been his mother's firstborn and her favorite, the heap of rice in his bowl second only to his father's. The most tender greens and the plumpest dumpling always piled before him. When he was very young, he followed her to the river, where she beat laundry against the rocks. How mighty she'd seemed! Warm mud squishing between his toes, sunshine heavy on his cheek, and the smell of the river, of wind on water and churned earth.

Little Treasure cleared the table, and he smelled the dank musk of her, straw and loamy soil, and all at once he remembered his boyhood, the life he'd left behind, and he was overcome with longing for this lost world. He closed his eyes, inhaling.

She tugged at the zipper of his pants, and he pushed her away, harder than he intended. She stumbled, crying out, and his cousin burst in, ready to catch Old Zhang deflowering her. Old Zhang pushed past him and found the car unlocked, the radio playing and keys in the ignition. He buckled himself into the passenger seat. He'd never learned how to drive.

His cousin told him to go back inside, with a smile that slid into a snarl. "We're not finished."

"We're late," Old Zhang said. "You don't want to keep Ma waiting."

Ma, the final arbiter of any marriage. His cousin called for Little Treasure, who climbed into the back seat, and they drove in silence for an hour in the land of the red earth laced with rivers, passing between centuries from one bend in the road to another. Farmers in straw hats tilled the fields with wooden plows and oxen, and at the next curve, squat factories interrupted. The pitted road was so narrow they had to drive into the oncoming lane to pass men pedaling carts loaded with sugarcane or sheet metal, before turning onto a dirt track that led to an arched gate marking the village entrance.

Money from relatives abroad and teenagers working in the cities, in factories and construction sites, as maids, security guards, and waitresses, had transformed the village. Crumbling mud bricks made way for concrete homes, a new schoolhouse, and a fishpond beneath a willow tree in the central plaza. But the village still lacked electricity, still lacked running water, still lacked opportunity.

Strangers, all. No one he remembered.

In his mother's house, Old Zhang discovered a photo in a dusty plastic frame in the family's shrine, beside a pot of incense and a bunch of lychees. In the overexposed snapshot, tinged in orange and brown, he appeared miraculously young. His hair was bushy as a fox's tail and his back straight as an iron rod, a man who should have had his pick of a wife. Shocking, to discover a piece of him had been here all along, in a village that had become abstract in his memories. He didn't remember who had snapped his photo in Chinatown, sometime in the 1970s, nor did he remember sending it to his mother, slipped into the translucent sheets of airmail, in which he never could reveal much of himself. She never learned to read or write, and her brief, sporadic replies came under a different stranger's handwriting each time.

For decades, she'd been a widow. If his mother expected him in his prime, she—and all the prospective brides-to-be—would be grievously disappointed. Only the brightness of his eyes remained, and a full set of teeth, of which he was exceedingly proud. If he'd stayed in the village, he might have become stooped, his hands shaky and his breath labored. He might have died. He was hardiest of the three siblings in his family and the sole survivor. He didn't remember Ma's face, only how she squeezed him so tightly he couldn't breathe the day he left the village. He'd been ten years old.

From the deck, he watched his father, standing still as a pillar on the waterfront, until the ship slipped out of sight. His parents had borrowed to pay for his passage to San Francisco, resting their hopes on his wiry frame. He entered under a false identity, becoming a Kwan, the alleged son of an American citizen. A name he repeated over and over to himself, a name that never felt right, that he never wanted to pass on to a wife or children. A name that prevented him from sponsoring visas for his true mother and father because in the eyes of the U.S. government, his parents-on-paper had already immigrated.

If he never saw Ma again, she could remain as vital and strong in his memories. Any minute, she would shuffle in here, her arms wide in greeting. She slept in here, beside the kitchen. She must be preparing his bed in the second room he'd paid for but had never seen. He'd bow to her, and present her the supplements she'd requested to help lower her blood pressure. "Ma?" he asked. She didn't answer.

His cousin eased Old Zhang into a chair, telling him that she'd died a week ago in her sleep. A heart attack, the doctor declared, and there had been no way to get a message to him before he arrived.

Ma—dead? In San Francisco, she rarely crossed his mind. Now he reeled, as much as if he'd witnessed a car plowing her down. Because Old Zhang didn't have a phone or an email address, it had been decided he should be told after his arrival. Who decided—his cousin? His cousin, who'd dined with him, offered a cigarette, pimped his daughter, but said nothing this afternoon. Old Zhang wanted to flip the table and shove him to the ground. Watch his cousin's ugly face twist in panic, in fear, a fraction of what roiled in Old Zhang.

No expense had been spared, his cousin was saying, and he scrolled through photos on his mobile phone, displaying wreathes and banners, top-quality, slow-burning incense and the loudest firecrackers. "Three layers of silk garments and a pearl in her hand," he said. To light her way into the next world.

Ma was here. She was everywhere in this house, in the musty herbs she boiled for medicine, in the mud-spattered rubber shoes by the front door, as if she'd stepped inside a moment ago.

"Why didn't you tell me?" Old Zhang's hands curled into fists.

"You'd had such a long trip," his cousin said. "You needed something to eat first. Bad news on an empty stomach, it's too much of a shock.

"You don't know what I need!"

"Don't I?"

Out by the car, Little Treasure was unloading Old Zhang's luggage, heavy with gifts. Children swarmed around her. Old Zhang staggered to his feet, knocking over the chair. Without Ma, he had no connection to this village. To China, his homeland alien as the moon. Dizzy, he hung his head, trying to get his bearings. His cousin tied something around Old Zhang's arm—a strip of black cloth, to be worn for forty-nine days of mourning. Unfilial son. If only—if only he'd booked an earlier ticket, if only he'd come back last year, or five years ago. "Take me there."

His cousin ushered him down the crooked path to the cemetery and to the burial mound, heaped with wilting flowers and the ashes of incense and hell money, burnt offerings so she could enjoy the wealth she never had in life. The smells coated his tongue like a vile pudding. His brother and sister had passed away years ago, and their children hadn't attended the funeral. They had grandchildren of their own and lived in distant cities after Old Zhang's remittances had afforded them opportunities to leave. His father's grave was beside hers, the grass clipped short and the stone marker wiped clean of mud. Other mounds were unkempt, overgrown with weeds, abandoned by forgetful, ungrateful descendants like Old Zhang.

More villagers were coming up the path now, curious to meet their long-lost cousin who lived in America. The crowd parted for a man whose body coiled with the power of a withheld punch, the headman who must have conspired to bring Old

Zhang here. A few young women—teenagers—had brushed on lip gloss, rouged their cheeks, and tied off their braids with satin bows. After he paid his respects to his mother, they probably would parade before him, like contestants in the Miss China-town pageant.

Did Ma have any say in the candidates? Were they kind to her, these potential daughters-in-law, to the poor granny who lived alone? He knew little of his mother's daily life. She must have relied on neighbors to fetch straw to light the stove, to boil water for her bath, and to weed the toughest patches. He couldn't have failed her more, no different than if he'd forced her to live in a pigsty. He couldn't stay here for a week. He couldn't bear to stay here overnight.

"Big Brother," his cousin said. Old Zhang bristled. "You'll never have to worry sweeping her tomb. We're family, and we take care of each other."

Family? He had little in common with his cousin other than the vaunted ancestor from ten generations ago, who'd settled and spawned in this damp patch of valley.

"I can't," Old Zhang said. "I can't stay."

"But you've just arrived!" His cousin put an arm around Old Zhang's shoulders, and lowered his voice. "The conditions at re-vered Granny's aren't up to your standards, but you can stay with me. I have a generator. A television. You'll have my bed. I'll sleep on the ground, Big Brother."

Old Zhang jerked away. The air was hazy and overcast, and the heat so intense he felt like an ant beneath a magnifying glass. "Cousin, take me to the airport."

"I promised revered Granny that I'd look after you." His cousin wore muddy loafers, with no socks, never able to escape his peasant habits, his peasant stink despite his boxy suit with the sales tag dangling from the sleeve—purchased for the funeral?—and his sickening cologne.

"I'll make a ghost out of you!" Old Zhang said. His cousin backed off.

"Stay." Little Treasure clutched an empty sack of the foil-wrapped premium chocolates he'd purchased at a Chinatown drug store. She must have opened his suitcase, dug through his belongings, and distributed his gifts to the children, whose mouths were streaked brown. She also must have tossed aside his yellowing undershirts and underpants stippled with holes, in front of dozens of onlookers. He wanted to clap his hands over his crotch.

"A good daughter," his cousin said. "She massaged revered Granny's legs every day and read her stories from newspapers." He paused. "It was Granny's last wish. For you to marry. To marry Little Treasure."

This entire trip might have grown out of this man's plotting. Old Zhang's mother could have been ailing for a while. If his cousin had feared the end of the remittances, he might have written the letter ordering Old Zhang to come home and marry. He couldn't trust this man with sly eyes and oily lips, couldn't trust anyone here not to tear the clothes off his back and the shoes off his feet.

The neighboring village wasn't far, a cluster of homes on the other side of the patchwork of tilled plots, and from there, he'd find a ride to the airport. He'd sleep in the departures hall if necessary until he could get a flight to San Francisco.

He lurched away from his cousin and Little Treasure and into a pack of children who clapped and spun and hugged him, all the descendants he'd never had and never would. Their faces offered glimpses of Old Zhang's lost siblings, his lost father and lost mother. Their common blood, their vitality that he might draw upon, as if from a well.

Though their welcome was a show, a shakedown, though he knew the children flocked to him out of survival and not out of love, he would never be received like an emperor again. For most of his life, he lived a lowly existence. For tonight, he deserved VIP treatment. Tomorrow he'd walk out of the trap they had laid. Their moist, grubby hands reached for his, and he followed.

THE CRESCENT MOON hung heavy and low in the sky, ripe enough to pluck on a warm night, of the sort that San Francisco never had, that kept people up and outdoors, that he hadn't realized he missed. Every table, chair, bowl, and plate in the village had been carried into the plaza and set for a feast grand as a wedding—grander. The villagers greeted him with claps and cheers, and he fought the urge to duck his head, feeling unexpectedly embarrassed.

He wanted to impress them. Not for his sake, but for Ma and her legacy. The headman served him first, the most tender fish, succulent beef, and broccoli green as jade. Everyone watched, perhaps worried that he might have returned with tastes too refined for the likes of their country cuisine. When he swallowed and took another bite, relief swept over their faces. Old Zhang was still like them, despite the years and the distance between them.

The headman poured the first of many cups of rice wine. Old Zhang spat silvery pinbones into his bowl. With a chopstick in each hand, the headman raised the fish aloft and Old Zhang picked off the filet underneath. The taste was sweet and faintly muddy as the pond where it had been raised. If you were Chinese, flipping a fish was bad luck—akin to capsizing a boat—no matter where you lived, no matter how long ago you left the village.

The lion dancers cavorted in threadbare, ill-fitting costumes, followed by a brass band with braying, out-of-tune trumpets and arrhythmic drums, and a children's chorus that sang a tune about a wise old man of the forest. Afterward, the performers marched by. He clapped until his hands throbbed, but the soloist's eyes glittered with tears, a girl no more than eight. She trembled, and he wondered if her parents had threatened to beat her, to deny her food if she failed to stir the heart of Old Zhang.

Little Treasure caught his eye and raised her hands, hinting he should stand. Only when he jumped to his feet did the soloist straighten. To his surprise, everyone else rose too, imitating him. He wasn't used to people watching him so closely, and the attention unnerved him. He smoothed his hands down his shirt and over his rumpled hair. All his life, he'd worked in the background, in the kitchen, the customers focused on the dish before them and never the man who chopped, sauced, steamed, and stir-fried—even if his hands at the gas stove were as fluid as a calligrapher's.

If he hopped on one leg, clapped his arms over his head, would they copy him? He took his seat. The breeze rattled the bare branches of the sycamore trees and carried the scent of burning straw from the stoves of the communal kitchen, where grannies emerged with the next course. A crone set a platter before him and pinched his cheek. "Little Zhang!"

He pulled away. "You don't remember me?" she asked.

He wanted to be generous, as the others must have been to his mother and other abandoned grannies in the village. He squinted at her. "I might."

"My brother shared a desk with you at school. We all played together."

Played together? She seemed as ancient as Ma. "That songbird, that's my granddaughter. Some say she looks just like me, when I was her age."

"Very talented." Old Zhang reached for his chopsticks.

"She'd earn her keep."

He hovered his chopsticks over his bowl.

"She could help with chores, washing and cleaning and cooking. And she could bring in money singing, too. If you adopt," she whispered. It seemed she didn't want anyone else to hear her scheme. "Little Zhang." Her gaze frank, and her smile suggestive, though missing most of her teeth. She leaned in again, her voice throaty and her scent musty. She placed her hand on his forearm. "Remember those afternoons in the apple orchard?"

The headman took her by the arm and all but shoved her

toward the kitchen. Apparently, Old Zhang had passed into legend. Everyone had stories about him, even those born decades after he'd left, stories that he himself didn't remember. Like the time he'd gone missing, and the village had fanned out with lanterns at sundown, calling his name. He'd been a handsome toddler, with a head round and hard as an iron bowl. Never still, headlong toward the horizon. His mother had feared he'd been carried off, sold to a childless couple who wanted a son, or captured by bandits who ate the flesh of the young to give them the strength of ten men. It seemed a miracle when the headman found him asleep, curled in a haystack. Later, he fell ill with a high fever, and might have died but for his mother, who begged a market customer for help, a doctor's wife, and procured a vial of an expensive medicine new to the country—penicillin. He could have, should have died a hundred times before he turned ten. In his mother's telling, he'd been fated to leave the village, and fated to remain abroad, the only way she could accept his long absence.

Dark blots whizzed across the sky, flapping their wings. Bats. He hadn't seen one in decades, not in Chinatown. To Ma, bats symbolized prosperity and good luck, and she had embroidered a flock onto the hem of the shirt, those knots and nubs he rubbed in the dark on his voyage to America. All at once, he remembered that she was gone.

He hung his head until dancers jostled before him, dropping any pretence of cooperation and coordination. Many of these teenagers might be candidates, faced with a choice of marrying him or leaving for the cities to find work. He knocked over his empty cup. Tipsy after too much rice wine, he tilted the cup toward the dancers, toasting their efforts, and a handful giggled.

They tried to jump higher than each other, as if the strength in their calves and the spring in their thighs might nudge them ahead in the competition. The scratchy strings ended on the cassette tape, and the dancers skipped off. Throwing backward glances at Old Zhang, a few crashed into each other like bowling pins.

He burped. His stomach swollen on his skinny frame, like a snake who has swallowed a chicken whole. He drummed his fingers on his belly, his shirt untucked, pants unzipped. He had no intention of taking a wife whose youth would only age him. He knew that now.

At the children's table, Little Treasure passed out steamed buns. She filled their bowls and wiped their faces with brisk yet loving ease. A maiden aunt who must long for her own brood. She noticed him watching and smiled.

After a night of performing for him, didn't the villagers deserve a show of their own? He tossed up a spongy bun and caught it with a flick of his hand, and added two more. He pushed through his intoxication, his hands remembering how to keep the buns in the air. Two up, one down. One on one on one. Something he'd picked up along the way, in his years alone. Juggling, another marvel from the village benefactor, and this time, when everyone clapped, he'd earned their applause.

Little Treasure brought him a cup of tea. His mouth puckered from the brew, which had been steeped for too long, but he swallowed.

———

BEFORE GOING TO sleep, he barricaded the front door with the kitchen table and two chairs. He didn't want to wake up to the midnight gropes of Little Treasure, or any of the wretched young beauties. He collapsed onto his mother's narrow bed, trying to find a comfortable position, too tired to change into his pajamas. His cheeks numb from the wine, and his belly bloated as carrion. Soon someone scratched at the front door. "Uncle."

"Go away," Old Zhang said. "It's late." Little Treasure's breathing was labored, and he pictured her slumped on the ground, pressed against the door.

"It's awful," she said. "You didn't get to say good-bye."

The first and only time that anyone had acknowledged his loss. His pulse was racing now, and he thought he might vomit. He tore off his sweater.

"Granny told me you never stopped sending money, not like most everyone else who leaves and forgets," she said.

Some months more, some months less, enough to build a house for his parents that didn't dissolve in the rain, to pay for medicine, the school fees of his niece and nephew, and a dignified funeral for his father. And for his mother too.

"Uncle, I have something you want."

"Go to sleep, Little Treasure."

She laughed a madwoman's laugh. "Let's go for a dip. The moon—it's bright as day."

She'd drown in the pond, her body bloated and her hair floating like weeds. He pushed aside the table and chairs, sweating from his exertions, his pulse frantic as oil on a hot wok. He opened the door.

Little Treasure set down an insulated bottle on the kitchen table. She sat him on his mother's lumpy bed, put a cool hand against his forehead, and he leaned against her until his breathing steadied. She reeked of liquor, of regret, sour and sharp.

"Too much," she murmured to herself. Too much food, too much drink at the feast?

She poured tea into two cups from her bottle. Hot and bitter, but he was thirsty.

"Granny said you had your own place, and that you ate all your meals in restaurants," she said.

He nodded but couldn't find the words to explain that by American standards, he was poor, and that the more you earned, the more you wanted.

"And that you had a mansion. Like this." She picked up a rumpled magazine that fell open to a picture of a grand estate with the white columns and ornate trim of the White House. What he'd achieved in America hadn't been enough for his mother, not compared to the other stories of riches from Gold Mountain. She had to invent the son she wanted, the son she deserved, and these lies explained the desperate interest of these families in marrying off their daughters. He apparently had enough wealth to support a wife, to support them all.

"A new car, every other year." She scooted beside Old Zhang, her thigh pressing against his. She poured him another cup of the bitter brew. "I like Teslas."

"I prefer Ferrari." He couldn't stop the lies from tumbling

out, the lies that would raise his mother higher in the village's esteem. Little Treasure touched his chest and heat stirred in him.

Who didn't want a rich American uncle, who filled you with a sense of possibility, of prosperity close enough to touch? In your dreams, you escaped the prison of your circumstances and danced on the streets paved with gold. Little Treasure put her hand on his, her fingers stroking, circling until he felt pooled in sunshine. She'd left her tea untouched. Tainted, sprinkled with powdered rhino horn or another sexual tonic to raise him from the dead? Her lips brushed against his, and he fell into her.

Just Like Us

It wasn't easy to get kicked out of Happy Trails RV Park and Camp. The owner put up with a lot, as long as you followed the rules. Put your fire out before turning in. Dump your trash each night and secure the lid to keep the raccoons away. No fireworks on the beach. Only if people fell to shouting and shoving—after a long day of drinking that slid into night—did the owner call the cops. I won't abide fighting, she said.

But she let us go without summoning the authorities.

Mama and I had arrived at Happy Trails the spring I turned fourteen. We drove north on Highway 101, past the green hills and herds of cows in Sonoma County, the billboards for the Indian casinos, the signs to Shelter Cove and the Lost Coast. Past Ukiah and Willits and Garberville and Phillipsville, each town smaller than the last. It seemed like we'd been driving forever in our truck camper and we were still in California.

We entered a grove of redwoods that kept the roads in a

cool perpetual twilight and not long after came upon a carved wooden cowboy sleeping in a crescent moon, the sign for Happy Trails. At the front counter, the woman studied our hair, our clothes. Our camper's shower had a lukewarm, faint spray, never wet enough.

"We're looking for a place to stay," Mama said.

"How many nights?" The woman wore a green velour tracksuit and a white visor tucked into her bobbed silver hair.

"Is there a discount for more nights?" Mama asked.

The woman peered at us. I didn't look much like either of my parents, with my tawny skin and dark brown hair that people mistook for Mexican or Italian or Native American or Middle Eastern. Mama had sandy-blond hair and fair skin freckled from too much sun. In photos, my Chinese father had been lean and dark enough to disappear into my mother's shadow.

A fat man in flip-flops came in and pulled out a cherry popsicle from the freezer case. "Thanks, Ma." He tossed the plastic wrapper toward the trash can by the door. He missed but didn't pick it up.

"That's my profit you're eating into," she grumbled. She must be the owner. "Alan. Alan!" He didn't acknowledge her and the screen door slammed behind him.

Fetching the wrapper, Mama asked the owner if she had any jobs around the campsite in exchange for a discount on the weekly rate. The owner leaned forward for a closer look, checking my mother's hand—no ring. Please, I asked silently. Let us stay. Just for a while. A place to start over, maybe settle for more than a few weeks. For the last five months, Mama and I had bunked down in RV parks, by warehouses and factories, and in superstore parking lots.

"I could use a little help around here," the owner said. "I'm Margie."

LAST WINTER, MAMA'S boyfriend, Roy, tried to get her to sell the 1983 Ford Conestoga truck camper that she inherited from Grandpa Milanovich. With the money, they could vacation in Rosarito, relax on the beach with margaritas, and feast on $12 lobster dinners.

Then Mama caught Roy cheating on her for the third time, after a slow night at the Jackson Rancheria, where she worked as a bingo attendant. She left early and let herself into his apartment, only to find him with his neighbor under the silk sheets Mama had driven two hours round-trip to Sacramento to buy.

I was asleep on the foldout couch when Mama returned home. She ripped open the closet and yanking out his belongings. A pair of jeans ripped at the crotch. A sweat-stained baseball hat. A stuffed bear with a red bow tie. I flicked on the television, and a travel show about the California coast flashed onscreen, the view swooping above jagged rocks, golden sand, bobbing otters, and surfers skimming waves without end. A red convertible zoomed along the cliffs.

We started packing that night.

My entire life, I had lived in Jackson, in the foothills of the Sierras. Mama left once, at eighteen, and returned six months later pregnant with me. She'd been waiting tables at a San

Francisco diner when she met my father, a merchant marine. Joe Chang. His stories about the ports he visited entranced her: Hanoi, Shanghai, Manila. Names that floated like soap bubbles. He mailed us postcards and presents: a hula girl carved from a coconut, a cone-shaped straw hat, a wooden cricket. His gifts stopped when I turned two, though our desire to be anyplace else didn't. Mama sent away for brochures for vacations in lodges in Greenland, cruises to Alaska, and resorts in the Bahamas. We tacked up free posters of mountain vistas and fjords, castles and cathedrals, waterfalls and jungles, and I checked out travel books from the library, memorizing maps of city centers and historical trivia. Someday, we hoped.

We drove to San Francisco on New Year's Day. After we parked at Ocean Beach, I explored the truck camper, the closet-size compartment that held a tiny shower, toilet, and dinette that folded into a sleeping platform beside a two-burner stove and small refrigerator. Everything was covered in a peeling dark wood laminate, and orange plaid curtains edged the narrow windows along the bed. This was what it must be like to live on a sailing ship, I thought. To be carried away by the wind.

That night, I listened to the rain pounding on the ceiling, inches from my face. I loved being in the middle of something big, yet still protected. My mother slept beside me, her right arm curved above her head. If I had looked more like my father, more Chinese, would he have stayed? Would our lives be easier? He could have been an asshole like Mama's other men. Maybe he'd been the original.

———

MAMA CLEANED THE communal showers and unloaded deliveries at Happy Trails. She also drove into towns along the coast finding work, sometimes waiting tables at a brewery in Eureka or cleaning rooms in motels and bed-and-breakfasts. At the local library she picked up books for me about life on other planets, the mysteries of the body, and histories of pioneers blazing trails to California.

One morning, before heading into town, she put her hair into a French braid, her hands hovering like hummingbirds. I stood behind her.

"How do I look?" She eyed my reflection in the mirror. The hollows under her eyes were deep and dark as thumbprints.

I tugged the end of her thick braid. "This will hold."

"I've gotten so used to being around you all the time." She tucked my hair behind my ears. "Do you want a braid?"

"Thanks," I said, "but . . . it always falls out." My hair was slippery compared to hers, and her handiwork would have unraveled after an hour.

That afternoon, thirsty for a soda, I went to the general store where Margie perched on her stool. A bell tinkled and a chunky woman walked in, followed by her husband, a short balding man with a groundhog's overbite. She signed and paid for an RV berth. When her husband asked for a candy bar, she scolded him, no, that would spoil dinner.

"I bet she's the boss," Margie said after they left.

We both laughed, and in that moment, I knew how we could be united—against others. I bought a soda. "Pull one out for me too, hon," Margie said.

She spread out a sheaf of brochures for local attractions: Fern Canyon. Trinidad Bay. Whale watching. Ferndale, the Victorian Village. I thumbed through them, remembering Mama's freebie travel guides. We had dumped them when we left Jackson, and now I realized how much I missed them and their possibility.

Within a week, I began helping Margie keep order at Happy Trails. She forced a family to pay for the damages after I reported seeing their son flushing handfuls of toilet paper that caused the bathroom to flood. She yelled at a father with a sticky mess on his picnic table, after I told her that he left out a bag of marshmallows that raccoons devoured. In return, Margie slipped me hard candies wrapped in gold foil, and let me borrow books and magazines from the rack if I was careful not to wrinkle them. She'd paid for Happy Trails from her divorce settlement. She'd made mistakes but made the best of it.

At the weekly movie night, I wheeled a twenty-five-inch television under the trees and set up cardboard tubs of vanilla ice cream and bottles of root beer.

"You're lucky to have a daughter like her," Margie said to Mama.

I looked down, embarrassed, but it felt good to pull my weight. Margie's son, Alan, fixed himself a root beer float, adding so much ice cream that foam spilled down the side of his plastic cup. He ran his tongue up the cup and licked his hand, studying me. "You want one?" he asked. He had his mother's rangy build, but with a paunch big as a sack of cement. After hurting his back working construction, he was laid up on disability.

"No, thanks," Mama said.

I said nothing, even though I knew he was offering the float to me. He'd been coming by the front office more often, awkwardly chiming into my conversations with Margie. The attention my body had started to attract both disgusted and thrilled me. I was developing my mother's body, her curvy hips and breasts. I felt clumsy, off-balance. Askew.

Mama and I spread out a blanket and watched *Star Wars*. I smirked when Leia kissed Luke and a goofy grin spread over his face. He wouldn't know it was his twin sister until two movies later. But what if they never found out, married, and had monster babies? It was a relief to see Leia and Han Solo flirting in the final scene.

Mama sighed. "I had such a crush on Han. Who's your favorite?"

"No one."

"You're not interested in boys yet?" she asked.

If I had to pick, it would be Han. Luke was annoying; Han knew what he was doing. But Mama and I couldn't have a crush on the same person.

Other nights, when Mama worked in town, I patrolled the campground. Margie had complained there were too many Mexicans jamming the site with their tents and cars. "How can they live that way?"

She asked where my father was from and when I replied New York, she'd clarified, but *where is he really from*. After I told her his family was Chinese, last name Chang, she seemed relieved, and I knew she would have hardened toward me if I told her something different. If I told her that he—I—was Mexican.

The Mexicans brought their living room outside, installing bright lights and televisions hooked to generators. One night, two boys kicked a soccer ball, the thumps stuttering into the darkness. A pair of young men played guitars, and the family started singing along, some mouthing, others belting out the words. One of the guitarists waved at me. He had smoky eyes and messy curls. I shook my head but after they widened the circle, I squeezed in. Mama would have loved this music—on the road, we had listened to yearning songs like these, even though we didn't understand the words. Although my butt went numb on the damp log, it was cozier than in the empty truck camper. Tomorrow, I'd convince Mama to stay in and bring her here.

The next morning, they were gone.

MAMA AND I snapped at each other when the weather was cold and foggy, and when the sink was piled high with dishes that neither of us wanted to wash. I was mortified when our periods synched and our single trash can overflowed with our used tampons. I had started my period a year earlier and my cycles had been sporadic—every five or six weeks. Now they were as regular as the moon, something to do with our sweat or hormones. Disturbing, what effect we had on each other when we weren't trying. As we slept.

My mother started staying in town a couple of nights a week, to work late, she said, and didn't want to drive back to the campground in the dark. She stayed with a coworker. A man, I guessed. Maybe the same guy or different ones, who offered to take care of her and expected her to wait on them in return.

One morning I caught her wearing my favorite T-shirt, a soft faded shamrock green. "That's mine!" I hated the whine in my voice but hated her in my clothes even more. It was like watching her try on my skin.

"Some jerk spilled beer on me," she said, "then tipped fifty cents."

"Not that one. Take this." I held up an ugly blue plaid shirt, torn at the elbow.

"I like this one. Didn't you have time to do laundry? I left you quarters. Or were you with Margie?"

"It's not her fault that your life sucks."

"It's our life, Nina. Our life."

In June, we picked up another passenger, my cousin Ritchie. Though technically speaking we weren't going anywhere. And technically speaking, Ritchie was not my cousin, but the son of Mama's best friend from high school who lived in West Sac. Susie had landed in jail, after getting pulled over driving drunk for the third time. It had been decided that rather than staying by himself or with his granny—with whom he fought—Ritchie would live with us. He would sleep on the other side of the curtain, on the bed that folded out from the wall. His father had long since disappeared, like mine.

Ritchie rode the Greyhound to Eureka, about thirty miles north of Happy Trails. At the bus station, Mama hugged him and he mumbled hello. At fifteen, Ritchie was a year older than me, with the oversized feet and hands of a Labrador puppy. He rode shotgun. From the bench seat, I stared at the whorls of brown hair curling down his neck.

He was half Mexican—something I didn't remember until now—with caramel skin and watermelon-seed eyes that could almost be Chinese. He and I looked alike, more so than Mama and I. The last time I saw Ritchie, I was eight or nine years old. Our mothers had blended mango margaritas while his father manned the grill. Ritchie and I watched television, not a word passing between us. He controlled the remote, flipping through the shows. Just as I started to understand, he was onto the next. That's not what bothered me, though. It was how he complained that he hated burgers without cheese. How he wanted Dr Pepper, not Coke. How he brushed off his dad's suggestion they play ping-pong. You talk that way when you think that the people in your life will always be there. No one should be so confident.

The following day, I gave Ritchie a tour of the facilities: the basketball court with no net, the sagging ping-pong table, and the horseshoe pit littered with cigarette butts. I brought him to the front office with the promise of free potato chips. Margie's eyes lingered on him, trying to catch him shoplifting. Fidgeting, he flipped through dusty guidebooks.

I watched the both of them watching each other.

"Did you see the family that drove in today?" Margie asked me. "At campsite forty-nine. Their truck bed was filled with scrap lumber! Talk about cheap. Can't even afford firewood."

Ritchie dropped a magazine, and when he retrieved it, the

cover ripped. He tried to hide it behind the others, but Margie had seen what happened.

"I'll take it," she said. "No one's going to want that."

He set it on the counter. "I'll be outside."

Margie shot me a look.

"I'll pay for it when Mama gets home tonight," I said.

She smoothed the cover of the magazine. "Just tell him to be more careful. You know how expensive these are, and people read without buying."

Through the window, we glimpsed Ritchie huddled on a picnic table, arms around his knees, his head turned toward the redwoods.

"What's his story, anyway?" Margie asked.

I held back because he was too much like me, I could already tell, and I had to keep our common secrets from getting out.

"Mama told me to keep him entertained. Keep him from getting lost in the woods."

Margie laughed. "Too late."

RITCHIE WAS DEAD in the water. He floated facedown, legs dangling, arms outstretched in the Eel River.

I counted aloud. ". . . fifty-six, fifty-seven, fifty-eight . . ."

He raised his head, sputtering. "Your turn."

I took a deep breath and dunked my head. The water filled my ears, muffling the screams of a brother and sister splashing in arm floaties. Their parents were sitting in lawn chairs in the shallows, keeping their beer cool in a net bag.

Two weeks had passed since Ritchie arrived, and this was

how we spent our days. We slept late, went swimming in the late morning, and hiked through the redwoods in the afternoon. We went cross-eyed, trying to see the tops of trees, immense and ancient, like the leg of a dinosaur. I had someone close to my age to hang out with after many months alone with Mama. I didn't miss the girls from school, who flashed fake smiles and whispered when I passed them, or else stared right through me. I'd been marked as strange from kindergarten, after I arrived swollen, scabby, and oozing from rolling in poison oak.

". . . sixty. One minute, two, three, four, five . . ."

My lungs burning, heart pounding, I lifted my head and gasped for air. I'd won.

He ignored me and floated on his back, drifting in the slow-moving current. I clasped my arms around myself and rubbed away goose pimples on my shoulders and belly. Looking up, I spotted Alan watching us from shore, sipping from a can in a foam insulator. I shivered. He waved and walked back to camp.

Ritchie threw a handful of gravel against the opposite shore. Most pebbles arced into the water, but a few clattered in the bushes. Drops sparkled in his hair. I felt a flutter in my chest, a silly rising excitement. He didn't flirt with me in that jokey, bullying way boys had, as if they deserved attention for whatever they said.

"There's nothing to do around here, is there?" His question was a kick to my gut.

I'd had more fun in the last two weeks than I had all summer, and I thought he felt the same way too. In his eyes, Happy

Trails was a run-down campsite in the middle of nowhere, and I must seem like a freak with no friends.

An idea, an impulse, flickered in me as we paced in front of a shady corner site, far from the front office, far from Margie and Alan. I unzipped the red tent but then hesitated, thinking of Margie's disappointment if she found out. She treated me like I mattered, and this was how I repaid her? Then I felt ashamed for thinking of Margie first. Getting caught would cause a lot of trouble, trouble I wasn't sure Mama could handle.

Ritchie dove in. "Are you coming?"

I followed him inside the tent. Scrambling through the sleeping bags and air mattresses, we found a headlamp, a pair of glasses, and a pocketknife.

"Cool." He folded open the pliers.

We were on our sides, admiring our finds, when he leaned over and kissed me. My eyes were open and his kiss landed off-center, taking in part of my chin. My first kiss. His sour-cream-and-onion breath. His heat upon my cheek. Should I move to kiss him square? Where should I put my hands? I gave Ritchie a tight smile and cleared my throat, remembering that Margie had warned me about him.

"We should go." He dropped the pocketknife and started crawling out.

"Take it." Maybe this would keep him with me.

He pocketed it, and that was the start of our spree. Soon we were hitting three or four tents or RVs a day. We took whatever we wanted. They would never know, and we would always hold that over them. We witnessed the lives of ordinary people who did not live on the road or flee bad boyfriends and debts. Tents were the easiest. Inside we found books, condoms, knit hats, and mittens. Our rule was to take only one item, without sentimental value, that would not be missed immediately. People always left the doors of their RV unlocked. We snacked from refrigerators, flipped through board games and playing cards. I figured them out from their smells—mothballs or sweat or grease or rotting orange peels, the sweetness of blood and the penetrating stink of shit, the thick sticky scent of sex. Everything magnified in close quarters. I saw them in the porn they stuffed in drawers next to self-help books, in the bags of marijuana and bongs tucked under the sink. Without their façade, people were disgusting. Just like us.

We were almost caught once. We watched three boys and their mother leave their RV, loaded with folding chairs and striped towels for a day on the river. As soon as we were inside, we heard someone pounding up the stairs, and we jumped into the bathroom, drawing the accordion door behind us. We held each other, Ritchie's feet between mine, trying to avoid falling backward into the room. The kid bumped around, opening drawers.

"Won't be long," Ritchie whispered.

"If he finds us, we'll say we mixed up their RV with ours."

At that, the intruder—for that is what it felt like, that he had invaded our private territory—farted. Three sharp bleats. I shook with silent giggles and though Ritchie clamped his hand over my mouth, he was holding back laughter too. The door slammed and then we were kissing, our arms tangled around each other, me pinned against the wall.

That kept us away only for a day.

Most people thought what we stole had been misplaced, left somewhere in the mess of the car or never packed in the first place. We eavesdropped when they were hurrying to pack. *It's got to be here somewhere. We'll find it later.* Others were more frantic, running around their campsite or rooting through their back seats, but they always ended their search, the call of home greater than possession.

WE HID OUR stash inside a hollow log in a clearing where the sun filtered through the redwoods. A creek flowed nearby, a quiet burbling that ended by some miracle in the Pacific—picking up size and certainty and direction along the way, though it started off as a trickle.

One afternoon Ritchie scrolled through the pictures on a digital camera, nude shots of a blond couple posing like statues in the woods. Bushes rustled and I sat up.

"Do you hear that?" I whispered. Ritchie and I had a cover story if we were caught: we had stumbled upon these items. No one could prove we had stolen them. I imagined Alan flat on his belly, peeking at us through the brush. His bad back aching. I hadn't seen him in days and assumed he had given up whatever it was he wanted from us. From me. We waited, listened, and heard nothing but the sound of high wind in high trees.

Ritchie rolled on top and kissed me. A week ago, we started groping each other on the outside of our clothes, which led to him resting his hand under my shirt. Now he guided my hand to his hard-on, which I squeezed before pulling away. I was beginning to see how Mama could want this, and how it would make Ritchie want me. What I liked best was his dead weight on top of me—comforting, like a heavy blanket or an old coat.

"Do you think your mom would like me?" I asked Ritchie.

"Mama likes you."

He rested his head on my shoulder, his mouth next to my ear, his breath the roar of the ocean. "So listen. Tonto and the Lone Ranger are riding their horses, when suddenly they're surrounded by enemy Indians."

"Who's Tonto?"

"The Lone Ranger is a cowboy and Tonto is his Indian sidekick," Ritchie said. "You never saw it? Grandpa's favorite show."

I nodded, picturing a bowlegged cowboy in a white hat, and a man in fringed buckskin and a single feather in his beaded headband.

"They're surrounded. The Lone Ranger says, 'Tonto, Tonto, what are we going to do?' Tonto replies, 'What do you mean *we*, paleface?'"

Ritchie started laughing, shaking on top of me. What did he mean? Our difference was all that mattered? I thought of the family of Mexicans, singing a song not meant for me. Ritchie was a boy and I was a girl. He was older and I was younger. He was half Mexican and I was not. Would he sell out his best friend to save himself?

I sat up. "We should get back."

"What do you mean *we*," Ritchie repeated, snorting with laughter.

The next day in the clearing, we stripped down to our shorts, our shirts off, even though I'd told myself I wouldn't go this far. That I wasn't like Mama. He pulled me on top of him and we rubbed, crotch to crotch. I felt an ache, a pounding between my legs. I opened my eyes and stared at him, his eyes closed and his chest pulsing with fast, shallow breaths. I could have been anyone to him. Anything. I was friction, nothing more. He started to knead my butt and ran his finger along the leg hole of my bikini bottom.

"Do you want to see it?" His voice sounded strained, as if he'd been running laps.

I nodded, my mouth gone dry, and he pulled it above the elastic waistband. Up close, it was hard, purple, veined, alien. I put my hand on it—smooth and hotter than I expected, like a feverish forehead—and then he came. Sticky wetness. Egg whites. Snot. His eyes shut tight, and his mouth hung open, exposing dark fillings that made his teeth look rotted out.

I wiped my hand on the grass, yanked on my shirt, and fled. He caught up with me by the time we reached the trailer, where Mama had lunch ready, ham sandwiches and fruit cocktail, and afterward, she suggested gin rummy. Work had slowed after Labor Day and she was spending more time with us than she had all summer. She was dealing the first hand when the knock came at the door.

Margie entered, her eyes lingering on the dirty plates in the sink, piled higher than the faucet. We'd run out of dish soap and Mama had forgotten to buy more. She informed us that Ritchie's mother was calling collect from jail to the office phone. Cell phone service at the campsite was patchy.

In the office, Mama relayed each sentence to us: Susie was fine, reading a lot of books. She handed the phone to Ritchie, who listened before replying, "No, I don't." He dropped the phone and darted out of the office. I suspected that Ritchie's mother had asked him if he missed her. Mama hung up soon after, offering to pay for the phone call, but Margie waved her off.

"I know how expenses can add up. Especially with kids," Margie said, and I flushed, feeling as if she knew exactly what Ritchie and I were doing together—the stealing, the groping—even if Mama did not.

Mama and I walked back to the truck camper. "Maybe," Mama said, "maybe we could move back in a couple weeks. Get you enrolled in school."

We never talked about what we left behind. Mama and I had seen so much, traveling around California, but life plodded on as usual in Jackson. While we were away, I figured they were the ones missing out. It aged you, to stay still. Like the twin paradox I'd read about. One twin rocketed at the speed of light and returned to earth younger than the twin who remained behind. Your life was set before you had a chance to figure it out.

"To West Sac. We could stay with Susie and Ritchie for a while."

I said nothing, unable to imagine Ritchie outside of Happy Trails. Would he still want me in any other circumstance besides one boy, one girl, alone in the woods? I let things go as far as they had because I knew our time here would end.

———

THE NEXT DAY, Alan came by the truck camper after dinner. Margie wanted to see us, he said, crowding the doorway and blotting out the last of the sunset. "All of you."

"If it's about the rent, I told Margie, I'm getting paid tomorrow," Mama said.

"Right now."

If we ran now, we would never have to face her. I glanced at Ritchie. His expression gave nothing away. If he stayed calm, then so could I. The fluorescent light in the front office stole our shadows, making everything flat like a cartoon. The stolen goods sat on the counter. Prickles burned on my neck, down my back, as though I'd fallen in stinging nettles.

"Well?" Margie stood in front of the counter while Alan waited by the door, blocking our escape.

"What is it?" Mama asked.

"Ask your daughter, and her friend. About what they stole."

Mama gripped her hands together and thumped them against the counter. "Nina could never do something like that," she said. "You know that, Margie. You told me how much she helps you out."

"Used to."

"I would have noticed." Mama would always defend me, because she loved me, yes, but also because she didn't want to acknowledge what she might have done to lead us here.

"You can't notice if you're not around," Margie said.

"Fuck you!" Mama said. Her shoulders sagged. She hardly ever swore, and this outburst seemed to exhaust her.

"Alan followed them and found these items piled in a log," Margie said.

Earlier that afternoon, as Ritchie and I set off for the clearing, I'd felt unseen eyes on my back. I'd almost stopped us from going, until Ritchie impatiently tugged on my elbow. Not on my hand, we didn't hold hands. I felt like a bird squashed flat in the road. A bloody pulp, with only the suggestion of a feather or a beak.

"That's nothing. That's no proof," Mama said.

Margie rested her hand on my shoulder—gently, as though she were about to praise me for a job well done. "Not until you admit if there's anything else you've taken. I understand someone might have put you up to it. Just tell us. Tell me."

It was as if we were the only people in the room. My thoughts flared, disintegrated like a log on a fire. I had to blame someone, someone Margie expected, not someone she trusted.

"It was the Mexicans," I shouted. "The Mexicans!"

Alan snorted and I wanted to swallow my words, even if they ate away my insides like toilet bowl cleaner, even if it meant I would never speak again.

"Please vacate the premises," Margie said, her eyes glistening. If I ever doubted she cared about me, now I knew.

We left. Ritchie did not look at me, not then, not while we were packing. Not while we hooked the camper to the truck, Mama cutting her hands in her hurry, and not after we pulled into the last available spot in an RV park about twenty miles up the road. Not when we put him on a bus the next day. He was gone, just like my father and all the men who had followed.

When we were on the road, Mama and I had only each other, and I might have told her how I felt: I was owed. Why should other people have casual accessories of permanence and stability? Look, these objects say, there is so much more where this came from. People don't know the worth of their possessions because they so easily replace what is lost.

Mama and I had tried to start over, and we wound up here, worse off, punished for wanting more. She turned on the radio, skipped past a Spanish pop station, and settled on classic rock. The lead singer wailed about a small-town girl escaping into a lonely world—the coincidence of a song about our lives. We burst out laughing during the extended guitar riff. If you were driving in the opposite direction and glanced into our truck, you might think that Mama and I were on vacation. Together, exploring the coast, no worries except what to see next.

You'd be wrong.

Room at the Table

Grace had the urge to introduce herself again, though that would be insulting. They were family, but it had been years since she and her cousin Daniel had seen each other.

"The volcano erupted right before we landed in Manila," he told her. With his spiky black hair, he appeared not much older than when they had roughhoused at family reunions, weddings, and funerals. "It was dark at noon."

"We tied bandannas around our faces to breathe," said his wife, Phyllis. After postings to Kenya, Thailand, and the Philippines, they had returned to the Bay Area to plant a church. They were also expecting. Their son, due next month, would be the first child of the next generation, the firstborn of the American-born.

Phyllis started coughing, and Daniel left to fetch a glass of water. Her cousin had become a stranger. Seeing him tonight, she realized how much she had missed him. On the radio, a commentator mentioned Saddam Hussein's trial, and holidays for the troops in Iraq. Grace searched the dial for Christmas songs, and then dug into the bulging brown grocery sacks of decorations she'd fetched from the garage.

"What year are you in college?" Phyllis unfurled a gold garland.

Grace winced. Her attempt at adulthood—her bobbed haircut and tailored shirt and trousers from a Williamsburg boutique near her apartment—had failed. "I graduated eight years ago. Class of '97."

"I'm sorry, I should have known." Phyllis brushed a strand of tinsel from her long black hair. Her hands were callused, imbued with a nimble flexibility. "I'm bad at remembering those things." She rubbed the small of her back, shifting in her ballet flats to find a comfortable standing position. Her slight frame seemed too fragile to support her swollen belly.

"You've been away," Grace said.

They'd left while the first Bush was president, and returned after his son came to office. They'd missed the Clintons, 9/11, MySpace, and other collective American experiences that had marked Grace's own entry into adulthood. She untangled an ornament, a project from elementary school, a red clay stocking with her brother's initials carved on the back in crooked letters. The first and only time she'd met Phyllis, at their wedding, Grace had still been in high school.

"You know the saying, 'Asian don't raisin'?" Grace said.

Phyllis laughed. "Still, though."

"I'll probably feel insulted once I stop getting carded," Grace said.

It was Christmas Eve, and Grace's father, as always, hosted dinner. The elders were in the kitchen, drinking tea. Grace called her father Baba when she was small and now when she was sentimental. He was First Uncle to her cousins, the elder of their extended family.

Indoctrinated from his college years in Indiana, Baba insisted on Western rituals for the holidays. Cranberry sauce with turkey, visiting church on Easter and Christmas, slices of canned pineapple on ham, and a fake Christmas tree—garnishes of propriety, of patriotism, as American as the stars and stripes, as the red, white, and blue.

Kneeling, Grace plugged in the Christmas lights, which reflected off the windows and winked onto their faces like a neon sign. As she stood up, Phyllis swayed and leaned on Grace's shoulder. Startled, Grace stumbled before steadying them both.

Phyllis apologized. "Standing too long, I guess. Blood pools in my legs, and then I get dizzy."

She didn't mind bearing her cousin's weight; it felt good to be sturdy. When Ma called them to dinner, Grace steered Phyllis to the dining room.

Baba sat at the head of the table, next to the turkey, and Ma at the foot. Phyllis and Grace joined Second Uncle, Baba's widowed younger brother, and Daniel, already seated.

The table delighted Baba with its promise of expansive hospitality. Tonight, though, for only six guests, he didn't need to pull out the extension. With her brother Frank missing, everything felt off-kilter.

At past family dinners, Baba had advised Daniel, and her

cousin in turn asked questions of the family elder. They were both the first sons of their generation, and Daniel had once excelled in this role, winning scholarships to cover his schooling at UC Berkeley. Grace had envied her father's interest in her cousin, paternalistic but given with the respect and knowledge that someday they would be equals. Upon graduating, though, Daniel became a missionary.

Now Baba asked him to say grace.

Daniel looked around the table. "Where's Frank? Is he coming later?"

"Work," Baba said a little too quickly.

Daniel couldn't hide his surprise. "On Christmas Eve? Even my parents closed early tonight." They ran a diner in Chicago.

"End of the year, he's finishing a project," Baba said.

Her cousin nodded. He looked down, seeming to collect himself. "Dear Father, thank you for blessing all of us this year. Let us thank First Uncle for having us over to share time with family. Thank you for this feast, and for bringing us safely together. Amen."

The family repeated after him, "Amen."

Baba carved the turkey, cutting the breast so that each snowy slice had a sliver of crispy skin. He speared a piece with the serving fork and offered it to Daniel. "You should use your education and write software. So many Chinese in tech. You can give money to the church and help out your parents. Use all your talents. A God-given gift."

Daniel held Baba's gaze. "The church is my calling."

Grace wished his prayer could have brought a god through

the ceiling and into their laps, that he could part the Red Sea or rain down frogs to demonstrate his powers to Baba—anything to prove that Daniel and their generation could succeed outside the decrees of their elders.

"Hao chi," Second Uncle said. Tasty. Even before he'd started going deaf, he'd always been a beat behind the conversation. His wife had died of a heart attack five years ago. They'd never had children, and he now lived alone in senior housing in Oakland Chinatown.

Because Chinese respect dictated that aunts and uncles were to be addressed in terms of birth order, Grace did not know his real name, in English or in Chinese. Though younger than Baba, he'd aged twenty years since becoming a widower, and seemed a withered replica—quiet, pale, and wispy next to the hearty solidness of her father. His green argyle sweater looked familiar; it was a hand-me-down from Baba, she realized, one she'd picked out for him years ago.

When her cell phone vibrated in her pants pocket, Grace jumped in her seat. She checked the screen: Andy. New York was three hours ahead and she would lose her chance to talk to him if she waited to return the call. Excusing herself, she went into the kitchen.

"Merry Christmas," Andy said.

"Happy Hanukkah," she said. This year the holidays coincided.

Tomorrow he and the twin girls he shared with his ex would drive to Tenafly and spend the day with her, her new husband, and their baby on the first night of Hanukkah. Grace pictured him shirtless in his striped pajama bottoms, pushing his horn-rims with the tip of his finger, his curly dark hair flecked with silver—on his head, and on his chest. Right now snow was falling, she was sure of it. She read the forecast before she left: a 90 percent chance of snow showers, temperatures in the thirties. Just as she checked Bay Area weather every day while in New York, mindful of the family left behind, mindful of the life she might have led had she stayed: dinners home on Sunday nights, ferrying her parents to social events, responsibilities her brother had handled until he sank out of their lives.

She'd moved to New York after college to take a recruiting job, promising she'd go for one year that turned into two and now eight. Her parents had never stopped pressuring her to move home. "Henry and his wife bought a house in the neighborhood," her mother would say, mentioning a high school classmate. Then she'd email Grace listings for starter condos. Her father sent news articles about stabbings and shootings in Queens, New Jersey, or anywhere else in a hundred-mile vicinity of her apartment.

They didn't yet know her landlord was tripling her rent, and her roommates had found places elsewhere. Andy wanted her to move in.

The phone crackled. The reception was bad, and she leaned over the kitchen sink, tilting her phone toward the window. Water soaked the hem of her shirt, the damp fabric chafing her skin. The morning she flew out, they'd taken a shower together at his apartment and flooded the bathroom. She had almost missed her flight.

"We just started dinner," she said.

"Put me on speaker, I can say hello," he said pointedly.

She didn't answer. She was thirty now, too old to be sneaking around, and not for the first time, her secrecy annoyed him. She cleared her throat. "I should go. I'll call you later."

As she hung up, she heard his tinny "I love you."

"I love you too," she whispered in return, a moment too late. She wanted to rest her head against his chest, listening to his heartbeat. Reach up and stroke the scruff on his cheeks and on the back of his neck. He was fifteen years older and divorced with children, not anyone her parents might accept: a son of Chinese immigrants who attended a top university, who worked in a respectable profession of medicine, engineering, or law. If she married him someday, it would blow up what remained of her family.

Half a year ago, her brother had proposed to Gabriela, and moved in with her and her son, a kindergartner. He'd said nothing to Baba and Ma until he knew he intended to marry her, but when he tried to introduce her, they refused. She was six years older, the daughter of immigrants from El Salvador, and a divorced single mother. Irredeemable. Baba said she was only after his money and, by extension, their money.

After Frank stopped answering their parents' calls and emails, Baba had taken to wearing his son's varsity cross-country letterman jacket around the house. She felt a pang, to see him in the jacket, as if a Frank of the future—saggier, slower—haunted the hallways.

Yesterday, Baba told her that they wanted to sell their house and use part of the money as a down payment on a condo for her.

"I can't take your money," she'd said.

"It's *our* money." He paused. "Mommy needs you."

He'd named her executor of his will. Last night, while looking over the paperwork, she discovered they'd written her brother out of the will. Staring at the page, she'd felt like she was choking. Did Frank already know, or did her parents expect her to tell him?

This Christmas was the first without Frank, and as much as she missed him, she also could not forgive him for leaving her alone with their parents. The burden of responsibility, hers alone, even if she'd done it to him first by moving across the country.

Maybe Baba might have been so insistent with Daniel tonight because he'd lost his own son. He could want to redeem himself as a father, as the family elder.

The answering machine blinked on the kitchen counter. Her parents never erased the messages, and the dozen in the queue bothered her. She played and erased them, one by one, keeping the volume low—much as she surreptitiously bagged up clutter around the house and dropped it off at Goodwill. There were several hang-ups, a couple of telemarketers, and an automated appointment reminder from a few months ago for her father. From a neurologist. She played it again, but the message offered no additional clues.

"Who was that?" Baba asked when she returned to the dining room. He straightened his glasses, which he had begun to wear full-time in the last year. The huge plastic frames made him seem dependent, at the mercy of something beyond his control. He was the kind of man who left nothing to chance, who practiced and timed driving routes before important events, who developed contingency plans to protect his family in every kind of emergency.

"A friend. From college," she said. The lie came easily after a lifetime of omissions and deceptions. She had learned how to balance her life against them, to bare only what they wanted to see, and yet their presence always shadowed her. "She's alone on Christmas."

"Is she Chinese?" Ma asked. She styled her hair in a 1960s bouffant, never tiring of the glamour she had dreamed was American. Grace suspected she was still trying to match-make with her brother, harboring the hope he might change his mind.

"No," Grace said.

"You should have invited your friend to come over," Baba said. "Always room for one more."

AT THE CLOSE of the civil war in China, her father's family fled across the strait to the island of Taiwan. Baba's youngest brother, Third Uncle, was Daniel's father. He and his wife were the last to immigrate to the United States, the least educated and the first to have children. Third Uncle and his family had lived in this house for a few months when Grace was eight years old. They slept in her room, and she'd been forced to bunk with her brother. She had resented them, their smelly foods and bad haircuts.

At fourteen, Daniel was supposed to be knowledgeable and cool, but instead she had to explain how to use a microwave. "No metal," she had scolded, after he heated up a tinfoil-covered dish, causing miniature lightning strikes.

Yet when she and her brother wrestled, knocking over and

shattering a vase, Daniel helped glue it together before their parents discovered what happened. He learned English from watching reruns of sitcoms like *Gilligan's Island* or *The Brady Bunch* and game shows like *The Price Is Right*. She and her cousin used to shout along with the host, "A new car!" In America, if you answered correctly, you could drive into the sunset that very day.

In time, she and Daniel confided in each other. She revealed the mysteries of the schoolyard: "*Hella* means 'very.'" "Don't be a dual-strapper. Only hang your backpack off one shoulder."

In turn he divulged the mysteries of the older generation, giving her tips on how to be *guai*, the Chinese concept of good wrapped up in obedience. "Make Baba his tea without him asking."

She didn't realize she'd needed his protection and guidance until his family moved to Chicago, where a friend of a friend had a restaurant job for Third Uncle. With the help of a loan from Baba, the family bought a diner, Junior's, where Daniel worked as a busboy, and later on, as a waiter and a cook. His parents had no savings, no future without him, and Baba still sent them money every month to cover their expenses

A few years later, Daniel had lived with Grace's family, taking classes in the summer to finish his engineering degree at Cal early. He studied for most of the day at the library, returning for dinner, when Baba quizzed him about what he had learned. Daniel, in turn, coaxed out stories about Baba's days in graduate school and the start of his engineering career, stories that Grace had heard only in brief or not at all.

If Baba had returned to Taiwan, he might have landed a

prestigious government post or become a professor, instead of getting passed up for promotions, forever the foreigner. If he'd returned, he might not have borne the weight of becoming the sponsor for his three brothers and two sisters. He might not have called her good-for-nothing or told her brother he was lazy and useless. He might not have pounded his fist against the dining room table, so hard the chopsticks jumped into the air. All this Grace had pieced together later, but back then, she never knew what might set off her father—if she scraped the car door against the curb, or if her brother played the television too loud during Baba's nap.

After such blowups, Daniel drove his cousins through the hills to the Lawrence Hall of Science, where they climbed on the fiberglass humpback whale and the double-helix sculptures on the plaza overlooking the bay. If it was windy, he slipped off his hoodie and tugged it over her, the fleece downy as a chick. She'd draw up her knees and tent herself in the baggy fabric. They didn't talk about what happened, but she always felt more steady and solid afterward.

His final year at Cal, Daniel picked up a flyer for an Asian American Christian fellowship. At the welcome barbecue, he met Phyllis, and neither of them was far apart from each other, or the church, after that.

Now Baba finished dividing the turkey into piles of dark and white meat. He would not stop until the bird was stripped. "I know you want the drumstick." He reached for Grace's plate while brandishing the leg impaled on the serving fork.

She shrank back, pleased that he remembered, though also

resenting the inescapable loop of his recollection. As a child, she had wrapped paper napkins around chicken legs and gnawed on them. Andy would have been surprised, for now, given the choice, she ate no meat, only fish. She jerked back her plate, causing the drumstick to slide onto the tablecloth. She nudged the leg with her fork and moved her plate to cover the grease spot.

"The wine!" Baba said. Her mother, a real estate agent specializing in Chinese clients, had received two bottles of Chardonnay from a customer. She was going to regift them until Baba had claimed the bottles, calling the wine a proper accompaniment to a holiday dinner. Slipping into the kitchen, he reemerged with a corkscrew and the wine. Grace could not recall a single occasion in which her family had consumed wine, and she was astonished her father had a corkscrew. The cork did not budge under his inexpert hand.

"First Uncle, let me do it," Daniel said.

"It's my duty. I'm the host." Baba pushed and pulled until half the cork crumbled into the wine.

Grace fetched a strainer and glass tumblers from the kitchen. Her parents didn't have wineglasses. She had come to like wine, which she had each night at dinner with Andy. She never had more than a glass—more, and she might vomit. If she drank too much, her heart pounded in her ears, and her throat seized up. Andy would knock on the bathroom door, checking on her while she splashed her face. She probably should stop drinking, but she couldn't give up the festivity, the feeling she had entered a wider world.

She asked Daniel if he wanted a glass, and to her surprise, he said yes. His wedding had been dry.

"Let us make a toast," Baba said. "To Daniel, who will start software consulting next year."

Daniel stiffened. The more Baba drank, the more he toasted. To his family, to his brother, but most of all to Daniel and to computer programming. Baba's cheeks flushed and his eyes turned bloodshot, small and red as holly berries. Grace had never seen her father drink but for the occasional Cognac toast at a Chinese banquet.

Her cousin kept up, glass after glass. Once Phyllis put her hand on his glass, as though to tell him to slow down, to stop, but he knocked back the wine without looking at her.

Grace's phone buzzed in her pocket: a text from Andy, telling her good night. She didn't write back. Another arrived from her brother. Her chest tightened. Was he imagining them at dinner? She'd see Frank the day after Christmas, before her flight back to New York. She had a gift for his stepson-to-be, the same age as Andy's twins, who had picked out the Lego set.

Baba raised his glass. Ma shook her head and said something in Chinese, something about medicine. He could be taking a drug that didn't mix with alcohol. Maybe when her father had told her "Mommy needs you," it wasn't that her mother ailed—he did, and he wanted to make sure that Grace would take care of Ma if he turned sicker.

"Da Ge," Second Uncle said. Big Brother. It could have been another gentle warning. Though his voice was creaky, Grace could imagine him as a boy, looking up to Baba then, now, and always.

Without a word, she pushed back her chair and hurried over to the coat closet, a few steps off of the dining room. She'd seen an old Polaroid camera hanging on a hook.

"I almost forgot," she called out. She knew how odd she must seem, getting up like that, but she had to put a stop to her father's next toast. "Picture time!"

She remembered the camera from her childhood, before the advent of slim silver digital cameras. Her fingers brushed against the black plastic casing, the device bulky and awkward to hold. But Polaroids provided a sense of occasion, with its technology that still astonished her—an entire processing lab crammed inside and spitting out a photo then and there.

"They still make film for that?" Daniel asked.

Baba nodded. He took the camera, and then gestured for her to stand behind Daniel. Baba snapped the shutter without giving a warning count. He wanted a natural-looking shot, he often said, but Grace suspected he liked to remain in control. He blew across the thin plastic square, breathing the image to life.

Grace sat back down. As they passed around the photo, the claims began. Second Uncle said her eyes looked like his mother's.

"No, her eyes are like mine." Ma tilted her head. "The corners."

Although Grace was present, they spoke of her in the third person. When she was younger, she used to dispute such statements, not wanting to look like anyone else. Now she understood that children were subject to discussion like other kinds of possessions. Her parents, aunts, and uncles never tired of playing this game.

She and Daniel both had close-lipped smiles in the photo.

She ached for her brother; he belonged in the picture too. "Daniel and Baba look alike," she said.

Everyone stared at the two men, searching for the similarities. They had the same round faces, broad noses, and parenthetical creases around their eyes. In unison they shook their heads in disagreement, adding to their likeness.

"Looks skip a generation." Baba reclaimed the photo from Grace. "Maybe his baby might look like me. But not Daniel." He swigged his wine. "You know, we learned English from the missionaries. In grade school. First they taught us how to count. That's the best place to begin, right?"

Eying Baba, her cousin must have wondered if the question was a friendly overture, an attempt to find common ground—or a trap.

"They taught us songs, 'You Have a Friend in Jesus . . .'" With a glass still raised, Baba emphasized every other syllable, in a jerky vaudeville beat, thumping his other hand on the table so hard that the glasses rattled. "And He will bring you home."

He set down his glass. "We learned another song too." He sang in Mandarin, about mountains and stars. Now the melody smoothed out, the roundness of the notes originating from low in his diaphragm, the song more beautiful than the original. Ma hummed along, and Second Uncle bobbed his head.

"Same tune, different song," Baba said. "They never knew our version was different."

He raised an empty glass, streaked with wine. Daniel picked up his fork and jabbed it into the remainder of the turkey.

———

THE LAST TIME Grace had seen Daniel, at his wedding almost fifteen years ago, Baba had warned her and her brother about the dangers of being duped by a cult. He fumed that they were throwing away a good education. Daniel and Phyllis sat by themselves at a sweetheart table beneath a red paper cutout of the double-happiness symbol, their heads bowed in private conversation, untouchable and dazzling as movie stars in their wedding finery. Pink tablecloths, paper napkins, gold-rimmed plates, and a bottle of apple cider adorned each table. Luxury, Chinese style.

The newlyweds were leaving for the Philippines, where they would begin their honeymoon and their missionary assignment. No one knew how long they'd remain abroad, or that they'd go from country to country. Third Aunt began weeping as the waiters served long-life noodles, the final course. Baba put his hand on the table beside his sister-in-law's, the most comfort that he could offer her.

"Can we leave?" Frank had finished his book, whose cover featured a woman in leather armor riding a dragon. Against his protest, Ma dished noodles onto his plate. If she kept his mouth full, he wouldn't complain.

At the next table, Phyllis's parents were stone-faced instead of smiling. Parents of both the bride and groom had united in refusing to shake the hand of the young minister, with a dimpled chin and an easy grin—blandly handsome, like a male model in a department store's Sunday flyers. Baba had advised his siblings not to give money as a wedding present as called for by tradition, because the stacks of red envelopes might wind up in the hands of the church. Better to give a savings bond, for the eventual grandchildren. According to Baba, as a missionary, Daniel would never make enough to support his family.

On the dance floor, Daniel lit up when he spotted Grace. He spun her around and hugged her tightly as the song ended. "Congratulations!" she blurted, wanting to say so much more, but another guest pulled him away.

Driving back from the reception, her father ran through a stop sign. A truck crossing the intersection skidded and honked, and Grace rocked against the seat belt and braced her hand on the door. Did he have anything to drink at the banquet? No—no alcohol had been served. It was his fury that made him reckless.

Closing her eyes, she rested her forehead against the window, imagining her cousin in an Edenic jungle—no, on a beach, in sunglasses—giving a sermon about paradise while blue-green waves lapped against a pristine shore. Daniel chose the spiritual over his obligations to his parents, his religion worth more to him than a career. His mutiny traded one form of rigid belief for another, but in the years that followed, Grace had admired that the choice remained his alone. She'd never been so brave. Never so selfish.

As she searched the kitchen drawers, looking for a knife to slice dessert, Daniel entered, offering to help. He marveled at the pumpkin pie. "It's as big as a wagon wheel!"

Ma had stockpiled it from Thanksgiving, buying it from a warehouse superstore and freezing it until now. It had been defrosting on the counter all afternoon.

"Thanks," she said. "We can carry it together."

She wanted to apologize for her father, though Baba had a duty to advise and command that Daniel must understand. That was why he endured this meal.

"None for Phyllis," he said. "She hasn't had much of an appetite lately."

"How's she been?" Grace had wondered why her cousin and his wife, both in their mid-thirties, had waited so long to have children. Maybe they'd wanted to focus on their missionary work, or wait until they returned to the United States, for better schools and medical facilities. "It's a lot of change at once."

"It's not the first," Daniel said. Grace understood then that Phyllis had miscarried, maybe several times. Not knowing what else to do, she took both his hands into her own, clasping his knobby knuckles and clammy skin.

"Now God has blessed us," he said.

She didn't know how to respond to such a naked expression of his beliefs, as if he'd broken apart his breastbone to reveal his raw wounded heart.

"I'm excited to meet my nephew." She released his hands and stared down at the glossy surface of the pie. "Or would it be my second cousin?"

"He'll call you Ayi," Daniel said. Auntie.

Her phone buzzed, a call from Andy. She let it go to voice mail, but when he rang again, she apologized to her cousin. Turning away, she picked up.

"Aren't you asleep?" she asked.

"I can't find their gifts."

The gifts that his daughters had been on the verge of

discovering the other day, that she'd whisked away while he distracted them. Grace wanted to have children someday too, but maybe she wouldn't be able to, if she waited too long to get pregnant. Maybe she might struggle too.

"Look under the bed," she said.

"Already did . . ."

"In the green suitcase. But save what I got the girls for when I get back," she said.

"I will."

"Love you too," she said, louder than before, to make up for whispering last time.

After she hung up, Daniel cocked his head at her, making no effort to pretend he hadn't been listening.

It could have been the jet lag or the wine, but she felt too weary to keep hiding. She'd convinced herself secrets were necessary. Yet the secrets also turned her into a stranger to her family—to herself.

"The guy I'm dating, Andy. His daughters, they're twins." The words rushed out with the force of a stubborn champagne cork popping off. He was from Boston, and worked at a tech company, she continued, unsure of what to say about him.

"Your parents . . . ?" He glanced back at the dining room.

"Don't know." She sliced the pie, wiping the blade after each cut.

He locked eyes with her. "They should," he said.

"I can't." Panic fluttered through her. He didn't know Frank had been disowned. Such information, once leaked, would spread through the family.

"They should," he repeated.

"Not now," she said.

"You shouldn't lie to them," he said, his tone righteous and scolding.

She clenched the pie server. "You—lecture me? You abandoned your parents!" They were alone at Christmas in Chicago, alone for a long while to come. She unstacked the dessert plates with a clatter and began to serve slices.

He slid plates toward himself. Their hands busy, they didn't have to look at each other. "God provided," he said.

"Baba provided," she said.

Daniel grabbed a handful of forks, and when one fell to the floor, she could tell he had to restrain himself from flinging the rest. He scowled, transforming himself: Baba's expression reborn on his face. Did he see Baba in her expression too, in her reproach?

BABA CALLED FOR another toast. "To your success in programming!"

"Maybe. Sure, sure. Whatever you say," Daniel said.

"Did everyone hear that? Congratulations for Daniel, who will start working in computers next year. Cheers!"

Everyone went through the musical ritual of clinking glasses. Phyllis had gone pale, her forehead furrowed in fatigue, but she gamely raised her water glass.

"Maybe Grace's boyfriend could help me find a job," Daniel said.

She almost knocked over her glass, hands trembling.

"Grace doesn't have a boyfriend," Baba said.

"Too busy," Ma said. The reason Grace stated, and her parents accepted, for her infrequent visits home.

"Andy," her cousin said. Grace opened her mouth but found herself unable to speak.

The knowing expression slipped off Baba's face. "Xiao Mei?" he said. *Little Daughter, how could you,* he didn't have to say. *Your brother, and now you?* Ma rubbed her temples, just as stricken.

Phyllis grabbed Daniel's hand, whispering in his ear. She rose to her feet. "Thank you for a wonderful dinner," she said. "But I'm exhausted. It's past my bedtime." She wobbled, and as her eyelids fluttered, she crumpled toward the floor.

Ma screamed as Daniel caught his wife. Her hair curtained her face, her head lolling against Daniel's chest. Her legs fell open, her hem riding up to reveal her knobby knees.

Together, he and Baba carried her to the living room couch, and after a moment, Phyllis revived. She traced her thumb along Daniel's jaw, through his tears, and he kissed her hand. They mesmerized Grace, their strength and their faith. The kind of love given wholly, taken wholly, that her brother must share with his fiancée, and that she yearned for with Andy.

Daniel touched his wife's belly. "He's kicking!" The light fabric of her dress twitched, drops of rain falling on water.

Baba appeared with a mug of tea.

"Chinese herbs?" Phyllis asked.

"Lipton." He showed the orange tag at the end of the string.

Everyone laughed. Baba locked eyes with Grace, to show he had not forgotten. After the guests left, he'd question her. She had questions of her own. She'd withheld so much, for so long, that letting go seemed a relief.

Phyllis took a few sips and swung her legs around to sit up. She smoothed her dress around her knees.

"We should go," Daniel said, stroking her hair.

Grace fetched the Polaroid of her and Daniel. "Here."

Daniel studied the photo for a few seconds. "I have pictures of him," he said. "My son."

Everyone turned to look at the high dome of Phyllis's belly. "We have printouts from the sonogram," she said. "In the car."

Daniel hurried outside, and through the bay window, they watched him fumbling in the front seat.

"What's his name?" Grace asked.

"We won't decide until he's born," Phyllis said. "You can't tell until then. What will fit."

After Daniel returned, he spread the sonogram printouts on the coffee table. He pulled out his digital camera, explaining he'd filmed the checkup. Everyone clustered around its palm-size screen, and suddenly they were plunged into the watery motion of life. The silvery blob—was that a fist or a foot? The baby's features might resemble his father's, his mother's, echoes of each generation from the beginning.

The heartbeat fluttered faster than thoughts, a hollow, whistling, croaking sound, a primal whisper. His head nodded to the music of the body, his face blurred in the murk, not yet visible to anyone. He was swimming, tiny hands swaying in the tides.

Harte Lake

The last step was to unload the unnecessary weight. Anna Murata looked at the brilliant blue, not a cloud in the fall sky. She set down her backpack, removed the heavy rain pants, waterproof jacket, and wool socks, and tossed them into the back seat of her car. She strapped herself into the lightened load and set out on the trailhead at nine o'clock in the morning. Her destination was Harte Lake, elevation 9,500, latitude 36° north, longitude 118° west. The date: October 10, the first anniversary of her husband Ken's death.

A year ago, as they pored over a map for their upcoming trip, Ken stopped talking midsentence and tumbled to the floor. She shook him, screamed his name, and crawled to the phone to call 911. While waiting for the paramedics, she put his head in her lap and straightened his glasses. She could not save him. She did not remember driving to the hospital, following the ambulance, parking their car, or filling out forms—only the moment when the petite Indian doctor told her that they were unable to revive him. An artery in his brain had burst. He was dead by the time the ambulance arrived, maybe by the time he hit the floor, and she was left alone after thirty years.

On this trip, Anna wanted to remember Ken as he was, on the last trek they were meant to take together. Out backpacking, they had depended on each other the most. She would spend three days on the twenty-four-mile loop, Friday through Sunday.

They met at UC Berkeley in 1969, squares among the hippies. Both their families had been interned in the camps during the war. She and Ken met in one of the first classes in Asian American Studies, and they were married the following year. They had stayed together for decades, despite—or because of— the losses and betrayals they had inflicted on each other.

She was more attractive at fifty-four than when she had been in her twenties—strong and sturdy while others her age sagged. If she had once been beautiful, she might have mourned the loss of her youth, but her plainness had sustained her. She kept a garden behind her lemon-yellow Berkeley bungalow, walked every day before work, and ate cruciferous vegetables and whole grains, redeeming herself with these small virtues.

The first half mile of the trail was flat, alternating between meadows and groves of trees before climbing steeply. Where the trail petered out, Anna checked the route against the topo map, trying to make sense of the rippling lines of elevation. Navigation was new to her.

Laughter and conversation came up fast behind her. She

stepped to the side and a family passed by: a mother, a father, a teenage girl, and a young boy. They weren't going far, judging by their thin sandals, fanny packs, and single bottle of water shared among them. The sandy-haired boy, maybe eight, with a narrow fox's face, trailed behind. He halted and picked up a stick, which he banged against the trees. After a few more steps, he used it to dig into the ground, flinging stones and clods.

His parents called for him—"Wyatt! Wyyy-at!"—and he dropped the stick and ran to catch up.

Anna waited until she could no longer see or hear them before she started walking. She picked up the stick and hurled it into the trees. She and Ken had no children. She'd mentioned the trip to a few friends, but couldn't imagine them or her siblings coming with her. She had to take this hike alone. She pushed forward with two spring-loaded walking sticks. Although she used to disdain extra equipment as unnecessary coddling, her knees and back ached without them. The pack bit into her shoulders and pulled at her chest. Winded, she rested, took a long drink of water, and looked at the steep switchbacks up the mountain. Was this a mistake? She and Ken trekked farther before, but she was older and slower now. She would have to hike faster or risk arriving at the campsite in the dark.

The winter after Ken died had been unusually rainy, and many sites were snowed in until late in the summer. Some had been closed for the entire season. She imagined the frozen campsites, never receiving the airy touch of spring nor the deep, still heat of summer nor the fading warmth of autumn. Come winter, fresh snow would fall on packed drifts untouched by the present. If she burrowed into the snowbanks, what remained of the past would be hers.

Several times, Anna climbed over fallen trees, grabbing their branches and hoisting herself, then jumping or sliding down. Each time she landed, she wobbled for a moment. With each jolt, she could see a flash of Ken in motion—the way he knelt to weed a tomato plant, reached for a platter high up, or pulled her head to his chest. She scraped the back of her knee on a tree. Wincing, she stopped to check the damage—two long scrapes, and a trickle of blood—when a ranger loped up from behind her and asked to see her wilderness permit. She turned around, showing where it was tied to her pack. He wore green shorts and a button-up shirt, with a hat clapped over a short brown ponytail. No wedding ring, and looked to be in his early twenties, with a scraggly goatee, which might have been an attempt to add a few years to his smooth baby face. *Billy* was embroidered on his shirt pocket. He needed nothing more than what fit into his small pack. Was endurance a test of how little you could survive on? Proof of how much you carried inside yourself?

"This is the best time of year to go," he said. "After the crowds are gone."

He said he was going into the backcountry for a few days, first to Pear Lake and then to Bodie Lake, to check the conditions. She realized that he might be the last person she would talk to for days, and she had to resist calling after him as he disappeared from view. That was the unspoken rule of backpacking: you kept to yourself. Each hiker strapped on forty pounds to escape the crowds, and the only permissible topic was trail conditions, asked in the most concise manner.

If the first day's hike wasn't too difficult, she might recommend it to the group that organized outdoor trips for girls, the latest in a series of nonprofits where she had worked. From her messy cubicle, she did the books, cut the checks, and clamped down on expenses. Ken had been a partner at a big law firm in San Francisco. He always said that she did enough good for the both of them, though each recognized they could live well on his salary alone. In the year before he died, Anna had come to believe that her noble calling was nothing more than a hobby. She resented his compliments about her good deeds, but how could she ask him to stop?

She poured water onto a handkerchief and wiped at the slashes on her leg. The thin scar would join the others from a lifetime of walking through brush. Going uphill on the last stretch, she slipped in the dirt, her right ankle rolling to the side. Shit. She yelped, using her trekking poles to catch herself. It was her weak ankle, the one that gave out on uneven ground, that she had sprained badly as a kid.

She dropped her pack and sat down on a boulder. She massaged the tender ankle, flexing and moving it from side to side. Anna hobbled her way over the crest, stopping every few yards, bracing herself against gnarled trees to keep from toppling over. She descended toward Harte Lake. This was her favorite part of every hike, when she caught the first glimpse of her destination. Here, Ken would move ahead, scouting for a campsite while she trailed behind. She had felt serene in the knowledge that he would find a safe, comfortable place for them. Even now, she could see his back, broad and muscled, exposed after he dropped his pack. The way his exquisite muscles rolled and pitched beneath his thin shirt. For a moment, she could not breathe, electrified by her desire.

She set up camp on a sloping patch of ground backed by pine trees. On the other side of the lake, a field of speckled granite boulders led up the ridge. A flash of green—a tent? A bush. The solitude made her uneasy, and she had to admit she had counted on neighbors who could help if anything went wrong. She assembled their battered two-person tent. The walls sagged, no matter how deeply she staked the pegs, but it would have to do. Their routine had been for Ken to raise the tent and put on the rain fly, and for her to inflate the air mattresses and unfurl their sleeping bags. She eased her boot off her swollen ankle and slipped on a pair of sport sandals.

Without the backpack, she felt light and nimble. She walked into the chilly lake, up to her knees, and washed off the grime. She trailed her hand in the water, watching the ripples spread to the other side of the lake. The luxury and dread of freedom opened before her.

Anna retreated into tasks, and grabbed the water filter from her backpack, throwing one end of the tube into the lake. She visualized the giardia, grit, and other foul microbes bunching against the filter, unable to reach her. Nothing tasted better than water that was out of reach of most people. She could pump all day, draining the lake.

To escape the thickening mosquitoes, she climbed into the

tent. She probed her ankle, puffy and sore, and tightened the bandanna. She checked her cell phone: no service, which was what she expected. She was drifting off when she heard a creature, a marmot maybe, knocking about her gear. It wasn't loud enough to be a bear. *Hey*, she shouted, *hey, hey*, and it shuffled off. Anna slept for an hour and awoke as the sun was starting to set. Alpenglow lit the granite above the lake gold-orange. She tried to start a fire, but the kindling flared and the logs never caught.

She pictured Ken lighting the fire, and all the little tricks he did to get it going. Anna snapped a stick in half and threw the pieces in the pit. She was able to light the fire when he coached her. Why hadn't Ken been a better teacher? No. She had been a poor student, following without understanding or memorizing. She hated him for undermining her. For acting like he would always be there. Anna gave up. She sat in the dark, waiting for her self-heating package of beef stew to warm. She took a few bites. The noodles were slimy and the beef chunks smelled like dog food. She dug a hole, buried the rest, and went inside the tent.

She curled into a ball, holding herself in the sleeping bag, when she heard a plaintive animal cry in the distance. Like a baby's wail. Now, and on other nights since he died, she longed for the child that she never had with Ken. She regretted not having some part of him that would live on. Not the genetics of it, his reborn puckish dark eyes or dimples, which she could revisit in photographs and memories. Not as a companion or a substitute, but for someone else who had experienced him, in private, without the world intruding.

Two decades ago, she had miscarried. During the ultrasound, the doctor said he could no longer detect the baby's heartbeat, and soon sharp cramps turned her inside out. Gray clumps and bloody clots. Broken helpless incomplete unfit.

They were already picking names. Michiko. Emi. Hitomi. Keiko. Ken, who was sure the baby was a girl. Within months, Ken wanted to try again, to help them to start over. She miscarried again and yet again, four times in all, her body unable to hold on to a child. Did the babies know she feared their all-consuming need? She grew up in a family of seven and saw how her parents had lived for their sons and daughters, and no longer for each other. She did not want to share her husband's love. Ken, the only son in his generation of cousins, wanted a child of his own blood. Anna had tried, for him, but never longed for a baby.

They stopped having sex.

She recoiled when Ken stroked her cheek, his touch a reminder of her failure as a woman, a wife, a mother. He began spending late nights at the office and going on weekend business trips. He took showers at night instead of in the morning. He confessed, after Anna found a crumpled receipt for a San Francisco bistro that she had wanted to try out with him. She had liked the looks of the black awning and cheerful red and yellow storefront.

That was what wounded her: he had experienced what she wanted, with someone else. He was giving up on the life they were meant to have together.

WHEN SHE AWOKE the next morning, her ankle still throbbed. She decided against moving on and went for a walk around the lake. She saw no other hikers. She wondered what the solo ranger was doing. Meditating at sunrise, smoking pot at twilight, and bounding cross-country, his life ahead expanding, not narrowing.

With each step, she expected to see Ken around the bend to greet her. She grabbed a handful of trail mix, his favorite, coconut, dates, chocolate, and peanuts. She could hear his low, delighted *mmm-mmm*s. She reached her hand out to the rough brown bark of the lodgepole pine behind her. The solid bulk comforted her at first, and then she trembled and dropped her hand—sickened by its solitary life. The trees lived for hundreds of years, alone, dropping cones that needed a forest fire to explode them and release their seeds. Their survival depended on forces beyond their control.

At sunset, the wind stirred and Anna could see fast, faint clouds overhead. A storm was supposed to blow in Tuesday, but she planned to be back home by Sunday evening. She would get an early start, gulp down a couple of packets of oatmeal, power down the mountain, and take a late lunch at their favorite hamburger stand. She buried the rest of her dehydrated spaghetti dinner and climbed into the tent.

She nestled into her sleeping bag. She delighted in her aches, even the twinge in her ankle, proof that she had pushed herself to the limit. She was too excited to fall asleep, anticipating her return. What she had looked forward to the most—before she set foot on the trail, before she left her house in Berkeley—was to get through the trip. She only had to last until the next morning to prove that she could survive without him. In the year since Ken had died, she marked off special dates this way: his birthday, their wedding anniversary, Thanksgiving, and Christmas. She focused on the end rather than experiencing the event itself. The day was speeded up, disregarded, and afterward she savored the accomplishment of getting through it.

IN THE MONTHS after she learned of his affair, they had pledged twice to make the marriage work. It fell apart each time. He could not forgive her for not wanting children, she knew. She could not forgive him for wanting more.

The other woman did not want a family, not until she made partner, and maybe not after, he told Anna. The knowledge burned her, to think that he might be with his lover if she had been willing to have children.

On the eve of their third and final reconciliation, they had camped in Desolation Wilderness. It was the first time they went backpacking in more than a year, after they began sleeping in separate bedrooms. They passed the first day with exceeding politeness, commenting on what they saw on the trail. They could agree on the beauty of a dead tree, struck by lightning, or discuss the geologic forces that shaped a granite peak, but could not talk about their past or their future.

At sunset, he said he was going for a walk around the lake. The low, slanting light turned him gold, his skin glowing and his black hair shining. He was hers to lose, she knew. He was almost gone.

"Back in a while," he said.

"Wait."

He stopped and turned.

"Can you go by the store?"

"What do you want?" He had a half smile on his face. An old joke of theirs, to ask for impossible foods in the middle of nowhere.

"Ice cream. Mocha fudge. With hot sauce."

"I'll do my best." He disappeared into the trees.

She put on her jacket and pulled out bags of couscous and dried mushrooms, and then packed and repacked their food in the bear canister, in the order of when they would eat it. She spent another fifteen minutes gathering twigs and fallen branches for the fire. Her busywork done, she walked to the edge of the lake. She could see Ken already on the other side, popping in and out of the bushes. She wished he would hurry. He returned a half hour later, his hands behind his back. He took out a capful of snow from a slow-melting patch under the trees.

"Will this do?"

She had scooped a loose handful, marveling at snow in June. "Thank you."

She put a careful measure on her tongue. He clapped his hands around hers, the heat melting the snow into rivulets between her fingers. Out in the wild, they would know nothing of a nuclear war, a terrorist attack, or an alien landing that ended civilization. They alone would hold on to the perfection of the world that existed before calamity. That night, inside the tent, they zipped the sleeping bags tight, past their heads, and pulled the drawstring on the hood. The mummy bag bound their arms and legs. Although she could not see him in the darkness, she sensed him looking at her.

"This is all I have to give," she said.

He sighed. "This is all I need."

They kissed and rested their foreheads against each other.

IT WAS SILENT the next day, on the morning of her departure. Anna fumbled for her watch—8:30 a.m.! Usually, while camping, she was up by 6:30 or 7 a.m., awakened by the discomfort of sleeping on the ground and her excitement to start the day. She unzipped the tent door and poked out her head. The sky was confusing, the color of dull, wet concrete. She looked up. Was that volcanic ash falling through the sky? Or pollen? She reached her hand out to feel the cold wet flakes. Snowing, drifting overnight to two feet or more around her tent. She had gone to sleep in a world of greens, blues, and browns but now everything was white flurries. She sat back, zipped the door shut, and sank into her sleeping bag to salvage the residual heat. The snow accumulated on the roof in a spatter pattern, filtering kaleidoscope shadows, and when she touched the side of the tent, it pushed back. Snow pressed against the walls.

She fumbled for her boots. A light layer of snow covered her backpack, which sat under the tent vestibule. Her food was tucked in the bear canister, a hundred feet away. Her stomach rumbled, and she scrounged in her pockets, where she found a half-eaten energy bar. They—she, now—had been lucky too long. She and Ken had gone over what to do in case of emergency. If a bear attacked? Stay on your feet for as long as possible, and then lie in a fetal position, using your backpack to protect vulnerable areas. Create a diversion by banging pots and pans. In a forest fire? Run into the lake or river. Take turns bobbing up to check when the fire has passed. Broken leg? Get the victim back to the tent, keep them warm, and elevate the leg. Run like hell for help. And even, what to do in a snowstorm? Stay put, stay dry. Zip the sleeping bags together for warmth.

In each of the scenarios, Anna now realized, the plan involved both of them.

By early afternoon, the snowfall had lightened and cracks of blue broke through the clouds. The snow was now about three and a half feet deep, judging by the height next to the tent. She checked her cell phone again, but she still had no signal. She decided to hike out the eight miles and leave behind her gear. Snow hid the trail, but she figured she would keep walking downhill. She struggled to break through the heavy, wet snow and within minutes she was exhausted and soaked. Her foot plunged into the powder and pain shot through her weak ankle. She pinwheeled and fell. Panting, she willed herself to rise before her clothes were soaked. After a half hour and progressing only three hundred yards, she turned back.

She spent an hour digging for the bear canister, using the lid of a pot to dig through the snow. She blew on her hands, but it did little to warm them. She thought of the stew that she buried in disgust. Hunger dug at her. She made many false starts before she heard the dull thump of metal on plastic. Yes. She cradled the black canister in relief, her hands wet and stiff, scratched and bloody from the ice. Her ankles and feet were numb but she could still wiggle her toes.

Back in the tent, she upended the canister and poured out a

packet of oatmeal, a few crumbs of trail mix, a couple of granola bars, scrapes of peanut butter, and one freeze-dried meal. She inhaled the musty, earthy smells and took a small handful of the trail mix.

She told herself that help was on the way, that it was an early winter storm that would soon pass. Besides, she had registered at the ranger station, indicating she had set out from the trail-head three days ago. But—they did not know when she was returning. What if the rangers thought she was already gone? There was no one to expect her at home.

No one had been expecting her at home, the night she started her affair.

A decade after he had betrayed her, Ken introduced her to the man who became her lover. He and Jack Olson, both playing singles at the Tilden Park Golf Course, had been paired up. The two lawyers had a beer at the clubhouse after their round, and Ken offered to take out Jack and his wife, Becky, who were both new to town. Ken and Anna were always looking for other childless couples who did not have to cut their evenings short because of the babysitter, who did not spend hours conversing about potty-training and summer camps.

Ken, Jack, and Anna were all in their forties. At twenty-eight, Becky seemed even younger, favoring overalls and brightly colored clothes and ponytails. She was adopted from South Korea and raised in Minnesota, where she said there was one lake for every adoptee. Jack, the son of a Korean war veteran and his war bride, looked almost fully Asian, with a strong jaw and a faint tilt to his eyes. His Swedish origins were manifest in his height, and his hair, the color of dark honey.

The Olsons were always game for whatever Anna proposed, though she caught them giving each other quick looks, raised eyebrows and set mouths, resigned to the evening's adventures: Ethiopian food. Pilobolus dance. Kronos Quartet. It irked her that they tolerated, rather than enjoyed, her suggestions.

"Why don't you ask them what they'd like to do?" Ken asked.

"I do! But then they ask what we're up to," Anna said.

"Maybe that's all they want," he said. "For you to decide."

His refusal to take sides or judge others had maddened her more each year. It made her feel low, unkind for having an opinion. Long after his affair, Anna held a part of herself back. She would never give herself completely to him again, and this knowledge had protected her.

The old fears of Ken cheating returned in the presence of a younger woman. Anna studied them together: Did their hands linger when passing the wine? Did they lean close when talking? But when Becky didn't understand a reference, it was Jack who smiled at Anna, their own little joke.

Becky had yet to find a teaching job because they were thinking of starting a family. "It wouldn't be right, to get hired, and then have a baby so quick." She could resume her career later, in a few years, after the kids were in school.

Jack called when his wife was visiting her parents and Ken was in New York on a business trip. "Why should we both eat frozen dinners?" he asked. They went to an Italian trattoria, his pick, where the food was bland, as she supposed he preferred.

She flushed in the candlelight, aware of his steady gaze. Afterward, he leaned down to kiss her by his car, hidden in the shadow of eucalyptus trees. In bed, she ran her fingers along his downy back, where the skin was young and smooth, in contrast to his weathered neck and his arms. For two decades, she had been with no one else besides Ken, and she reveled in discovering a new body. She stroked the hairless patch on his thigh, rubbed bare by blue jeans. This was also where she caressed Ken. Disorienting, to see the same purring effect on another man.

The thought of having children panicked Jack, she suspected, just as it had stricken her. He married a young wife to put off fatherhood and never suspected Becky would be so eager to start trying. Anna had long tried to understand her husband's infidelity and was learning through this deception. The first encounters were excitement and pleasure and discovery. Without commitment or expectations, you had none of the problems in your marriage. You despised the person you were cheating on and blamed your spouse for driving you away. She wanted Ken to see Jack look at her with longing. To remind him of what he had and of what he stood to lose. Ken was as powerless as she once was. As lacking.

EVERY FEW HOURS, she left the tent to dig the snow away from the sides and to pack it to shield the walls from the cutting wind. Snow slid into her boots, melting and soaking her feet. The wind knifed through her; each gust pushed her further past the limit of what she thought she could endure. Each slap proof that her numb face could feel still more pain. Snow fell faster than she could keep it away. She feared the tent would break, collapsing into a blue shroud onto her face.

Stupid, stupid. Why did she leave behind her foul-weather gear?

She ran her tongue behind her teeth, across the roof of her mouth, but could summon no saliva. She tilted her water bottle back, desperate for a few drops. Unable to wait for the snow to melt in her bottle, she stumbled to the edge of the lake, where she broke through the crust of ice with a kick. She drank deeply, shuddering from the chill. For dinner, she ate a bit of dry oatmeal and a lick of peanut butter. Her stomach knotted in hunger and she turned her head away from the dwindling food, resisting the temptation to eat it all. Now she regretted what she had wasted on this trip, the spilled trail mix and the two dinners she did not finish. She craved a vanilla milkshake, cheeseburger, and curly fries from Ikeda's, the roadside stand along I-80. And to share the meal with Ken, who let her eat his fries. Indulging her. At this, she wept, the tears stinging her marble cheek.

WEDNESDAY AFTERNOON, AFTER the storm let up, snow drifted higher next to the tent. As night fell, the temperatures dropped, and ice, her condensed breath, built up inside and outside the tent. She tried to be still. When she touched the wall, ice fell and melted, making everything wetter. She thought of her parents, who died three years ago, within months of each other. Her mother of stomach cancer, her father of a heart attack. They died without ever speaking of what happened at camp. Not until college did Anna discover stories about the barbed wire fences and the tar paper barracks in the high desert. Searing summer heat. Bitter winter wind. Snow swirling on frozen mud. Pain swallowed. She had learned her silences from them, the silences that lengthened like shadows between her and Ken.

She rubbed her hands along her cheeks, her neck, her ribs, her thighs, and her feet, to check the wholeness of her body. Each breath, a second. Sixty breaths, a minute. It was impossible to judge how much time had passed. How much longer she would remain clenched. How close she was to dawn. She watched individual drops of water track down from the roof and along the side of the tent, wiggling snakes.

An airplane whined above. She ran out of the tent, waving her orange sleeping pad in the air, and shouting. She unscrewed her flashlight and held the mirror to the sky, trying to catch its attention. The airplane flew past. Too high. She staggered back. She was going to die. Snow would drift over the tent, and she would succumb to sleep. Hikers would find her body in the spring. Rotten, bloated, black—or the bones picked clean.

She tried to conjure specific memories of Ken. To bear witness. The first time they met in college, when he asked to borrow her notes. His shy smile. His concentration when he made gnocchi, the fat larvae falling off the spoon into boiling water. How defeated he looked after his father died.

SOME DETAILS, SHE will never forget.

Just before she began her affair, her periods sometimes dragged on or skipped altogether. She'd stopped filling her prescription for the pill. When she went in for a checkup, her doctor told her that she was pregnant, almost two and a half months along. Since she was forty-four years old, she and her husband should consider genetic testing. Her husband. Judging from when the baby was conceived, it was not his. They had not slept together in October; they were down to having sex once a month or every other, and on special occasions.

She did not want to mislead Ken, to play father to a bastard, nor did she want to escape into a life with her lover that seemed much like the one she already had.

"You seem distracted," Ken said. They were in bed, spooning for a few minutes before they went to sleep.

Her appointment for the procedure was the next day. She felt the baby roll and spin within, even though she knew it was impossible at this stage. Less than two inches long, but with a miniature brain, fingers and feet and lips and eyes—eyes!— beginning to develop. Though she could not be certain, she sensed she wouldn't miscarry this time. It was her last chance to be a mother, to reverse her losses a decade ago. Maybe Ken knew about the affair and was waiting for her to tell him. She imagined the bolt of anger ripping across his face. Her tears. She would have said she wanted to hurt him. To make things even. She was sorry and now knew that they belonged together.

"It's nothing," she said. Although she kept this secret to protect him, she hadn't realized it would distance them. How she would flee from him, over the years, into other rooms, for a walk, into the car for long drives. At times, she despised him for not guessing and leaving her heavy with this burden.

In the last year, she had come to wonder if Ken's early death was retribution. Why was he taken from her? A life for a life. It seemed the only reasonable explanation.

What if she kept the baby, and never told Ken who the father was? Her boy would have been nine this year. She had decided it would have been a boy. He may have even looked like Ken. He and her lover had the same broad shoulders and broad noses. She and her son would huddle to outlast the storm. Or her son, back with friends in the Bay Area, would alert authorities that she was lost in the snowstorm. Or the three of them would still be together. Ken, with a son, would be more cautious, would have gone in for more checkups to catch the condition that killed him. But no. She had made different decisions that led to today.

Her attempts at an explanation were misguided, Anna had come to see. Foolish. Her miscarriage—divine will, or nature's? His affair—whose fault? Her affair? Her abortion? Impossible, to judge if her good intentions hit their mark, or the worth of her sin. She could not imagine who was keeping track, and why she would matter. Only this she knew: she would die alone.

FRIDAY AFTERNOON A helicopter *whump-whump-whumps* in the thin mountain air. Weak as she is, she climbs out on wobbly legs. "Help, help!" She beats the pans together. The helicopter passes again overhead. It circles twice, and she knows she will be OK. She sinks to her knees. The reflected sunshine is blinding and beautiful. Snow glistens on tree branches and boulders, soft, fluffy, pristine, and harmless as cake frosting. The granite peaks in the distance are tipped in snow, in sharp relief against the sky, as if outlined with a black pen. A ladder falls down from the sky and a man is helping her get in a basket. He is wearing mirrored sunglasses in which she can see a tiny haggard reflection of herself. He extends a hand covered in a puffy blue glove, and as she reaches up, she stumbles and falls against him. She feels the moist heat of his breath against her ear. "Easy now," he says. "We got you." Up, up they go, up the beanstalk, up the charmed rope into the sky.

Strapped into her seat, she gulps down an energy bar and a sports drink. The rescuer covers her with a blanket and slips headphones over her ears so she can hear them above the shaking roar. They are talking about the lost ranger, who set off from the same trailhead. He is missing.

"Where to?" the pilot asks.

"Not sure. The ranger told the station that he was going to check out some lakes, and there's several in the area."

"I saw him," she says. "On the trail."

The rescuer turns to look at her. "What did you say?"

"I saw him. Billy."

"Where?"

"To Pear Lake. Then Bodie Lake."

He nods and points out to the right. The helicopter wheels back around, and she closes her eyes. The rumbling whirling is rocking her to sleep. She is slipping away when she hears him cry out—"There, there!"

A life saved. Surely, it meant something.

The Deal

They were besieged upon arrival.

"Sir, sir," the touts shouted. "This way, sir! Come with me! I will carry."

Pastor David Noh scanned the airport, looking for a driver with a sign. Perhaps the man in the orange baseball cap, or the one in aviator sunglasses? Their guide, Justus, had said he would meet them, emailing David the final details along with a photo of himself, but he was nowhere to be found.

It was three weeks before Christmas. They had been traveling for twenty-eight hours, on flights departing from San Francisco and connecting through Amsterdam to Dubai. Already they had lost a day, Saturday skipping straight to Monday, before they even started their mission.

The volunteers swept past the touts, lean men in rumpled button-down shirts and narrow ties, who fell upon other deplaning passengers. David felt unsteady, his head foggy from travel. "Get a shot of this." He swept his hand over the crowd.

Gene panned the video camera over businessmen toting laptops, tourists in khaki safari jackets, matrons in embroidered velvet sweatsuits, and advertisements promoting wildlife tours and beach resort hotels on the Indian Ocean. Clad in rugged boots, lightweight hiking pants, and moisture-wicking shirts, the volunteers would have blended in with the international tribe of backpackers but for their suitcases and duffels piled on the luggage carts. They weren't traveling lightly. Their guide had promised to take them to a village in East Africa unreached by other missionaries. David and his four volunteers would install water filters, teach English, and introduce the word of God. With stirring footage and photos from the trip, he could convince his flock to pledge their stock options, tithe their salaries—and rescue their church.

Bountiful Abundance had taken root among Korean American lawyers, software engineers, college students, and activists, the children of immigrants: strivers, all. The church had a different style of worship, not so serious, not so *Korean*.

"We're here!" Lily had applied powder and lipstick just before landing.

Eunhee flung her hand into the air. "Group high five!"

"Sir, sir, what's the name of your tour company?" A tout jammed his face into David's. He was wiry, with a scar shaped like a fishhook carved across his right cheek. His pungent scent was overwhelming, and David pushed the man away. The tout fell backward to the ground.

"Hey, hey, hey!" the other touts shouted, and a few lurched forward, fists raised. Someone screamed—Lily maybe. David braced himself, squaring his shoulders and lowering his head, ready to take the nearest one down. He had been an excellent wrestler, with the right build and temperament. A shrill whistle sounded, and the crowd parted for two policemen in sunglasses.

"We have a few questions for you. Come with us."

The tout David shoved had slipped away, and those who remained glowered, shaking their heads and shouting what sounded like accusations.

"Unless you want to pay the fine here."

"How much?" David had heard bribes were common here, and he prayed it wouldn't be much. Their trip money, kept in a heavy pouch around his neck, was barely enough to cover their expenses.

"Twenty dollars U.S." Considerate, as if the policeman did not want to inconvenience David with a visit to the currency exchange counter.

David paid, trying to keep his hands from trembling, and ushered his volunteers to a cafeteria. At the counter, where the tile floor was sticky with spilled drinks, he ordered sodas and sandwiches. "My treat."

The cashier swiped his credit card. Once, twice, it didn't go through. He had been financing the trip on that card, and his debts had caught up with him at last.

"Try this one." He took out his emergency credit card. This one failed too. He imagined his wife, Esther, trying to buy groceries. She would stare at the declined card with her head cocked, biting on her lower lip. So she would pay with cash. Maybe she would have to leave certain items behind. Naomi would fuss, demanding that dried cranberries and apple juice be put back in the cart. "No, Mama, no!" At home, Esther would put Naomi down for a nap, call the credit card company, and discover his secret.

"Sometimes credit card companies block charges in other countries." Immanuel opened his wallet and slid out two $20 bills. "I can get it."

One crisis solved. Or at least postponed.

Much bigger problems loomed. Bountiful Abundance had been forced to leave a site David leased in a residential area, after neighbors complained to authorities about the traffic. He hadn't obtained the proper permits and, as a result, incurred a substantial fine. The church moved into a vacant storefront flanked by liquor stores. After multiple muggings and car break-ins, the congregation relocated to an office park by the Oakland Coliseum. In total, Bountiful Abundance owed more than $100,000 in rent, equipment, renovations, and other expenses. $100,000! A debt that multiplied while collections from the congregation dwindled. The previous two sites sat empty because David was unable to find anyone to sublet. Worse yet, fund-raising for the mission trip hadn't gone well, and he'd financed the shortfall. He told no one, not even Esther.

At the table, Immanuel pulled apart the gummy pieces of white bread and tore out the pale lunch meat. "Airport food is terrible in any country." At thirty-five, the doctor was the old man of the volunteers—five years younger than David—and he spoke with a gravitas that made people listen closely.

"You can have mine." Lily pushed her sandwich at David and ripped open the gold wrapper of an energy bar. "My dad gave me a box."

David tried not to fume. The sandwiches were each $5, the bribe $20: wasted money they could have spent on supplies.

Lily was watchful and gentle, with a round face and pale skin, a traditional Korean beauty.

"I can't wait to try local dishes." Eunhee flipped to a list in her guidebook. She was worldly in a way that Lily was not, although they'd had an almost identical upbringing, blocks apart in Oakland. The difference was that Eunhee had graduated from Cal with a streak of social justice—and purple hair. She had a radical's self-assurance that David often envied.

"I always go local when I travel. Nothing's worse than craving something from home and getting a bad version of it," Immanuel said.

"Like hamburgers in Iceland," Gene said. "This one place seemed like they re-created everything from a photo. Instead of tomato, they used slices of red pepper. Instead of pickles, cucumber."

A bite of sandwich stuck in David's throat, and his palms felt papery, dried out from the long flight. The three of them were well traveled, and he felt small, naive as Lily, unworthy somehow. He had been to Mexico three times on missions, but what did he know of the wider world?

After lunch, David changed $30, enough for the taxi ride and tip. He'd read that the money counters at the airport were a rip-off, and he would ask their guide where to exchange the rest. He looked around one last time, but did not see Justus. Maybe the guide had had a last-minute emergency, or suffered an accident? Or had David misunderstood the instructions? No. He'd memorized the email during the flight, not wanting to fumble with the printouts like a tourist upon arrival. Justus had been the only guide available on short notice, and at a bargain price, after the original one canceled.

At the taxi kiosk, they piled into a battered Peugeot station wagon. David sat in the front with the driver. "The Jacaranda Fairview," he said. "Downtown."

"Closed for renovations," the driver said. "But I can take you to a better hotel, even cheaper. The Parklands. Very nice."

"Fine, fine." David's head throbbed, his eyes sticky. He might have been more upset at the guide if Justus hadn't already failed to meet the group at the airport. "Take us there."

The Peugeot inched through traffic, crawling beside lime-green buses and trucks packed with goods and people, and whole families aboard puttering motorbikes. The air inside the station wagon was stifling.

"Can you turn on the air-conditioning?" Lily's voice sounded faint. Sweat beaded on her forehead.

"It's broken," the driver said. "You can roll down the windows."

The stench of diesel fumes flooded in, along with the sound of coughing motors and futile honking. The dashboard held pictures of a small boy in a red bow tie, maybe five years old, and a baby girl, her hair knotted in pink ribbons. He wondered if the driver sent his wages to a distant village to feed his family, or if he was able to tuck these children in each night. A laminated portrait of the Virgin Mary in a blue mantle hung from the rearview mirror. Her peaceful expression, lowered eyes and beatific smile, calmed David. He exhaled, allowing himself to sink into his exhaustion.

"You're Catholic?" David asked.

"My grandfather converted."

They introduced each other. The driver's name was Amos. David asked him if the children in the pictures were his.

"My sister's. I have no time to have children right now. No time to find a wife." Amos chuckled, the lilt to his words soothing.

David couldn't tell how old Amos was. Sometimes, with unwrinkled skin and bright eyes, Africans and Asians shared an ageless quality. Amos squeezed the car behind a truck loaded with sheets of tin and concrete blocks. "You Korean?"

"We're from America," David said. "My parents are from Korea."

"Lots of Koreans come here. Good people. I can take you to a Korean barbecue right now, if you want. Misono."

"Maybe later. Thanks for the offer." After the shakedown at the airport, David was relieved to find someone friendly in this country.

Then he noticed they were passing the Jacaranda Fairview, the hotel where their guide had made reservations. A bellman in a tan uniform stood in front beside a pile of luggage. The hotel wasn't closed for renovations. If anything, the Fairview needed them still, with its cracked cement walls, dirty windows, and namesake trees shedding wilted purple flowers.

"Stop!" David shouted.

"We're almost to the Parklands," Amos said.

"Stop the car. We just drove by the Fairview—it's open."

Being tricked by the driver, who was probably getting a kickback from the Parklands, was intolerable, a symbol of everything that had gone wrong so far. Soon the whole car was shouting. "Stop, stop, stop!"

Amos did a U-turn, buzzing through oncoming traffic, and screeched to a stop in front of the Fairview. They grabbed their luggage, while Amos glowered in the front seat. David threw the bills, scattering them on the driver's lap and on the floorboard. No tip. That was what cheaters deserved. He stumbled over the broken asphalt, the smell of smoke and rotting garbage making him dizzy. Eunhee and Immanuel hung a few paces back, and David slowed to eavesdrop.

"I wasn't down with that," Eunhee said.

He glanced over his shoulder to see Immanuel give the driver a handful of dollar bills. David didn't like being questioned. He strode into the lobby, where Justus was reading a newspaper.

"Welcome!" Justus rose to his feet. He was dark as an espresso bean, with a diamond-shaped face, close-cropped curly hair, and slanted eyes.

"You were supposed to meet us at the airport." David had to keep himself from grabbing Justus by the shoulders and shaking him.

"The driver wasn't there?" Justus asked.

"No."

"I'll call him," Justus said. "Something must have happened. He's usually very reliable."

"He's not taking us to the village, is he? We can't have someone like that, who would leave us stranded at the airport," David said.

"Everything will be fine," Justus said. "Let me help with your bags."

They registered at the front desk. David had his own room, Gene and Immanuel were sharing a room, and the women were in another, all on the fourth floor.

"Enjoy your stay." The clerk handed them keys on plastic fobs. "I put you in the renovated rooms."

David halted. "What do you mean?"

"A pipe broke and flooded the rooms. We were closed for a week."

Toting his bags, David took the punishing walk alone up the stairs, leaving everyone else to the elevator.

A DECADE AGO, just before his conversion, he had been a history teacher and wrestling coach at a prep school in Providence. From across the country, his parents nagged him in weekly phone calls, insisting that he obtain his doctorate, although they knew that it was too late for David to become a rising star in academia. Those who won tenure at prestigious universities had to proceed directly to graduate school, publish papers in top journals, and present at conferences. But to his parents, attending graduate school was superior to David's teaching position, even if at the end of the program he would have no better job prospects than he currently held.

His parents were professors at a top-ranked science and

engineering college in the foothills of the San Gabriels, in a leafy, prosperous enclave less than an hour's drive from the largest Korean community outside of Seoul. However, the Professors Noh had no use for other Koreans, nor for Christ, despite their own Protestant upbringing.

Instead of studying for graduate exams and writing essays, David was lured by another calling: professional poker. He'd come across a televised tournament featuring players stoic and solid as totem poles. They never betrayed their doubts—never had doubts at all. Nobodies emerged to win by their wits. Why not him?

In pursuit of poker, David drove an hour to southern Connecticut, to the Foxwoods Casino, a sprawling labyrinth in the forest, on the weekends and eventually, every night. Surrounded by the elderly clientele—who were hooked to oxygen tanks and to slot machines—he never felt more alive, young and perfect. Powerful and possible.

At first he won. He felt blessed by a preternatural understanding, as if he could see through the cards, through everyone at the table. His losses were momentary and quickly reversed. He loved the crack and riffle of the shuffling deck. The click of the chips, heavy and hypnotic. An accretion of risk, luminous and great. One night, a crowd gathered, pointing at him and whispering, "Hot hands." David knew better—he owed his success to his skills, not luck. When he returned home, he fanned the $100 bills and tossed them into the air, giddy with the scent of all who had lost to him. He made plans for Vegas.

Then he lost. His fingers became clumsy, thick as cigars.

Always a minute behind what was happening, realizing too late the way the cards had fallen. When he won, it was by chance. By accident. He drained his savings and maxed out three credit cards, fell behind on his rent, called in sick at work. He wrote none of the college recommendations he'd promised his seniors, played documentaries from the History Channel rather than teaching, and by the end of May, the school had fired him. His wallowing worsened in the summer. He rarely left his stuffy apartment, rarely left his bed, and lived on saltines, tuna straight from the can, and cheap whiskey. His portable fan cranked at full blast in a numbing buzz. With sticky red plastic cups piled on every surface, his apartment resembled a carnival game: win a goldfish, if you can land a ping-pong ball inside the rim.

After months of doubts, he woke early one morning with the overwhelming urge to pray. He knelt on his bed, wobbling and sinking into the mattress, before he climbed onto the dusty hardwood floor. Was this how? He didn't know how long he could hold himself up. Head bowed, he began. "How much longer? Tomorrow? Next month, next year? Why not now?" he had whispered, his eyes wet with unspilled tears.

A shaft of sunlight expanded, filling the room, and David felt light enough to levitate. He no longer had to worry: he was in the Lord's hands. On his shelf, he found the Bible—from his college days, a reference book—and read it as if for the first time. *For it is with your heart that you believe and are justified, and it is with your mouth that you confess and are saved.* In search of God and a community, he joined an immigrant Korean church, the Holy Redeemer in Boston, where he met Esther and, to the continued disappointment of his parents, devoted his life to spreading the Good Word. Guiding others, he kept his own life under control.

He never confided in Esther about his gambling, telling her only that God had filled a void in his heart. He had his reasons. She would despise him, and he had to admit, keeping the secret allowed him to cherish certain memories, jewels he could admire in private rather than submit for public reckoning. God already knew.

THAT AFTERNOON, THE men headed to an open-air market, where Justus bargained for shovels, PVC pipe, and other supplies. He shielded them from the beggars and the trinket vendors, sending them away with a flick of his chin. Reggaeton thumped beneath the haggling of shoppers and the rustle of plastic bags. They passed a stand that sold nothing but used T-shirts emblazoned with the logos of imploded tech companies.

This is where failure finds another life, David thought.

He bought his daughter a knit doll, a baby monkey with cream-colored paws that he waved at Gene's video camera. She was daddy's little girl, all rosy cheeks and sturdy legs, preferring him when she got into a scrape. He stroked the monkey's head and imagined Naomi's delighted laughter, her gap-toothed smile—and behind her, his wife. As a pastor's kid, Esther helped legitimize him. She knew how to befriend women no one else wanted to talk to—the shy or prickly ones—and how to word the most difficult part of a sermon.

Five years ago, he and Esther had moved from Boston to

Southern California, where he'd served as an assistant pastor at a Korean megachurch. Two years passed, and the Lord called on David to plant a new church in the Bay Area. He went from backyard barbecues to breakfast meetings to win over KA professionals who wanted to start a new church, galvanized them into joining a radical startup that would go public in a very big way. Calling himself a social entrepreneur, a change maker, a thought leader, he had positioned Bountiful Abundance as a revolutionary movement to transform not only their lives but the world around them. *Let's go after a God-sized dream!*

After so many frugal meals, his evenings and weekends away from home attending to endless emergencies, their cheap cars, and cheap vacations, Bountiful Abundance had seemed a success worthy of their sacrifice.

Yesterday—or was it two or three days ago?—on the way to the airport, Esther had asked if he'd remembered to cancel the bills. Yes, David said, though he hadn't, too preoccupied with last-minute preparations.

"I still don't understand why we're getting utility bills for our old church space. Water. Phone. Garbage," she said. A sheaf of bills, stamped with their apartment as a forwarding address, had arrived that week.

He cursed himself for forgetting to cancel the utilities. More debt. A few times, he had waited on hold, but hung up before customer service came on the line. Urgent matters had interceded: Naomi wailed after a spill, or an email or call arrived from someone in crisis.

"While you're gone, I can sort through all the bills." She

pulled away from the toll plaza. The sky was boundless, and sunshine shimmered over the bay. "What's your password for the church's online bank account?"

"I told you, I took care of it." David swiveled around and wiggled Naomi's nose. She giggled and grasped his arm, and he licked his thumb and wiped off a streak of dried milk around her mouth.

Both sets of grandparents had wanted a firstborn son. Esther too. "A big brother, to look after his siblings," she had said. But David had wanted a daughter, Esther reborn, whom he could watch grow up from the beginning. Naomi would flip off the arm of the couch, bounce on the bed so high that her head almost hit the ceiling, and ran off naked after her baths—as hard to catch as a greased pig, glistening with salve to treat the eczema she'd inherited from him.

"Where are we going?" she asked.

"To the airport. You'll get to see the planes," David said. Takeoff and landings mesmerized her.

"Why?" She nibbled goldfish crackers from a plastic cup.

"Daddy's trip." Yesterday, she'd come into the bedroom and seen him packing. They looked at the map, and he showed her pictures of the village. Now he clicked a few tracks ahead on the album, to a song in Swahili, from a world music compilation for kids. "I'm going to a place where they speak this language."

Her cheeks and fingers were still chubby, and her hair fine, but her features were sharpening into the girl, into the woman she'd become. Someday, he'd bring her on a mission trip and raise her as his parents did not—to love others. He reminded her that they'd prayed for the children who weren't as lucky as her. She nodded sleepily, and a Goldfish slipped out of her hand. David blew her a kiss. "I love you, sweetie."

When he turned around, Esther was clenching the steering wheel, her mouth a thin line. He stroked her face, but she did not reply.

"A pastor's wife has more important duties," he said. "Don't worry about the bills."

Esther had dropped him off at the curb—which stung because he thought that she and Naomi would wait with him in the departures terminal before the flight. He took out his satchel and his suitcase and set them on the ground. They had only a minute before the airport police would tell them to move. He opened the back door to kiss Naomi, strapped in and starting to cry. She smelled of baby powder and shampoo from the bath he had given her last night. Esther waited for him on the curb. They hugged, and in his grip he tried to make her understand what she meant to him, how difficult and terrible it was to leave her. He kissed the top of her head and rubbed his cheek against her silky hair.

"Do good," Esther whispered.

He watched their silver hatchback disappear around the bend.

The vision of Esther taking off with Naomi seemed ominous now, maybe prophetic. David blinked in the bright sunlight, trying to dismiss his doubts. Bountiful Abundance didn't yet have a board, although some members had spoken of forming one. An exploratory meeting was scheduled for the first week of

January, after the missionaries returned. Although he dreaded opening the books, he was convinced a successful trip would ease the shock. "The church can pull together," he'd say. "Look at this footage, look at the good we're doing."

As he turned toward the sound of a car backfiring, he noticed posters for prayer meetings. He sidestepped a murky puddle leaking from a restaurant. "There are many Christians here," he said to Justus, and pointed at a rusty cross marking a shanty church.

"When did you accept Christ?" Immanuel asked.

Justus told them that he had been saved as a teenager, when missionaries visited his village, and an overseas church provided for his schooling before he moved to the capital. Their guide was proof of the good work missionaries could do here. David hoped to change a child's life in the same way. He knew he shouldn't try to predict how many villagers might come to Christ—he couldn't divine God's plan—but he ached for at least one on this mission.

At the hotel, they found Lily crying in her room, with a bump on her head and a bloody gouge on her knee. "I want to go home," she sobbed.

They'd gone in search of a place for dinner, walked a couple of blocks, and opened the guidebook to check a map. A pair of men shoved Lily to the ground and took her backpack.

David had promised her parents that he'd protect her. Immanuel went to his room and returned with antiseptic and bandages that he wrapped around her knee, while Gene held her hand. They discussed reporting the crime to the police, but Lily didn't want to leave the hotel again.

"I'm so embarrassed." She fingered a frayed tassel on the worn gold blanket. "I'm sorry to be such a baby."

Together they prayed for her recovery and a successful mission.

That evening, from a pay phone in the lobby, David dialed Esther with a cheap calling card he had purchased at the market. He knew she wasn't home, because she'd be taking Naomi to preschool at this hour, morning in the Bay Area. He told her they had arrived safely and that he loved her. He rested his forehead against the faded velvet roses of the wallpaper. What did she know? He pictured Esther dropping off Naomi, going into his office and opening his filing cabinet. He never bothered to lock it. She would find the stacks of rental contracts and the credit card bills he could not pay, spread the bills on the kitchen table and tally them up, writing down the grand total in her neat, round script. Esther would take Naomi and fly to her parents in Boston the next day.

Lord, please let this mission be a success. Only then would Esther understand his lies and withheld truths. She loved the prestige of being a pastor's wife, the deference and attention. She had grown up in the church, the sparkling child of its feared and respected leaders. Take the church away, and what would be left? Nothing but him.

THEIR PLAN WAS to depart the day after their arrival, heading west to Lake Alexandrina. They would stay overnight in Port Kemba before driving another four hours to the village. One day in the capital dragged into two, then four, as Justus told them about each new delay. The Land Cruiser broke down, and they needed to wait for a part. The driver wanted more money. David agreed to the demands, for what else could he do? They would have to cut the English lessons short and maybe build fewer water filters.

They spent their days watching old American sitcoms and conducting Bible study. One afternoon, as they discussed forgiveness, Immanuel admitted his pain, after his rush to diagnosis left a patient paralyzed. A teenage girl, a promising diver, who now couldn't breathe on her own. He'd come on the mission to atone. David admired him, the doctor's willingness to be honest and vulnerable before them. Before God.

Privately, David questioned why they were here, and wondered if the trip had been a mistake, like the many others he had already made.

"This is safe to drink, isn't it?" Lily asked on the fifth day. She cracked open a can of Coke. They had tried everything on the hotel's short Western-style menu: gray hamburgers, soggy French fries, and watery scrambled eggs. Lily was too scared to go outside the hotel, and the others would not leave her behind. She ran out of energy bars and wasn't eating much at meals, although Gene prodded her. David was tired of all of them. Why did Lily have to add to his worries? Couldn't she just grow up? Gene didn't know when to shut up with his wisecracks, and Eunhee made sanctimonious speeches about suffering in the third world.

After lunch, Immanuel pulled David aside. "Can we talk?"

"What's up, brotha?"

"In your room."

He tasted his burger rising in the back of his throat. He smiled, unwilling to let Immanuel see him unnerved. In his room, dirty clothes leaked out of his suitcase, and books and papers were scattered across the nightstand.

"Sorry for the mess." David threw the cover over his unmade bed, realizing how sour the room smelled.

Gathering himself, Immanuel told David the group had voted and wanted to volunteer at a church in the capital. "I know you put a lot of work into this."

They had turned on David and chosen Immanuel as their leader. He had been losing them since the first day, maybe before then, and he had to put a stop to it.

"That's not the point." Years of training on the pulpit—and his months at the poker table—did not leave him now, and David spoke with an authority he no longer felt. "We can't give away the church's money to anyone off the street. Justus vetted this for us."

Immanuel nodded. He seemed to have anticipated such arguments. "I can get online and look for other options."

"Online?" David scoffed. "You don't know who's on the other end. If it's a swindler."

"We could meet them," Immanuel said.

"That's not enough to make a decision on. Justus made site visits. Met with local leaders. He spent weeks. Months. He worked up reports about each village."

David wasn't certain of the truth of these assertions, though he'd asked Justus to do those things. He had promised, but never sent David the status reports.

The television next door clicked off and David pictured the volunteers clustered in there, eavesdropping against the wall.

"I'll call some friends from my old church who went on missions here," Immanuel said.

David sensed something shifting in Immanuel. Maybe the doctor didn't want to be a leader, the others might have thrust the role upon him, and David seized upon this hesitation.

"We don't have time," David said.

"Can't we ask Justus if he knows of anything local?"

"I already have," David said. Another lie. "He hasn't heard of anything that fits our skills. Or our supplies."

He studied Immanuel, remembering what the doctor revealed during Bible study: the hasty diagnosis of his patient, the rush to treatment, and the tragedy that followed. "We can't act too quickly," David said. "Beware of feet swiftly running to mischief."

Immanuel sat on the bed and bowed his head—defeated as David had ever seen him, less of himself, unable to fill out his contours. A flat tire.

He had violated Immanuel's trust. What frightened him most was that he knew he would do it again, do much more, to gain control. To win. He counted the seconds, praying for a sign within the next minute that he might return to God's favor. He closed his eyes, listening to his labored breathing, feeling as if crushed on the ocean floor, tons of pressure squeezing air and motion out of him. The phone rang, and David lunged for the receiver. Justus. David murmured *yes, yes, yes*, and hung up. They would leave tomorrow.

———

ON THE ROAD to the lake, they passed by trucks and busloads of tourists in safari gear. People walked alongside on a red-dirt path and pedaled on bicycles loaded with straw baskets and sacks. Brilliant greens, infinite blues, and livid reds painted the scenery of lush fields, palm trees, and the occasional tin-roofed house. At sunset, they walked a few blocks from their hotel to the lake. A blaze of orange and pink reflected over the placid waters. For the first time on the trip, David felt this country could be a place of miracles.

The next day, they piled into two Land Cruisers and drove south on a rutted road along the lake and its bounty. The air was wet and heavy, scented with mud and steamier than in the capital. They rode by a crested crane with an orange mohawk. The deep, dark nostrils of hippos. A crocodile, jagged and ancient, sunned itself on a rock. A long canoe painted with teal and yellow geometric designs. A bare-chested fisherman. The hacking of machetes and the cackling call of birds echoed over the shoreline. David wished Esther were beside him. She had an eye for the fleeting.

Gene and Lily napped in the back seat, their heads lolling on each other, their faces shiny with sweat. David wondered if he might marry them. Other couples had emerged from the church, and he could not help but feel that he had a hand in their happiness. Soon, one of the couples would name their first child after him. This would be his legacy.

That afternoon, the road dipped down a ridge and they pulled into the village, which perched a few hundred yards

above Lake Alexandrina. Children flocked around them, pointing and giggling and pulling their eyes into slits. Justus spoke
with a teenager, who darted into one of the huts. The village
elders understood some Swahili and English, but preferred
their own tongue. Justus didn't speak the local language, and
so the teenager would interpret for the missionaries. Their message would be twice translated before reaching their recipients,
which seemed like a children's game of telephone.

A boy rubbed his hand on David's bare arm, fascinated by
the smooth, pale skin. Justus gently shooed him away. A gray-
haired man strolled out. He looked well fed—paunchy and jowl-
cheeked—and wore a bright orange T-shirt and a brand-new
pair of sport sandals, which puzzled David. He had imagined
the villagers living in unbelievable poverty, with rheumy eyes
and, if not the swollen bellies of starvation, at least gauntness.
The elders ushered them into a grassy clearing.

"Thank you for meeting with us," David said. "We've come a
long way. Our church has a lot to share."

Justus spoke with the teenager for several minutes, which
seemed odd because David's opening statement had been short.
The guide's tone turned sharp and his hands sliced the air. He
gestured for David to join him, and they walked out of earshot.

"They've already been saved," he said, unable to meet David's
eyes.

Impossible. This couldn't be happening, not when they had
traveled so far, survived so much, and come this close. Justus
meant the neighboring village, or he'd misheard the chief,
or he had misheard Justus. If he could come up with enough

explanations, he might hit upon one that negated Justus's words. But his dreams, once imminent, had become a Polaroid reverting: vivid to ghostly to blank in seconds.

"Some Baptists came through." Justus dropped into a whisper. "Last week."

"You said they were unreached. You promised. You promised." He shouldn't have picked such an inexperienced guide. Or had Justus known all along?

"Can we go somewhere else?" What he prayed for must exist out there, beyond the next bend or next hill. "Somewhere else unreached."

"Missionaries over the years have covered villages all the way to the border, they say. People here would welcome your church's help."

Pride, not love of God, had pushed him to lead this mission, to found his church, to gamble with people's lives and their faith. Pride: the root of sin, or sin in its final form. He was going to lose everything for his sins. An empty church, an empty apartment, an empty life beckoned. Unless.

"I take care of you, you take care of me, right?" David asked.

Justus nodded slowly. The trip—without the unreached—would fall short of the inspiration that would open the pocketbooks of his flock and soften the hearts of the board. He pictured the villagers beaming and singing a hymn, their arms raised high as they encountered the Lord. If not truly, then the appearance of it would be just as moving on film.

"We'll help, like we planned. But don't tell the volunteers that the villagers have already been saved. They need to think we did it. And tell the elders . . . well, tell them to act surprised when we share the Gospel with them. Like they've never heard of Jesus. Or at least, they've never been touched by him. Not like with us. The word of God came through us. That's the deal."

"We cannot lie," Justus said. "We can remind them of God's love."

Deliver my soul, O Lord, from lying lips, and from a deceitful tongue. And to convince others to lie, was that not even worse? *The lip of truth shall be established forever: but a lying tongue is but for a moment.* Donations would pour in. These people would be saved, as would Bountiful Abundance and his marriage. But for a moment.

If Justus refused to help, David would make sure he never screwed anyone over again—and the guide could pray to the god he held superior. He'd attack the guide's greatest weakness: his sense of responsibility. "If you don't work with me, the villagers will get nothing," David said.

The guide's face twisted, and David glimpsed the skinny teenager forced to sacrifice a life with his family for a life with the church. That struggle. David wanted to kneel and ask for forgiveness—from God, from them all—but he could not force the words from his lips.

Justus had escaped the poverty of his village for a reason. Call it instinct. Call it God-given, but Justus could see possibilities, practicalities, where others could not. "No problem. I will tell them."

They returned to the clearing. After winning over the villagers with their good works, the missionaries would spread the

Good Word. But first, an omen: a flock of cranes rose from the lake, startling them all. Their magnificence proof of God. Necks extended, pointing like arrows to the heavens. Wings powerful and beating in time to his heart. Why shouldn't soaring precede every fall? The cranes wheeled in the sun, blinding David for a moment before they lit out toward the horizon.

Acknowledgments

===

I wrote these stories over a decade and a half. Like the rings of a tree, the stories mark many significant events—the year I married, the year I gave birth to my twin sons, the year my father passed away—and reflect my passions past and present.

With this reissue, my stories have found another life. Thank you, Margaret Sutherland Brown and Emma Sweeney, my warm and wise agents whose insights have guided me at every turn. I am grateful to my brilliant editor, Dan Smetanka, and his savvy assistant, Dan Lopez. I am indebted to Lena Moses-Schmitt, Dory Athey, Katie Boland, Wah-Ming Chang, Miyako Singer, Megan Fishmann, Jenn Kovitz, Andy Hunter, Donna Cheng, Hope Levy, and everyone at Counterpoint and Catapult who has welcomed me into your family.

My deep gratitude goes to my writing group—Maury Zeff, Jane Hannon Kalmes, and David Baker—who read draft after draft, challenging and cheering me on.

The Rona Jaffe Foundation, the San Francisco Foundation,

and the Steinbeck Fellows Program at San José State University—and in particular Paul Douglass, Nick Taylor, Tommy Mouton, and Dallas Woodburn—have provided vital support.

Much love to my professors at UC Riverside, Susan Straight, Michael Jaime-Becerra, Chris Abani, Andrew Winer, Reza Aslan, and Robin Russin; and to my classmates, Andy Sarouhan, Carly Kimmel, Adam Pelavin, Eva Konstantopoulos, Holly Gaglio, and Jackie Bang, among others, who continue to encourage and inspire me. Teachers Michelle Richmond and Karen Bjorneby sent me back on the path of fiction.

A huge thanks to the conferences at Bread Loaf, Aspen Summer Words, the Community of Writers at Squaw Valley, Napa Valley, and Voices of Our Nation for your support and fellowship, especially the Waiters of 2009—you inspire me with your amazing work, and I cherish your advice, support, and friendship.

Angie Chuang has been an invaluable reader, with a careful eye and a big heart. Dawn MacKeen has been a virtual watercooler buddy—our near-daily calls are a lifeline, providing laughs, support, and strategy.

Friends and fellow writers who read drafts of these stories, recommended me for opportunities, and encouraged and advised me along the way include Yalitza Ferreras, Jessica Carew Kraft, Bridget Quinn, Alicia Jo Rabins, Reese Kwon, Harriet Clark, Dara Barnat, Kirstin Chen, Frances Hwang, Angie Chau, Beth Nguyen, Aimee Phan, Ky-Phong Tran, Pia Sarkar, Josue Hurtado, Ryan Kim, Irene Chan, Jason Husgen, John Stevenson, Mary Ladd, Ali Eteraz, Toni Mirosevich,

Valerie Miner, the Taylors, the Freedes, the Cooper-Jordans, the Nilsens, Rob Schmitz, Mei Fong, Kevin Allardice, Kaitlin Solimine, Tyche Hendricks, Joe Garofoli, and the Love Boat Crew.

I'm grateful to the Writers Grotto in San Francisco, a community where we commiserate and celebrate, and to editors and reporters at the *San Francisco Chronicle* who helped shape me as a writer.

When I disappeared to finish just one more story, just one more paragraph, just one more sentence, Jaqueline Perez took wonderful care of my twin sons.

Many thanks to the following magazines that published earlier versions of these stories: "The Deal" in *The Atlantic*; "VIP Tutoring" in *The Sun*; "Just Like Us," in *Calyx*; "Line, Please" in *Daily Lit*; "Loaves and Fishes" in *Kweli Journal*; "What We Have Is What We Need" in *American Literary Review*; "For What They Shared" in *River Styx*; "The Responsibility of Deceit" in *Cream City Review*; "Accepted" in *Crab Orchard Review*; "Harte Lake" in *Hopkins Review*; and "The Older the Ginger" (as "Uncle, Eat") in the *Los Angeles Review of Books Quarterly Journal*. Outpost 19's *California Prose Directory* anthologies and Baobab Press's *This Side of the Divide: Stories of the American West* republished stories, and the New Short Fiction Series and Stories on Stage Sacramento brought my fiction to the stage.

With all my heart, I treasure the libraries and independent booksellers who have championed my work, and have helped me and so many writers find our way in the world.

Special thanks to C. Michael Curtis at *The Atlantic*, and to the editors at ZYZZYVA, Laura Cogan and Oscar Villalon, who have generously opened many doors in the literary world.

I owe much to my mother, Sylvia, and my late father, Lo-Ching, whose determination and hard work have always inspired me. Their pride and faith spur me on. My sister, Inez, and my brother, Lawrence, were the earliest audience for my storytelling, and my nephew, Declan, among the latest. I deeply appreciate the support of my in-laws, Robert and Patricia Puich, and my sister-in-law, Kristine Puich, and her partner, Jeff Elmassian, and my brother's partner, Carenna Willmont. My husband, Marc, is my rock, my love, and father to our twins, who teach me so much about life and its wonders every day.

© Andria Lo

VANESSA HUA is a columnist for the *San Francisco Chronicle* and the author of *A River of Stars*. A National Endowment for the Arts Literature Fellow, she has also received a Rona Jaffe Foundation Writers' Award, the Asian/Pacific American Award for Literature, the San Francisco Foundation's James D. Phelan Award, and a Steinbeck Fellowship in Creative Writing. Her work has appeared in publications including *The New York Times*, *The Atlantic*, and *The Washington Post*. Find out more at vanessahua.com.